MW00583584

SAY YOU LOVE ME

EVA RAE THOMAS MYSTERY - BOOK 4

WILLOW ROSE

Books by the Author

HARRY HUNTER MYSTERY SERIES

- ALL THE GOOD GIRLS
- RUN GIRL RUN
- NO OTHER WAY
- NEVER WALK ALONE

MARY MILLS MYSTERY SERIES

- WHAT HURTS THE MOST
- YOU CAN RUN
- YOU CAN'T HIDE
- CAREFUL LITTLE EYES

EVA RAE THOMAS MYSTERY SERIES

- DON'T LIE TO ME
- WHAT YOU DID
- NEVER EVER
- SAY YOU LOVE ME
- LET ME GO
- IT'S NOT OVER
- NOT DEAD YET
- TO DIE FOR

EMMA FROST SERIES

- ITSY BITSY SPIDER
- MISS DOLLY HAD A DOLLY
- RUN, RUN AS FAST AS YOU CAN
- CROSS YOUR HEART AND HOPE TO DIE
- PEEK-A-BOO I SEE YOU

- TWEEDLEDUM AND TWEEDLEDEE
- EASY AS ONE, TWO, THREE
- THERE'S NO PLACE LIKE HOME
- SLENDERMAN
- WHERE THE WILD ROSES GROW
- WALTZING MATHILDA
- DRIP DROP DEAD
- BLACK FROST

JACK RYDER SERIES

- HIT THE ROAD JACK
- SLIP OUT THE BACK JACK
- THE HOUSE THAT JACK BUILT
- BLACK JACK
- GIRL NEXT DOOR
- HER FINAL WORD
- DON'T TELL

REBEKKA FRANCK SERIES

- ONE, TWO...HE IS COMING FOR YOU
- THREE, FOUR...BETTER LOCK YOUR DOOR
- FIVE, SIX...GRAB YOUR CRUCIFIX
- SEVEN, EIGHT...GONNA STAY UP LATE
- NINE, TEN...NEVER SLEEP AGAIN
- ELEVEN, TWELVE...DIG AND DELVE
- THIRTEEN, FOURTEEN...LITTLE BOY UNSEEN
- BETTER NOT CRY
- TEN LITTLE GIRLS
- IT ENDS HERE

MYSTERY/THRILLER/HORROR NOVELS

- SORRY CAN'T SAVE YOU
- IN ONE FELL SWOOP

- UMBRELLA MAN
- BLACKBIRD FLY
- TO HELL IN A HANDBASKET
- EDWINA

HORROR SHORT-STORIES

- MOMMY DEAREST
- THE BIRD
- BETTER WATCH OUT
- EENIE, MEENIE
- ROCK-A-BYE BABY
- NIBBLE, NIBBLE, CRUNCH
- HUMPTY DUMPTY
- CHAIN LETTER

PARANORMAL SUSPENSE/ROMANCE NOVELS

- IN COLD BLOOD
- THE SURGE
- GIRL DIVIDED

THE VAMPIRES OF SHADOW HILLS SERIES

- FLESH AND BLOOD
- BLOOD AND FIRE
- FIRE AND BEAUTY
- BEAUTY AND BEASTS
- BEASTS AND MAGIC
- MAGIC AND WITCHCRAFT
- WITCHCRAFT AND WAR
- WAR AND ORDER
- ORDER AND CHAOS
- CHAOS AND COURAGE

THE AFTERLIFE SERIES

- BEYOND
- SERENITY
- ENDURANCE
- COURAGEOUS

THE WOLFBOY CHRONICLES

- A GYPSY SONG
- I AM WOLF

DAUGHTERS OF THE JAGUAR

- SAVAGE
- BROKEN

Chapter One

SATURDAY, SEPTEMBER 28TH

10:45:07 PM

DISPATCH: Nine-one-one. What's your emergency? Hello?
    Allyson: Hello, I want to talk to the police.
    Dispatch: What happened? What is your name?
    Allyson: I'm Allyson. I've been kidnapped.
    Dispatch: How old are you, Allyson?
    Allyson: Fifteen. Please, hurry. I don't know where I am.
    Dispatch: What do you mean you don't know where you are? Don't you have a town name?
    Allyson: I think I'm still on the island, but I'm not sure. It was dark ... I don't know where I am exactly.
    Dispatch: Is there anything, any landmarks that can help us?
    Allyson: I ... I don't think so. It's so dark where I am.
    Dispatch: Is anyone there with you? Are you alone?
    Allyson: Yes. Right now, I'm alone in the room.
    Dispatch: Are you in a house or a condo?
    Allyson: It's a house. I'm sitting in the closet upstairs. He's

1

walking around downstairs. I can hear him. He's gonna come back up here soon. You must send the police to help me. Please, hurry.

Dispatch: Okay, okay. Problem is, your phone is not showing me any location. Is it a cell phone?

Allyson: Yes. I found it. It's probably his.

Dispatch: And that is the man that has kidnapped you?

Allyson: Yes ... he came ... he's coming ... come quickly, please!

Dispatch: Has he hurt you?

Allyson: Yes, he's hurt me. He beat me up!

Dispatch: Are you injured? Are you bleeding?

Allyson: Yes, I'm bleeding. Please, just send the police!

Dispatch: I would if I knew where to send them. Could you please help me out here? Is there anything that can help you find an address? A street outside the window that you can see the street sign?

Allyson: He closed the hurricane shutters. I can't look out. Please, please, send someone.

Dispatch: Is there any mail lying around with an address on it?

Allyson: No. Please. I can hear him. He's gonna come for me. I'm scared. I can't get out. Please!!

Dispatch: I'm working on it. I'm working. Is there any way you can get out of the house?

Allyson: No. He locked the door, and the window is closed by shutters.

Dispatch: Does he have a weapon?

Allyson: He used a taser when he took me. He was wearing a ski mask.

Dispatch: But no gun?

Allyson: I-I don't know. I remember something, though. There was a creek. We drove over a creek before I was blindfolded. And his car is blue. Yes! He brought me here in a blue car.

Dispatch: Okay, this is good. Now, try and look around and see if you can get any idea of where you are, anything that can give you an address.

(A long pause. There's fumbling. Allyson is moving around; then there's heavy breathing.)

Allyson: I went outside the closet, and I found something in a drawer. A card. There's an address on it.

Dispatch: Perfect. Give me the address, and I'll send a patrol out to get you. We'll find you, Allyson; don't worry, okay? We'll find you before he gets back up to you. Just give me the address from the card.

Allyson: T-twenty-three Breakers Drive.

Dispatch: Bakers Drive? Allyson? Was it Bakers Drive?

Allyson: (screams)

Dispatch: Try to remain calm. You're doing an excellent job, Allyson. I'm connecting to the police now. They'll come for you as soon as possible. Stay on the line. Hello? Hello? Allyson, are you there? Hello?

Chapter Two

SATURDAY, SEPTEMBER 28TH

10:50:07 PM

DISPATCH: Nine-one-one. What's your emergency?

Allyson: Help!

Dispatch: Allyson?

Allyson: Please, hurry! Did you send help?

Dispatch (breathes relieved): Yes, Allyson. I did. The police are on their way. Stay where you are. Are you all right, Allyson? Did something happen?

Allyson (breathing agitatedly): I'm so scared. Please, come quick.

Dispatch: They're coming, Allyson. I promise. A team will arrive in a few minutes. Try and relax. I heard you scream. Did he come up to you? Did he hurt you again?

Allyson (sniffles): I'm so scared; please, come and help me.

Dispatch: A team will arrive in a few minutes. Stay on the line with me.

Allyson (crying): Okay.

Dispatch (voice cracking slightly): Don't worry, sweetheart. They're coming now. You gotta hang in for me now; can you do that? I need you to be the strongest you can be; can you do that for me?

Allyson (crying and desperate): But I'm so scared ... please, are they coming?

Dispatch: They are coming, honey. Shouldn't be long now. They're on their way. Just stay with me.

Allyson: Okay.

Dispatch: Take a couple of deep breaths, okay?

Allyson (breathes): Okay, that helps. Thanks.

Dispatch: Keep breathing for me, okay?

Allyson (whimpers): I can hear him. Please!

Dispatch: Talk to me, Allyson. What's happening? Where is he? Is he upstairs where you are?

Allyson (almost whispers): I think so. I can hear him ... I hear footsteps.

Dispatch (nervously): Just stay calm. Don't make a sound; you hear me? Just keep the phone close to your ear so I can hear you breathing. The police are closing in now. Won't be more than a few seconds. I need you to stay calm now, baby. Stay on the line with me, and just stay completely still.

(Line goes dead.)

Dispatch: Allyson? Are you there? Allyson? Hello?

Chapter Three

SATURDAY, SEPTEMBER 28TH

10:52:03 PM

DISPATCH: Nine-one-one. What's your emergency?

(Heavy breathing)

Dispatch (gasping): Allyson? Is that you? Oh, sweetheart, I am so happy to hear from you again. Are you all right?

Allyson (whispers, crying): He's in the room now. I'm in the closet again. I can hear him. Oh, God, he's right outside the closet now.

Dispatch (sounding agitated): The police should be there by now, Allyson. It can't be many seconds ... (mumbles) why aren't they there yet? This can't be right!

Allyson (crying): Please. He's standing right outside the closet now. The handle is moving, oh, dear God. He's coming; he is coming for me!

Dispatch: Can you see anything in the closet that you can use as a weapon? All we need is a few seconds. Try and stall him. Talk to him if you can.

Allyson: I ... I can't. He's so strong. He's coming to kill me. I saw it in his eyes earlier. He was only downstairs to get ready for this. He is going to kill me, oh, dear Lord.

(The sound of turmoil. Someone yells. Allyson screams.)

Dispatch (crying): Allyson. I … I they … should be there; they should be right outside the house now. I … I … Allyson? Allyson? ALLYSON?

(The sound of someone breathing heavily into the phone, then the line goes dead)

Fernandina Beach High School, Amelia Island

MONDAY, SEPTEMBER 30TH

Chapter Four

SOMETHING IS NOT RIGHT.

Lauren had felt it all morning through her first three periods. Something was off. Whether it was just a feeling, or something in the air, or something she had forgotten to do, an assignment she had forgotten to turn in, or something completely different, she didn't know. But nothing about this day was the way it usually was.

Lauren looked around the cafeteria at the kids who were eating, chatting, and scrambling with their trays. Everything seemed to be normal to the eye, but something was definitely off if you asked Lauren. And it made her nervous.

"Where's Adam?"

Lauren looked up at Chris, who was sitting across from her and was unpacking his sack lunch. Lauren shook her head with a light shrug.

"I don't know."

She had seen Adam this morning before classes. But only briefly. He had been standing by the lockers with his backpack. She had waved and wanted to approach him, but he hadn't seen her, and then the bell rang, and she had to go to class. But when second period came along, he wasn't there. Usually, Adam and Lauren sat

9

together in US History. It was her favorite time of day. She'd had such a crush on Adam since the sixth grade, but he didn't know that. They were neighbors and best friends. And they usually sat together at lunch too.

That's it. That's all that's wrong. You're just sad that Adam isn't here.

"I saw him this morning," she said. "But he wasn't in US History. Maybe he felt sick and went home."

Chris shrugged and took a bite of his sandwich. "I just hope he hasn't forgotten our math paper that we did together. We have to turn it in today, or we'll get a zero, and I can't afford that. Maybe I should call him."

Chris pulled out his phone from his backpack, but just as he did, Lauren looked up and saw Adam standing by the doorway to the cafeteria. Seeing him made her face light up and her heart begin to race.

"There he is," she said and waved. She was blushing slightly and cursed her treacherous face for always revealing how she really felt. "Adam? Over here!"

But Adam didn't even look in her direction, and her heart sank. He seemed different somehow, she realized. There was something in his eyes, a look that seemed so strange that she doubted for a second whether it was really him.

"Adam?" she said half mumbling, then looked down at what was in his hand, still covered mostly by his jacket. At first, she didn't believe her eyes. She simply refused to. There was no way this was happening. Not at her school. Not by the hands of the boy she had loved so deeply for years.

No way.

All those stories she had heard came back to her in that instant. All those eyewitnesses she had heard tell their stories on TV, about a shooter coming into their classroom and shooting, about hearing shots somewhere and then barricading the doors to the classroom or rushing for the exits, of friends and fellow students falling to the ground dead.

All those times, she had watched chopper footage of children being escorted outside to safety while others remained trapped inside. All those scared, shaking voices, all those crying eyes, and desperate parents. So many times, she had thought that one day this could happen to her, at her school, but deep down, she had always believed that it wouldn't.

You never really think anything like this is going to happen to you, do you?

As Adam lifted the AK-47 from his jacket and fired it, Lauren was amazed at how frozen in place everyone in the cafeteria was, including herself. It was like time stood completely still, and no one moved, even though they knew deep down inside that there was no time in their lives that they needed to move more than in this second. Their lives depended on it. Yet, they didn't. It was like they couldn't fathom what was actually happening, that *this* was actually happening to them. This was no longer one of the million drills they had during the school year or something they were watching on TV while their parents held them a little closer, thinking, *next time it could be my kid.*

This was it. This was real.

This was painfully real.

One Week Later

Chapter Five

"How's he holding up? Any improvement?"

I barely looked at the man standing next to me. He cleared his throat, his eyes avoiding mine, then shook his head.

"No."

The man was my father. And the boy in the hospital bed in front of me was my brother that I didn't know I had until two days ago.

I hadn't seen my dad in thirty-six years, not since he kidnapped my sister, Sydney in a Wal-Mart and took her to London when she was seven and I was five years old. I grew up not knowing what had happened to her, with an emotionally distant mother, thinking I had to become an FBI-profiler to redeem myself for not having saved her on that fateful day.

Now, my father was back in my life. Not with my goodwill, but because of the boy lying in the hospital bed in front of us, tubes doing the breathing for him. Adam was my brother's name; I had very recently learned. My father was nothing like I had imagined he would be. He was small and stubby and had nervous blue eyes that made him look like he was afraid of me.

At last, now I knew where I got my red hair, the shortness, and the rest of my looks.

Thanks a lot, Dad!

"I brought coffee."

The voice belonged to my sister, Sydney. She handed me a cup and then gave one to our father as well. Their relationship wasn't much better than ours. Even though she grew up with him in London, he had told her that our mother didn't want her, that she had sent her away back when he took her. Once she grew up, she left London to find us in Florida, but our father wouldn't help her track us down or even tell her our real names, so for years, she lived very close, but we never found one another. We hadn't succeeded in reconnecting until about six months ago, and everything was still very new between us. Yet I already felt like Sydney understood me better than anyone in this world. Even better than my boyfriend, Matt, who had known me since we were in preschool. He was a local detective back in Cocoa Beach where we lived, and we had recently found our way back to one another after years apart.

Sydney and I had made the drive to Amelia Island to visit our brother, who was in a coma. It was our dad that had called and asked us to come.

Neither of us knew of our brother's existence until that moment.

And we still didn't know much since he hadn't been awake at all. All we knew about him was that he was fifteen years old and had been in a coma for a week … since the day he decided to bring an assault rifle to school and start shooting in the cafeteria. A school resource officer designated to the school had reacted quickly and shot him in the chest.

I still thought about the call from my dad two days ago. At first, I hadn't believed him and hung up. Several times actually. I kept telling him I didn't have a father, and to stop calling me, that it was a sick joke.

It was my sister Sydney who had convinced me to go with her up there. Our dad lived with his mother — our grandmother — in a house on Amelia Island, a three-hour drive from Cocoa Beach. And they needed my help.

"He's fifteen, for crying out loud," Sydney said when I told her there was no way I was going, that I didn't owe our dad anything, that I never wanted to meet him or his son. Ever.

"He's just a kid," she continued relentlessly. "It's not his fault our dad is such a fool. He didn't ask to be born just as little as you and I did. He didn't choose his family. We could be that for him; we could be his family or at least help him out of this trouble he's in."

I stared at her, mouth gaping open. I could hardly believe her. Was she seriously suggesting that I help them?

"He brought an AK-47 to school and started shooting at his classmates and friends. And you talk about him like he's some innocent child? He sounds like just as big a fool as our father. If you think I am going to help him get out of the grave he dug for himself, then you're just as much a fool as the rest of them."

"He's in a coma, Eva Rae. They shot him. Dad doesn't believe the police. He says our brother would never do such a thing."

"Yeah, well, he's his dad. Of course, he'd say that."

"What if he's right?"

I rose to my feet, but Sydney stopped me.

"Just a few hours away from here, you have a brother that you have never met; you have a grandmother that you haven't seen since you were a baby probably. Don't you want at least to meet them? Aren't you curious? Aren't you the least bit curious?"

It took me some time to admit it, but of course, I was, and here we were.

Our father, David Clarke, didn't believe his son would ever do what the police accused him of, and he wanted my help to prove it. After two days in Amelia Island, I still wasn't sure I wanted to help him. If the kid was dumb enough to take a gun to school, he kind of had made his own mess and needed to lie in it, right?

"Have the doctors said anything?" Sydney asked. "Does he still have a fever? Has the swelling gone down?"

I looked at my beautiful sister, the movie star, who was adored by the entire world. I couldn't believe I was so lucky to have her back in my life after thirty-six years, and I still felt so angry at our dad for stealing those years from us that it made it hard for me to look into his eyes without wanting to kill him. I refused even to call him dad or refer to him as my father.

To me, he was just David Clarke and nothing else.

"No. No one has been in here yet," David said. "I'm still waiting for the doctor to make his rounds."

He gave me a brief nervous look, and I sat down in the chair with a sigh. I closed my eyes and rubbed my temples.

What am I even doing here? What did I expect to find by coming?

Chapter Six

"I'm gonna head on home. It's late, and I need to get Elijah to bed."

Matt peeked inside of Chief Annie's office. She lifted her glance and looked at the clock on the wall.

"I didn't even know you were still here," she said, then sighed. "Finding it hard to be without Eva Rae again?"

He nodded. "Yeah, well, she needed to do this. I totally get it. Her father and a brother she didn't know she had. I can't blame her."

"But you still miss her," Annie said.

"It's hard not to," he said, then nodded, "Goodnight."

Matt walked to the car and got in. He sat for a few minutes and just stared into the darkness. Why was he dragging it out? Was it really that hard for him to go home?

Matt started the car up with a deep sigh. It *was* hard for him. His son, Elijah, waited at home. Matt's mother had taken care of him all day, and now Matt was supposed to put him to bed. He had promised his mother that he'd at least come home in time to do that. She wanted him to prioritize the boy more, to spend more time with him, but Matt found himself trying to find excuses to stay at work. Why? Because Elijah hated his guts. The way he spoke to him or even ignored him tormented Matt.

Matt hadn't been in the boy's life until recently when his mother died. And since the boy now blamed Matt for the death of his mother, things didn't exactly go down smoothly at the house. Matt found himself taking on more work and dragging out the day just so he didn't have to deal with him when he came home.

It wasn't a good way to deal with this; he knew that much, and Eva Rae kept telling him so. But he didn't know how else to deal with it. He felt like he had tried everything, yet nothing made things better. With Eva Rae out of town, he had no reason to leave work at all.

Matt thought about Eva Rae as he drove down A1A and stopped at the Sunoco on the corner. He wanted to buy a few beers to take home and maybe some candy for the boy. Maybe he could buy his love with some sweets.

Matt parked and walked inside to get the stuff, then came back out just as a black Lincoln Navigator drove up. Matt sighed when he saw Chad step out of it. Chad — Eva Rae's ex — had landed some very high-paid sales job and the brand new 2019 Navigator was leased to him by the company. He wore that smirk on his face as he approached Matt, giving him a casual wave.

"Hi there, buddy."

Buddy. It made him cringe every time Chad called him that. It was patronizing just like everything else with Chad was. Matt didn't understand why Eva Rae had ever married the guy.

"Just stopping by to get some candy for our kids," Chad said. "I see you got the same idea."

He looked at the bag of candy in Matt's hand.

Our kids. Chad always made sure to rub that one in Matt's face every chance he got. Making sure Matt knew they shared a family, while he and Eva Rae didn't. Matt loathed that this man had been married to Eva Rae and had three children with her. He hated even more that Chad was back in Eva Rae's life again. It was good for the kids, but not for Eva Rae. Matt feared he'd end up hurting her again. The guy cheated on her for more than a year of their marriage. In Matt's book, that's not something that is easily forgotten. How anyone could ever do anything like that to Eva Rae was a mystery to Matt. It showed the guy's character, and men like him weren't very likely to change. At least not in Matt's experience. Eva Rae didn't see it in quite the same way. She believed in giving people second chances, she said when they discussed it. Besides, it was only for the children's sake that she let him back into her life again.

But Matt wasn't so sure it was that easy. He was certain that Chad was trying to get Eva Rae back.

"Anyway, I should be going …" Matt said.

"Of course, yeah. Well, it was nice seeing you again, buddy. I'll tell Eva Rae I bumped into you when she calls to say goodnight to the kids. See ya."

Matt stared at him, nostrils flaring lightly as Chad entered the shop.

"Or maybe I'll tell her when I talk to her…first," he mumbled, then got back in the car and took off, slamming his fist into the steering wheel.

Chapter Seven

"Who said dumpster diving can't be classy?"

Evelyn looked into the camera of her phone and smiled. She was wearing a black and white striped dress and a fake pearl necklace with earrings and a bracelet to match. Her black hair was straightened and pulled back in a ponytail, also held up by white plastic pearls, as she stepped out of her car, holding the phone up so all of her viewers could follow her every move. She always recorded what she did with her phone and then uploaded it to YouTube later. She had twelve thousand subscribers who loved to get good advice on finding stuff in other people's garbage.

"Remember how I found a set of brand-new kitchen towels last week? This was the place I found it, tags on and everything. Nothing wrong with them, just tossed because people didn't like what they looked like or whatnot. Who knows why 'em rich folks throw out stuff that is brand new and unused?"

Evelyn grabbed her tote bag and walked to the dumpster, still filming herself. She stopped in front of a big green dumpster.

"Now, the best places to go, I think I've said this before, but I'll say it again to all of my new viewers who haven't been around so long and seen all of my earlier videos. But the best places to go dumpster diving is first of all affluent neighborhoods like the one I am standing in right now."

Evelyn turned the camera so her viewers could see all the big condominiums surrounding the park.

"All of those condos over there are oceanfront," she continued. "And owned by lots of rich folks from up north who come to Amelia Island and throw out all of that good stuff that I show you. Y'all remember the tablecloth with the nice skirt on it, the silver one I showed you a few weeks ago? Also from this dumpster. It had never been used, nuh-uh. Taken out of its original packaging, but never used. Some folks are just pigs, throwing out all that good stuff. But you know what I say; one woman's trash is another woman's treasure; yes, it sure is. Now the second-best place to go is behind retail stores, like behind Bealls or JJ Cooper. All those returns that they can't re-shelve, they go straight into the dumpster, did you know that? I haven't bought new clothes in ten years. I find all of my clothes behind these stores. Stick around, and I'll show you later on."

Evelyn turned the camera to face the dumpster in front of her. "Now, let's see what this baby has for us today."

She lifted the lid till it was fully open, then filmed inside. "Now, what you see here is mostly trash bags, and some of it is worthless, but if you just lift one bag and then look further in … *ah-ha*, see here."

Evelyn pulled out a roll of wrapping paper. "See, this is brand new. Never even been unwrapped. Perfect for my son's birthday that is coming up. I haven't bought wrapping paper in years. I always find these brand-new rolls. Now let's see what else is in here."

She put the roll on the ground next to the dumpster, then looked down again. She grabbed a plastic bag and pulled it open. She looked inside, then grimaced. "Nope. Nothing but trash, yak. All right, let's look a little over here."

She moved the stinky trash bag to the side, then looked underneath it. She grabbed a grey trash bag and pulled it up toward her.

"Now, this looks promising. It's long and seems hard. Something big inside of that one, I'm sure. This looks like a scoop. Let me just see what it can be," she said and pulled it upward. But it was heavy, and she had to give up. Instead, she pulled it open and peeked inside.

"What's in there?" she mumbled, still holding the camera so the viewers could follow along. "What is that? Is it a mannequin doll? Now, who would throw out a ..."

Evelyn went quiet. She stared at the head inside the bag, heart pounding in her chest. Then she turned to the camera and felt like she should say something, yet she couldn't. There simply were no words for this. Instead, she turned the recording off, then called nine-one-one instead.

Chapter Eight

THEN:

"I don't understand. Why am I here?"

Marlene looked at the two law enforcement officers in front of her. They had come to her house earlier in the morning and asked her to go with them. They were wearing badges, but she didn't know if they were police officers since they were in civilian clothes. They had presented themselves as criminal investigators and nearly given her a heart attack. They had told her nothing about why they were taking her to the station or what was going on, even though she asked again and again during the car ride there.

"What is this regarding?" she asked again. It felt like a terrible song playing on repeat. "Did something happen?"

The one on the right leaned forward and cleared his throat. She couldn't remember if he was the one that had presented himself as Rivers or if it was the other one. She was pretty sure he was Rivers and the other was Waltman.

Marlene shook her head. It didn't matter. She just wanted to get out of this place as soon as possible and get back to her kitchen. She was supposed to make chicken for dinner tonight and had left it out on the counter when they came for her. She feared the dog was going to eat it before she got back, and then she'd have nothing to serve tonight.

"It's regarding your son," the one she was pretty sure was Rivers said. He had a goatee that he kept rubbing.

Marlene looked at him, baffled. Her heart started to pound at the mention of her son.

"My son? He's in school. Did he do something? Did he get himself in trouble? Did something happen to him?"

"Now, I need you to calm down, ma'am," Waltman said and stretched his hand out toward her like it would help her feel less agitated. "We're here to conduct an investigation. Your son is all right. He's in safe hands."

"What do you mean he's in *safe* hands?" Marlene asked. "Of course, he is. My son is always in safe hands."

"It means he's with protective services and they'll keep him there till we have conducted our investigation."

Marlene wrinkled her forehead. What on Earth were they talking about? It had to be some mistake. All of it. Her being taken there, what they were saying now.

"Investigation? But … why is he with protective services? I don't understand," she said, feeling frustrated. She was wasting her entire day doing this, being there, and frankly, was just waiting for them to realize there had been a mistake. It was the wrong woman or the wrong child. Something. "Could someone please tell me what is going on here? What is this investigation?"

Rivers cleared his throat again and sipped from his coffee cup. It took forever before he put it down, and Marlene felt like screaming at him.

"We're investigating your husband," he finally said. "We have reason to believe that he is abusing your son."

Chapter Nine

"Mom, Christine and Alex aren't helping with the bunnies at all. I'm the one doing all the work."

I held the phone close to my ear while listening to my daughter, Olivia. She was the oldest of the three with her fifteen years to Christine's thirteen and Alex's seven.

"What do you mean?" I asked, not very interested, but just enjoying hearing my daughter's voice. It was Chad that had promised them they could have bunnies, and I was never asked about it, probably because they knew I would have said no. I knew it was going to cause problems, and so it did. The kids were constantly fighting about them and who was supposed to do what.

"I cleaned the cage three days ago, and now it needs to be cleaned again," she continued. "I feed them in the morning and give them water, and Christine and Alex never do any of it. I don't want to have to clean the cage again."

I was sitting in the waiting room, in a lonely spot where no one could hear me, taking a break from what went on in the hospital room. The kids were staying with their dad while I was gone for a few days.

"How's the boy doing?" Olivia asked. "Your brother? My … uncle? Gosh, it sounds weird to say that."

"Especially since he's the same age as you," I said, shaking my head. "I don't know, to be honest. The doctors don't know much either."

Olivia went quiet. "So … did he really take a gun to school and start shooting?"

"Mm-hm," I said.

"Who does that?"

I shrugged with a sigh. It was a thought that kept bothering me as well. What kind of a kid was my brother? "Someone who is mentally ill, probably."

"But … is he that?"

"I don't know, to be honest. I don't think he has a diagnosis. I am not sure he was ever evaluated."

"Did he show any signs? You know … before he did it?"

"What do you mean?"

"You know … you hear these stories about the shooters, how they've talked online about doing it or written something on social media about it."

I took in a deep breath. "I haven't … I haven't actually talked to his dad about any of this."

"Maybe you should," she said like it was the simplest thing in the world. I hadn't spoken to my dad for thirty-six years, and I could barely stand the sight of him or be in the same room as him. Why didn't I just talk to him about the brother I didn't know existed for fifteen years?

"It's not that easy, sweetie," I said.

"Why not?"

I exhaled. "It's complicated. Listen, kiss your siblings for me, will you? I need to get back."

"Bye, Mom."

We hung up, and I stared at the display on my phone. I found Matt's number and was about to call him when Sydney came into the room, a distressed look on her face.

"Something has happened," she said. "You need to come."

Chapter Ten

THE MAN in the blue car drove up in front of the liquor store and stopped the engine. He stared in the mirror at his own reflection, and at the alligator-shaped scar on his cheek, then let out a deep sigh. He stepped out of the car, looked over his shoulder to make sure he wasn't seen, then rushed inside the store.

The store's manager behind the counter didn't even look up from his phone as he entered. The store was nearly empty, only some older guy standing by the beers, wearing a hat and his jacket covering half of his face.

The man grabbed a bottle of vodka, then sighed when thinking about how he ought to stop, how this bottle was definitely going to be the last one. The man with the scar paid the cashier and grabbed the brown bag, then turned around when the man from earlier in the brown jacket stood right behind him, and he knocked into him. The man dropped his phone from his hand.

What an idiot. He doesn't deserve to live.

"Here, let me give you a hand," the man with the scar said. He picked up the phone and handed it to the man with the six-pack in his hand. The man smiled underneath his hat.

"Thank you. That is very kind of you."

"No problem."

He's nothing but an object to you — a means to an end. You kill him and receive your reward.

The man with the scar smiled and let the man with the hat pay for the beer. The man with the scar walked outside and was smoking a cigarette as the other came out, holding his beers in a bag. Rain had started to pour down.

"Just gonna wait it out," the man with the scar said as smoke emerged from between his lips. His eyes lingered on the other man. He had opened the bottle of vodka inside of the brown bag and took a sip while thunder crackled above them. "Just the walk to the car is gonna soak me."

"Me too," the man with the hat said. He looked at the cigarettes. "Say, do you mind?"

"Not at all," the man with the scar said and handed him a cigarette. He lit it with his lighter. The man with the hat blew out smoke with a relieved sigh.

"Been a while, huh?"

He's nothing but a piece in a puzzle. An object to reach your goal. You kill for one reason only.

"Yeah, you could say that."

"I know how it feels — been trying to quit for years. Same with this," he said and lifted the brown bag to his lips.

The man with the hat nodded.

To get famous.

"I'm Jeff, by the way," the man with the scar said and reached out his hand.

"E.T," the other man said with the cigarette sticking out between his lips and his eyes half-closed to avoid the smoke.

"E.T, huh? What an unusual name."

They shook hands. Two men waiting out the rain. Two men meeting by coincidence. All of it was quite ordinary and boring really if it hadn't been for the fact that one of them was a killer who had already begun filming his future victim using his phone.

Chapter Eleven

"I'M GOING TO KILL HIM!"

I rushed back from the waiting area when I heard the loud voices. Outside of my brother's hospital room, I saw a man in his mid-forties, his face red. He was being held back by Deputy Corel from the sheriff's office, who had been guarding Adam's room. David was standing by the door, a look of terror on his face.

"What's going on?" I asked and stepped closer to David. "Who is he?"

David's nostrils were flaring, and he looked at me, terrified. Tears were springing to his eyes, and he could hardly speak.

"He's Allyson's father," he finally said.

"And ... Allyson is?"

David stared at me, shaking his head. I could hear Allyson's dad still screaming and yelling. Deputy Corel was talking to him in a strained manner.

"You need to calm down, Ryan, or I'll have to take you to the station; you hear me? You have to calm down."

Ryan nodded and stopped fighting him. The deputy eased up. Ryan stared at David, his lips quivering.

"He killed her, you bastard; your son killed my daughter!"

"I ... I'm ..." David said, holding a hand to his chest. Allyson's dad held up a phone where some video was playing.

"See for yourself. This went viral this morning. She was pulled out of a dumpster. Your son killed her and threw her out like she was trash! Trash! My daughter, my beloved Allyson!"

"Was she killed at the school?" I asked, confused, looking from one to the other.

David shook his head. "She wasn't in school that day. She's been missing since ... since two nights before, and no one knew where she was. We'd all hoped and prayed that she'd turn up alive ..."

"Oh, save it," Ryan said. "We don't want your prayers. We want justice for our daughter."

"And justice you'll get, once the courts ..." Deputy Corel tried, but Ryan interrupted him with a loud roar.

"You think that's justice, huh? He'll get a couple of years, and me and my wife we'll get ... nothing because nothing will bring her back. Do you know where my wife and I have just been, huh? Do you know?"

David shook his head.

"We were at the medical examiner's office, IDing our own daughter. Can you imagine? Can you imagine what that's like? Knowing that your son ... your bastard son did this to her."

David's head slumped. "I don't understand," he said and glanced toward Adam, who looked like he was sleeping peacefully. "He loved her. They loved one another."

"Love?" Ryan hissed, while Deputy Corel held him back once again. "You call this love? Your boy sure has a strange way of showing love. But mark my words, David. I will kill your son if I get the chance; you hear me? I will kill him in cold blood for what he did to my girl, and I'll gladly take the jail time for it. Gladly!"

Chapter Twelve

WE DROVE BACK from the hospital in silence. Sydney was sitting in the passenger seat next to me, and David was in the back seat where I couldn't look at him. Just his presence in the car made my skin crawl. There was so much I wanted to say to him, so much I needed to say, yet the words didn't come. This wasn't the time or the place. The man was lying down — which was good; I needed him to be down — but I didn't like to kick him while he was still down there.

I parked in front of our grandmother's house and killed the engine of my minivan. David got out first, and we followed him. As we walked up on the porch, David sat on the porch swing and covered his face with his hands. Sydney and I just stood there, not knowing what to do.

"I just can't believe it," he said. "I can't believe he would do any of those things. Not my boy, not Adam."

It became awkward really fast. Sydney and I stared at one another, then at our father, who sobbed and cried. Neither of us wanted to comfort him. I felt anger rise in me as I couldn't stop wondering why he never cried over me. He could cry over his son, who was most likely a murderer, but never shed a tear for me?

It was selfish, but I couldn't help myself. I couldn't stop

wondering what made Adam so special that his dad wanted to see him grow up and not me.

Are you seriously mad because he kidnapped Sydney and not you?

I guess I was.

"He was a good boy; he *is* a good boy," he continued. "He would never kill Allyson. Of all the people in the world, she was the one who loved him and that he loved. He adored the very ground she walked on. It makes no sense!"

He lifted his glance and looked straight into my eyes for the first time in the two days I had been there.

"Please, Eva Rae. Please, help him. You're the only one who can."

I shook my head with a snort.

So, now you want me, huh? Because I can be of use to you?

"Please, sweetheart?"

I shook my head in anger. "You don't get to call me that. You hear me? You don't get to call me that!"

I stared at him, my nostrils flaring.

"This is ridiculous," I said and stepped back, emotions stirring in me like a tornado. It felt like my blood was boiling, and I found it hard to breathe properly. This was just too much for me.

I saw that the garage door was open, and I turned away from my sobbing excuse for a father and walked in there, finding my grandmother, Eileen, underneath her Harley, wrench in her hand. She was eighty years old, yet still rode her bike, refusing to act her age.

"I take it that Adam hasn't woken up yet by the look on your face," she said with a sniffle. Eileen had been with us to visit Adam the day before but had to leave because she couldn't hold it together. I had heard her pacing around in the living room all night, and this morning she said she didn't want to go with us; she said she'd go later. She said she had work to do, but I sensed she just couldn't take it, that seeing Adam like that was too unbearable for her.

I stared at her and shook my head. I had never had a grandmother before. The one on my mother's side cut my mother off when she decided to have children at a young age, and they never reconnected, and since I never knew my real dad, I had never realized Eileen even existed. She had told me that she had been down to visit a few times when I was just a baby, but I couldn't remember that, naturally.

The strangest part was that ever since I saw Eileen for the first time two days ago, I felt like she was someone I could talk to. Not to mention the uncanny likeness in our appearances. We both had those same light blue eyes, and the red hair — well, hers was mostly gray now, but still had some redness in it — the pale skin, the shortness, and stubbiness. We had a connection that I had never felt in my life, except maybe with my sister. But with Eileen, it was different. It was like she understood me, and she knew me, like really knew me. It was like she was some sort of older version of me.

She pulled out from underneath the bike, wiped her hands on a stray rag, then approached me. She was wearing ripped jeans with oil stains on them, a white T-shirt with a Harley logo on it, and a bandana on the top of her head. She still had long unruly hair, despite her age, which I liked. I never understood why people cut their hair short just because they rounded fifty or even sixty. Why weren't women allowed to have long hair just because they were old?

Eileen went to the fridge, grabbed two beers, and handed me one.

"Spill it, kid. What's going on?"

"David ..."

"Your dad," she said.

"Yeah, well ... he's asking me to help Adam. He says he doesn't believe Adam would do what he did."

"Well, David has followed your career closely. He knows how good you are at what you do. That's why he called you to come. You are the only hope for Adam, like it or not."

That was a surprise to me. My dad had been following my career? Didn't make me feel better about him, though. If he knew where I was, he could have come looking for me. It didn't have to take a murder case for him to do that.

"But ... what is it exactly that he thinks I can do? There's like an entire cafeteria full of witnesses who saw Adam come in with that gun and open fire."

Eileen sipped her beer and shook her head. "It's just not like Adam. I've known the kid for fifteen years."

"But still, the case is pretty clear … the evidence overwhelming. And now they say he killed his girlfriend too?" I said.

Eileen almost choked on her beer. "Allyson? Oh, dear God. They found her?"

I nodded. "In a dumpster at a place called Peter's Point."

Eileen sucked in air, and I could tell that her eyes were welling up.

"You knew her well?" I asked.

Eileen nodded. "She used to come here all the time. They'd hang out with me out here by the bikes, or they'd be in the house doing homework together. Those two were the cutest couple." Eileen shook her head and drank more from her beer. As she lowered the bottle, she snorted angrily. "Nope. I'm not buying it. This is the drop. Adam would never hurt her, never!"

She gave me a look. "You have to look into this. I know how you must feel about your father …"

"I don't think you know the half of it," I said.

"Maybe I don't, but this is not about him. I'm not asking you for your dad's sake. Do it for Adam's. He's innocent; I'm telling ya. He would never do any of these things. I know my grandson. He loved that girl. He was a good boy and always kind to his classmates."

"Did he have any history of mental illness?" I asked.

She shook her head. "No. Nothing of the sort. You must believe me."

I sighed and finished my beer, then put the empty bottle down. My eyes met Eileen's.

"You know … you could have looked for me," I said. "You could at least have tried."

With that, I turned my back on her and left, while mumbling, "Thanks for the beer."

Chapter Thirteen

"Hello-o-o, everybody. I'm back. Now, last time you saw me was earlier today when I took down a guy at the liquor store. Remember that? I hope you got a kick out of seeing me beat him senseless in the alley behind the dumpsters. I sure got a kick out of it; I have to say. My knuckles are still sore and swollen, look."

The man who called himself E.T. lifted his hand to the camera in front of him. It was hooked up to his computer, broadcasting everything live. Four users, Heinz45, Geogina211, superstar333, and hushnow5 were already commenting on his video, cheering him on. Now was the time for him not to disappoint them. They had come to listen to his words and to watch him as he lived out the fantasy that they could only dream about.

"I know that no one knows my name right now, but one day, I aspire to be really famous," he continued. "And this guy will help me achieve just that. Come and see."

E.T. took the camera with him toward the car parked in the garage. He opened the trunk so the viewers could better see.

"This is Jeff," he said and filmed the guy with the alligator-shaped scar. He was crying behind the gag, trying to scream, pleading for his life probably. "Jeff, say hello to everyone."

E.T. trembled with satisfaction, and he was certain his viewers did the same. The number on the computer screen of the people watching right now rose to almost a hundred, and it pleased E.T. immensely. This was what he needed to make it big. Now, he was reaching people all over the world with his achievements. It was odd how easy it was to become famous in the world today. And he hadn't reached nearly enough yet.

More came too, and soon he was closer to two hundred. E.T. filmed the guy in the trunk, placing the camera very close to him.

"There you go," he said. "Smile for the camera, Jeff. You're being watched from all over the world. They're commenting and liking this as we speak. Look, there's one guy from the Philippines, and one from India. Isn't it exciting, huh? Being seen by the entire world. Aren't you the lucky guy?"

E.T. put the camera back on the tripod, then reached down and grabbed the man with the scar by the shoulders and pulled him out of the trunk. His heavy body landed on the concrete with a loud thud. He could hear him whimpering behind the gag. The sound made him feel powerful.

More viewers had joined the broadcast, and more were commenting.

"Kill him with a hammer," hugo789 wrote. *"There's one right behind him on the wall. Take that and smash his face in while we watch."*

"I would like to see him get stabbed," IWunYu wrote.

"How about a good old-fashioned strangulation?" JulienP34, wrote. *"I always enjoy those."*

"Now, everyone, you must have patience. As most of you know, I have plans for this guy. Big plans. Plans that will put me on the map, and make people talk about me with a shiver in their voices. He's not here to just be killed savagely, even though it is tempting. No, I say you go big, or you go home. Am I right?"

The man with the scar was lying on the cement floor, whimpering behind his gag, while trying to fight the strips holding his hands. E.T. let him squirm till he got tired of watching him. He then grabbed the pliers from the shelf and turned to look at his new friend, Jeff, tapping the pliers repeatedly on the palm of his hand.

Then he squatted next to him and stroked him gently across his hair, making sure the camera captured everything. It was almost a shame. Jeff was so young and pretty still. His skin was so smooth and had no wrinkles.

At least he'd never get any.

Chapter Fourteen

"CAN I ASK YOU A QUESTION?"

I stared at the computer screen in front of me. I was scrolling through my brother's Instagram feed, trying to find anything that would give me an explanation as to why my brother would want to shoot his classmates and kill his girlfriend. A manifest, an angry post, a cry for help, anything.

But there was nothing but happy pictures of him and the girl Allyson, who they believed he had killed. He wasn't a gun lover; he wasn't angry at the world like I had expected him to be.

At least not publicly.

"Eva Rae?"

"Huh, yes, of course, you can ask me a question."

I had finally called Matt. I was sitting at the desk in the guest room where Eileen had put Sydney and me up while we were there. Sydney was reading a book while I kept going through my brother's social media accounts, tapping annoyed at the keyboard. I wanted my brother to be guilty so badly because that meant I would be off the hook; that meant I could leave here and go on hating them all for the rest of my life.

But nothing showed up, nothing. And deep down inside, I didn't believe he was guilty either. It was nagging at me.

I hated being in this house; I loathed even the smell inside of it. Because every second I spent there reminded me that I could have known these people, that these people who were supposedly my family, they didn't try to reconnect with me even though they knew perfectly well where to find me.

Three darn hours in a car was all it took. Three. That's all.

"What did you expect to find when you went up there? Why did you go?" Matt asked.

I looked up and leaned back in my chair. I was getting a little tired of this conversation.

"What do you mean? They asked me to come. David called me, and Sydney asked me too."

"But you could have told them no. If it wasn't to help them out, then why did you go? Just to look at them and let them fry in their own grease? Just to make them suffer? Or what?"

"I'm not following you," I said, even though I was. I just didn't like what he was saying. It hit a little close to home.

"I'm saying that it's not you, Eva Rae," Matt said. "I don't believe you went up there just to make them sweat, and I don't think you intend to leave them in their misery and go back to your own life. Because that is not who you are. I think you went because, deep down, you wanted to help. Because it's what you do, even if you don't feel like it, even if they make you angry beyond anything in this world, even if they hurt you, you want to help. You want to help them, Eva Rae. Besides, if it turns out that your brother didn't kill Allyson, then there's a murderer out there who did."

I exhaled and rubbed the bridge of my nose. Matt was right. Why did I keep dragging it out? If David and Eileen were right, then outside those old windows, on this forsaken island, there could be a murderer that needed to be caught.

Chapter Fifteen

THE DETECTIVE in charge of Adam's case had his office at the Nassau County Sheriff's Office in Yulee on the mainland. Sydney drove us there, while I looked at the beautiful scenery through my window. Amelia Island was a gorgeous island with lots of creeks and marshland, not to mention the beaches that seemed to have endless white sand. It was way further north than Cocoa Beach, and the winters could get cold, I was told. It wasn't at this time of year, though, so it was hard to imagine. The island was located close to Jacksonville and not far from the border to Georgia. It was about as far north as you could get in Florida, and still, it was a blazing eighty-nine degrees in October. I had dressed nicely in a black skirt and a light green button-up shirt. It wasn't how I usually dressed, but I wanted to make a good impression. I wanted to be taken seriously.

Sydney parked in front of the one-story red brick building. *Nassau County Sheriff's Office*, it said in big letters above the entrance. None of the three flags outside were moving. The wind had completely died down and made it feel even hotter.

I had called ahead and set up a meeting with Detective McMillen, and he greeted us slightly indifferently the hallway, then led us down to his office. He sat down, then folded his hands across his desk.

"And what can I do for you, Miss Thomas? Or is it Mrs.?"

"Miss," I said, feeling a stab to my heart. I still hadn't gotten used to the fact that I was divorced. I touched my finger gently where my ring used to be, then thought briefly about Matt before finding my focus once again.

"I'm here about the Clarke case, Adam Clarke."

He leaned back in his chair with an exhale. His fingers drummed on the desk. "I know who you are and what a mess you caused down in Miami a few months ago. Why are you really here? I know you left the FBI, so it's not the bureau that sent you. Are you writing a new book? I read one of your previous books; didn't find it very enlightening … basic stuff almost anyone could have written if you ask me."

Okay then.

"I just have some questions about the case," I said, doing my best not to be offended by this guy. McMillen was the type that obviously didn't think women could teach him anything.

He looked at his watch, then exhaled. "All right. I have a few minutes, but remember, it's an ongoing investigation, so there won't be much I can share."

"That's fine. I'll take what I can get. First of all, I need to know if Adam Clarke has been charged with the murder of Allyson Woodland."

"He will be. We believe the two cases are connected."

"How so?" I asked.

"Well, she was his girlfriend. She disappeared two days before he showed up at the school carrying an AK-47. He was on a killing spree. He wants to be famous like the other school shooters, or he's angry at the world or both. He kills the girlfriend first, and after that, there's no way back. Until our school resource officer, Conroy stops him and shoots him in the chest. If he hadn't been there, right on the spot, it could have ended a whole lot differently. All it takes to stop a bad guy with a gun is …"

"… a good guy with a gun. Yes, I hear that a lot around here lately," I said. "Have you confirmed that she was, in fact, murdered before Adam Clarke went to the school with his gun?"

"We haven't gotten the exact time of death yet, but we're pretty convinced she was, yes. Preliminary examination suggests she was killed the night before, but as I said, we need to wait for the ME to know for certain."

I wrote on my notepad to contact the ME office and get that as soon as possible. It would take a few days. If she had been killed before Adam went to the school, then she had been dead for more than a week, and the general rule was that the sooner after death occurs that the body is examined, the more accurate the estimate will be. There was no telling how long she had been in that dumpster since it was emptied once a week, and when she was found, it was the same day the renovation company did their rounds, I had read. She could have been in there for a week in the blazing heat, and that would speed up the decomposing of the body, making it harder to determine precisely. But in this case, it was vital to get it as accurately as possible. If she was killed later than 11:47 a.m. on October 1st, then it couldn't have been my brother since at that time he was lying on the floor of the cafeteria at his school, gunshot wound to his chest. It was as simple as that.

"And the cause of death?" I asked. "Do you have that yet?"

"We don't know that yet either. Still waiting for the autopsy to come through. Should be in in a couple of days, a week maybe."

"Any bruises? Any blunt-force trauma?" I asked.

"She was bruised up all right. He had his way with her before she died, the sick bastard. Removed all of her nails. Used some kind of tool to beat her up, which we haven't determined yet. Listen, I have work to do …"

"I'm almost done; I just need to ask you about something else," I said and looked at my notes that I had made the night before while researching the case and running through what did and what didn't make sense so far.

McMillen clicked his tongue. Sydney was waiting outside in the hallway, and he gave her a dirty look that made my skin crawl.

"Of course, you do," he said.

"There is something that has been bothering me. I spent the night researching this, and I keep coming back to the same thing."

"Of course, you did," he said, clicking his tongue again, then leaning back in his chair, placing a black shoe on top of his desk.

"In the days after she disappeared, the media printed the transcripts of several nine-one-one emergency calls coming from Allyson. According to them, she called from inside her kidnapper's house. Three times, she called and told the dispatch that she was in trouble and pleaded with them to send police to help her. This is one of the things that bothers me; there are several, actually. But first of all, she didn't know where she was; she didn't know the address. If I understand it correctly, Adam Clarke and Allyson Woodland had been dating for a year. Wouldn't she know his address?"

He shrugged. "He could have taken her somewhere else, an abandoned house somewhere out of town. We have a lot of those on the island. One of the summer cabins by the beach, maybe. Besides, he was wearing a ski mask, she also said, so maybe she didn't know it was him."

"But he took her there in his blue car, she said. Adam is fifteen; he doesn't have a car or even a license."

"He could have stolen a car. Lots of fifteen-year-olds can still drive, even without a license."

I paused, then looked up at detective McMillen. "She kept calling him a man. When she talked about who was coming for her, she specifically referred to him as a man. Not a boy."

He shrugged. "A fifteen-year-old is a man in my book, especially if he decides to kill. Then, you are no longer a child. Not where I come from."

"But don't you think she would have at least used his name?" I asked and gave him a look of distrust. This wasn't adding up. In my experience, if there were too many things that needed explaining or didn't make sense, there was something you were missing.

"When they asked her who was coming for her?" I asked, getting agitated. This guy didn't seem to care at all about the things

I pointed out. "Wouldn't she have said it was her boyfriend or called him by his name?"

McMillen looked at his watch, then sighed while rubbing his face. "He was wearing a mask."

"Still, if it was her boyfriend, she'd have known; don't you think? There are other ways of recognizing people than by their face. She would have known his hands, his stature, his eyes."

"Listen. I don't have time for this."

I rose to my feet. "It'll only be a minute. I have one final question. Let me ask you this, then I'll get out of your hair," I said. "According to the nine-one-one transcripts, you — the sheriff's office — sent out a patrol car to find her, to the address that she told dispatch on the phone. But no one ever showed up, did they? You can hear that the dispatch is frustrated and anxious because the car hasn't shown up yet when she calls the third time. The call ends when someone else is on the line, and Allyson is screaming in the background. What happened?"

"That's none of your business, lady."

"You sent it to the wrong address, didn't you? You messed up, and now you don't want the public to know. You missed your opportunity to save Allyson because you sent them to the wrong darn house. Am I right? What went wrong? Did dispatch hear it wrong? Did the deputies? Did you find the right house eventually and then it was too late? Did you trace the phone Allyson called from?"

McMillen stood to his feet. He was leaning on his knuckles on the desk, his nostrils were flaring, and he was speaking through gritted teeth.

"I don't need you to come here and tell me how to do my work. It doesn't matter that you used to be FBI. We have a way of doing things down here, and we're sticking to it. Besides, don't you think I know who you really are, and why you are really here? The boy is your brother, isn't he? Adam Clarke is your little brother. That's what I heard around the island. That's why I agreed to talk to you in the first place because I felt sorry for you and your family, but now I'm done. Please, leave my office; the door is right behind you. Please make sure it hits you on the way out. Thank you."

Chapter Sixteen

E.T. LOOKED at the redhead as she got into the car and took off. He grabbed his knife, then peeled an apple while opening his laptop and starting a search. He found thousands of articles about her that he skimmed through. He saw titles of books she had written about serial killer profiling and read through articles about the many killers she had caught while working for the FBI, based on her excellent skills as a profiler. After that, he settled on a YouTube video telling the story of her merits when taking down the domestic terrorist, the Iron Fist, responsible for three nerve gas attacks in Miami. He watched her as she spoke at a press conference, being all humble and saying that it wasn't all her doing, but also the great help she had received from Miami Dade Police and the support from the FBI.

Next, the speaker returned and spoke about how Eva Rae Thomas's own daughter had been among the kidnapped girls that were used in the attacks and how the woman, the former FBI-profiler, refused to give up in her relentless search for her, finally rescuing her from the claws of the terrorists and saving hundreds of lives in a hotel downtown, stopping a planned attack.

"A true hero, huh?" he mumbled to himself. "Coming all the way up here? For me? Now, what do ya know?"

E.T. watched a little more, then moved the cursor to speed it up, then watched the end, where you'd see Eva Rae Thomas reunited with her family. He stopped the video there. He looked closer at the three children, then at the man they said was her boyfriend, and also a detective. He placed a finger on the man's head and tried to wipe him away.

"A nice little family you have there, Eva Rae," he said as he closed the lid and took a bite of the peeled apple, slurping the juices as he ate and finished it. "Nothing more beautiful than a family, am I right? I guess since you're here anyway, you and I might as well have some fun; shouldn't we?"

With a deep sigh, E.T. turned on the camera on his phone. While recording it live for the broadcast, he rolled up the sleeve of his shirt, then lowered the knife and placed it on his skin. He closed his eyes and pressed down, carving four letters into the skin, while blood dripped onto his pants below.

Without pain, there would be no pleasure. In all pain, there is a purpose.

Chapter Seventeen

"THE CAFETERIA IS STILL CLOSED off, but the rest of the school is back to normal."

It was Mrs. Green, the principal at Fernandina Beach High School who showed me around. Sydney and I drove directly there after the sheriff's office. I had filled Sydney in on what Detective McMillen had told me and how I was beginning to get that nagging feeling inside my stomach that something was definitely off.

"So, you're saying our dad might be right?" she had asked in the car.

"I'm not sure I'd ever go that far," I said, "but I'll admit that something smells fishy."

That was why I had decided to go to the school. I needed to see for myself where Adam had shown up with the gun and started shooting. When reading the articles and watching the news broadcasts about it, I always came back to the same thing … the fact that no one was killed or even injured during the shooting. Not one single bullet hit a person. To the media, that was a miracle, and of course, due to the SRO-officer who reacted quickly. It was even used in the gun debate nationwide when discussing whether or not it was a good idea to allow the carrying of concealed weapons on school grounds. But to me, it was a mystery. If Adam fired an assault rifle into a crowd of people, how come not even a single bullet at least grazed someone?

Again, it made no sense, miracle or not.

"This door leads to the cafeteria," the principal said. She was a short woman, wearing black pants and a school team shirt. "We've kept it locked since it happened for the police investigation. We've served lunch in the media room instead, and the kids have been eating in the gymnasium or the courtyard. Many of them haven't returned yet, and we're cutting them some slack. Lots of trauma-tized kids have found it hard to return to the school at all. Can't blame them. It was quite a scare. But classes had to resume at some point, right? And lots of the kids find comfort in a return to the familiarity and controllability of their day. We've had therapists in the library for anyone who needed to cry or who was overwhelmed by uncontrollable fear."

I had told the principal a lie. I had said I was an FBI agent, and that I was looking into the case. I figured I might as well since there was no way I'd get access to the school or the students otherwise. I'd get in a lot of trouble if someone found out, but I was hoping they wouldn't. The principal had then told me that she really wished it wasn't true — that Adam was innocent.

"He is such a sweet kid. Always takes care of everyone. Espe-cially those that are needy, the ones no one else will talk to, like the Asperger's kids and the autistic kids, who often end up sitting alone. He is known to hang out with them too. He has a heart for the needy. That's why it came as a big surprise that he'd do anything like this. It's quite shocking, really. Just shows you that it could be anyone these days."

I didn't agree. A school shooter usually had a profile, and from what I had seen so far, Adam Clarke didn't match any of it.

"Do you know of any students who were close friends with Adam? I'd like to ask them a few questions as well," I asked.

· · ·

"I'LL ASK AROUND," she said. "But, as I said, many kids are heavily traumatized and don't want to talk about it."

"That's okay," I said. "No one will force them."

The principal smiled with a sad sigh. "Okay, then. I'll be right back."

The principal disappeared down the hallway. As in most Florida schools, the hallways were outside, only covered by a roof to keep the kids from getting wet when it poured during the rainy months from May to October. Even the lockers were outdoors.

I grabbed the door to the cafeteria and pushed it open. The light was turned off in there, and it smelled like day-old chicken nuggets. I turned on my flashlight that I had brought from my car, then walked in, Sydney coming up behind me.

I lifted the flashlight to shine it across the room and walked closer. I looked at the long tables and benches. I could tell the police's crime scene techs had been there, by the dust and signs with evidence numbers. I shone the flashlight toward the back wall, then to the wall to the right of me. Then to the left.

"Huh," I said.

"What?" Sydney asked. "What are we looking for?"

"According to the eyewitness accounts, Adam came in through the doors where we just entered. He stood for a few seconds as the door closed, then lifted his assault rifle and began to shoot, right?"

"Yes. That's right."

"So, he would have been standing right where you are — give or take a little."

"Probably," she said. "What are you getting at?"

"The kids were all sitting here, on the benches, eating when it happened."

"Yes?"

"So, if he shot at them, there would be bullet holes behind them on the walls, wouldn't there?"

Sydney looked where the beam of my flashlight landed on the white walls behind me.

"But there aren't," she said. "Not a single hole."

"Nope. The walls are as clean as if they had just been painted."

Sydney wrinkled her forehead. Most people would look ugly when doing that, but not Sydney. She was always so annoyingly cute to look at, while I always looked like I had just woken up with my unruly, impossible-to-control hair and pale, freckled skin.

"So, what happened do you think?"

I shone the light across the room, letting the beam slide across the walls. "Beats me. But it almost looks like no shots were fired at all, doesn't it?"

"Yet all eyewitnesses say there were."

"You're right," I said, then lifted my flashlight upward and to the right until I reached an area of the wall almost underneath the ceiling as far away from the seating area as possible.

"There you go," I said. "That's where all the bullet holes are."

"That's odd," Sydney said.

"It sure is," I said and took a picture of it.

"Why would he shoot in that direction all the way up there?" she asked. "It makes no sense."

"I know. It's a mystery," I said and took more pictures, then lowered my phone. "It's almost as if he was trying to *avoid* hitting anyone, isn't it?"

Chapter Eighteen

THEN:

"My husband? W-what ... I don't understand. Where is this coming from?"

Marlene looked at the two men in front of her. Her heart was beginning to race in her chest as the seriousness of the situation dawned on her.

It had to be a misunderstanding; didn't it?

"Have you observed any extraordinary behavior from your son recently?" the one to the right, Rivers asked.

"Extraordinary, what do you mean? He's seven years old. His behavior changes all the time."

"Let's just say in school then."

Marlene bit her lip. "Listen, I know he has been causing some trouble, but I hardly think ..."

"What kind of trouble?"

She exhaled, already getting tired of this.

"Well, I got a couple of calls this week from his teacher about his behavior," she said. "But it wasn't anything really ..."

"What did she say?"

"She asked me to come and meet with her."

"Did you go?"

"Yes, of course," Marlene said. "I wouldn't ignore a request like that. What mother would?"

"Some mothers do," the one to the left, Waltman said.

"Well, I don't. I went and I had a meeting with her, and that's it."

"What did you talk about?"

"She told me that my son had been yelling at her in class. That she had asked him to do his project, something about Henry Flagler, I don't know, but then he had responded that he wouldn't do it, and then he had left the class without saying anything about where he went. It really was no big deal."

"It says here that he uttered several disrespectful words to the teacher and any adult who tried to get him to go back to class. He seemed aggressive, and they were frightened of him."

"Yeah, well, I don't know why they'd feel that. Jack is the sweetest of kids."

"There was also a teacher who talked to you privately, wasn't there? Rivers said. His round face with a narrow set of eyes lingered on her. Marlene felt deep resentment toward them both. She felt so trapped.

"She took you aside when you came to pick up your son a few days later, right?"

Marlene sighed. What was this about? Her son using profanities in school? Hardly a crime the last time she checked.

"Yes, she said my son had said some disrespectful things to her during music class, using profane language, and that his behavior needed to change if she was to keep him in her class. I told this teacher that we were working on it with his homeroom teacher and that it was being taken care of."

"But then she said something else; didn't she?"

"Listen, if you already know all this, why do I have to repeat it?" Marlene said, raising her voice. "It's all in your papers there; isn't it? You already talked to the teachers yourselves, so why am I here?"

"Because we want to hear it from you as well," Waltman said. "Please, continue. What else did she tell you?"

Marlene sighed again and closed her eyes for a second. Her hands were beginning to get clammy, and she wiped them on her jeans. She still wondered about that chicken and whether or not it would go bad on the counter or if the dog had eaten it. What would she feed her family is she couldn't make the chicken?

She opened her eyes and looked at the two of them.

"She said that when she addressed Jack, when she tried to talk to him about his behavior, he began to cry."

"And what else?"

"And he said that he was scared he would get in trouble at home for this."

"What were his exact words?" Rivers said.

"His exact words were … my dad is probably going to beat me."

Chapter Nineteen

I MET Lauren and Chris in the media room, where Principal Green had brought them. I had sent Sydney back to the car so she wouldn't be recognized. She was wearing sunglasses and her black wig as a disguise, but I wasn't sure the young kids would be as easily fooled as the principal.

Lauren was a tall, skinny girl with brown hair and green eyes. She seemed nervous as she sat down and looked around. Chris was a small guy who was using crutches. He smiled at me pleasantly, then explained to me that he suffered from a hereditary disorder called Cutis Laxa and that it was okay to stare; he was used to it. He knew he looked peculiar.

"Adam was one of those that didn't see it. He saw me for who I was inside, without these stupid sticks," he said and came toward me, leaning on the crutches. "He could even joke about it and tell me I was just faking it, that I didn't even need them, but I refused to walk on my own because I was so lazy. He never treated me like everyone else does, like I was fragile and could break any second."

Chris went silent for a second. I sat down on a couch in a small reading corner. They both followed me.

"Tell me about Adam," I said and looked at Chris. "You were close?"

"He was … is my best friend. I keep reminding myself that he's not dead, but then again, if he wakes up, we'll probably never see him." Chris stopped himself with an exhale. It was obviously hard to talk about him.

"I feel like I should have stopped him," Lauren said. "Like I could have stopped him somehow."

"Why do you say that?" I asked.

"That's exactly how I feel too," Chris said. "That I should have seen it, seen what was going on with him somehow. Maybe I could have said something to stop him?"

"I saw the gun in his hand," Lauren said. "When he pulled it out. I could have said something. I could have stopped him. Maybe even when I saw him earlier in the morning, I could have said something to make him feel better. That's what I keep thinking in my mind. Over and over again."

"But now that they say he also killed Allyson," Chris said. "Then maybe he had just lost it, you know? He kidnapped her first and then killed her. He wasn't well."

"Why didn't we see it?" Lauren said, tears welling in her eyes. "We were his friends. We were the ones closest to him."

"You can't do that to yourself," I said. "You can't blame yourself for this. Adam made the choice to bring the gun to school. There was nothing you could have said or done to stop him. But did you sense any change in his behavior leading up to the shooting? Did anything happen in his life that might have caused him to snap?"

Chris and Lauren looked at one another, then shook their heads almost simultaneously.

"Adam was … a happy kid," Chris said. "He was always fun to be around. We'd go fishing and goof around together. He knows a guy who has a boat we can borrow from time to time. Those are some of my favorite memories with him. I didn't notice anything change in him; did you, Lauren?"

She looked at me pensively. "No. I can't think of anything."

"When did you talk to him last?" I asked.

"I saw him in the hallway on the morning before the shooting, but we didn't talk. He seemed lost in his thoughts, and I was late for class. So, it has to be on the day when Allyson disappeared," she said. "It was on a Saturday. He texted me and asked me if I wanted to go to the beach with him and Allyson. I told him I had to do my project for French class, so I didn't have time. He said they'd stay there all day and maybe make a bonfire at night. From what I heard, it turned into a party with lots of other kids from school."

"Were either of you at the party?" I asked.

They both shook their heads. Chris pointed at his crutches. "Doesn't really go well with sand. Unless someone carries me, I usually stay away from the beach."

"Of course."

"I didn't have time to go," Lauren said, "but from what I heard from others, Allyson never came home. The other kids told me she and Adam walked home together. The police later came to Adam's house, but he wasn't there. He came home early in the morning, and the police interrogated him about her disappearance, but they didn't arrest him. As far as I've heard, he told them that he had dropped Allyson off at her house and that he then walked back home. But he doesn't live that far from her, and everyone wondered what he was doing in those hours. Still, no one ever thought he could have hurt Allyson. But we didn't think he'd show up at the school and try to kill us all either."

Lauren paused to gather herself. Tears were rolling down her cheeks, and she was fiddling with her student ID card between her fingers.

"We have to make sure they are visible at all times now," she said. "So, no one from the outside can come into the school. No one dares even to go close to the cafeteria. Just a car that backfires on the street outside makes people jump inside the classrooms. We're constantly on the lookout, constantly suspicious of one another, ready to report even the smallest change in behavior. They've made a hotline for us to report suspicious behavior anonymously. It's Hell.

I still just can't find it in my heart to understand how someone like Adam could lose it like that. I thought I knew him. I've known him since Kindergarten. How did I not see this?"

Chris reached over and grabbed Lauren's hand in his. "We both thought we knew him, but we didn't."

"I just don't get it. I just don't," Lauren said, tears dripping onto her ripped black jeans. She wiped them away with the back of her hand.

"Did he have any suicidal thoughts?" I asked. "In the weeks leading up to it?"

She shook her head. "No. He never said anything about wanting to kill himself. He was always happy, you know? Always trying to make the rest of us happier too, always goofing around."

"Often, depressed people try to seem like the happiest," Chris said.

"But he loved Allyson," Lauren said. "It makes no sense to kill her. I just don't get it."

"None of us do. I mean the guy didn't even like guns. He hated them, and I don't understand how he got ahold of an AK-47," Chris said and looked into my eyes. He seemed confused, frustrated even. I sensed he too doubted Adam's guilt deep down. He was struggling with it because common sense told him it was foolish. He had seen Adam with the gun; he had heard the shots and felt the fear in his chest.

"Tell me about the morning in the cafeteria," I said addressed to Lauren.

"I was eating my lunch, wondering where he was," she said with a sob, "when the door opened, and he stepped inside. I was so happy because I thought he'd come sit with us, but then I saw it; I saw the gun, and next thing I knew, he lifted it, closed his eyes, and began to shoot."

I leaned forward. "He did what?"

"He began to shoot," she repeated.

"No, the thing you said before that. You said he closed his eyes?"

She sniffled and nodded. "Yes. That's the last thing I remember.

Next thing, I'm screaming because Adam is on the floor, shot by Officer Conroy. It all went by really fast."

"But you say he closed his eyes before he started to shoot?" I asked. "You're certain of that?"

She thought it over for a second, then nodded.

"Yes. I'm sure."

Chapter Twenty

"HE CLOSED HIS EYES. Can you believe it?"

I was speaking with my mouth full. Sydney and I had driven to downtown Fernandina Beach and found a place with views over the Intracoastal waters where they served fish burgers.

"I mean that doesn't sound like someone who wanted to kill a lot of people, does it? If you want to kill people, you look at where you shoot. That's pretty basic. It sounds more like he was scared."

"It also explains why he didn't hit anyone if he didn't aim," she said and grabbed a fry. She looked at it, turning it in the light. "You know I actually used to eat really healthy. Lots of greens and smoothies keeping myself slim and my skin radiant. Since you came back into my life, I've been eating so unhealthily; I'm not sure I'll ever get another movie … looking like this."

"Ah, come on, you look amazing," I said and took another bite of my burger, grinning. "Just admit that you like it."

"I'm afraid I do," she said and ate the fry, then reached for another one. "So, what are you saying with all this?"

"I don't know," I said and stopped chewing. "But something is off. Adam didn't bring that gun to kill people; that's for sure."

"Could he have regretted his intentions in the last minute? Been unable to follow through with it after all?"

"That's one theory," I said and sipped my Coke. "But there's also the thing about him not fitting the profile of a school shooter at all. No suicidal thoughts, no obsession with guns, no mental health concerns, no signs of depression, or even anxiety. There was no identifiable crisis in the weeks or months leading up to the shooting."

"We don't know if he had a crisis with Allyson," Sydney said. "She might have broken up with him that night when he walked her home, and after that, he could have snapped."

"Fair enough," I said. "That's true. But usually, it takes time to plan for this type of event. They don't just wake up one morning and decide to do it. It is known that most school shooters have studied the actions of other shooters and sought validation for their motives. There was no fascination with mass shootings. I've gone through his Internet history on his computer and social media. There's nothing there to indicate he was obsessed with other school shooters, and he didn't frequent online fora that talked about these things like most other school shooters have. That's the thing about school shootings; they tend to come in clusters. They are socially contagious. Perpetrators study other perpetrators and model their acts after other shootings. And they usually do it online in their search for validation from others that their will to murder is justified. They are often suicidal and decide that life is no longer worth living and that murdering others would be a proper way to go, and at the same time get their revenge and become famous, be somebody. Often, their crisis is well known to their friends and family before they perform their act. You often hear people say afterward, *I knew something was wrong, that something was off, but I didn't do anything.* These kids and his parents all say it was a total surprise. They still struggle to believe he really did it, even though they saw him pull out the gun. And you want to know why? Because he never intended to shoot anyone. He came in, lifted the gun and closed his eyes, then shot right under the ceiling until someone stopped him like he knew they would. I want to know why he did what he did. I think our brother is a victim here, and it's related to Allyson's murder. I just have no idea how to prove it."

"It sounds like crazy talk," my sister said and finished her burger with a satisfied sigh. For years, she hadn't been able to eat food like this, and even though I envied her for her good looks and complexion, I could never live the way she did.

"It *is* crazy talk," I said. "But there is something here; I just know there is. And I intend to get to the bottom of this, no matter what."

Sydney smiled. "I love a good crazy talk, especially when it comes from you. Count me in."

Chapter Twenty-One

"Hush now, baby; don't you worry about a thing. Momma is here."

E.T. crawled closer to her body and put her arm around him, spooning in the bed. He was supposed to sleep, but couldn't find rest. His arm was still hurting from where he had cut himself. The skin was swollen where the knife had gone through the skin. The four letters stared back at him, reminding him forever never to forget:

LOVE

E.T. ran a finger across the cuts while humming to himself. He thought about Eva Rae Thomas and fantasized about her. At first, it had scared him a little that she had shown up in town, especially when he found out who she was and that she was known to have taken down some of the biggest murderers in the history of the country. But then he felt kind of flattered.

Had she come here for him? To chase him?

The more he thought about it, the more he realized that she was only going to make everything so much more spectacular. Her chasing him could end up making headlines like it had down in Miami. He would be famous. He'd finally be a somebody. They'd talk about him with awe and shake their heads in fear like they did when talking about the Iron Fist. People would fear him. They'd shiver when mentioning his name. Others would be inspired by him. They'd study him and his methods for years, then try and do the same. Books might be written about him, maybe even one by Eva Rae Thomas herself? Like the ones he had found online that she had written about the worst serial killers, those that were so gruesome that they made your skin crawl.

Just like those.

E.T. wanted to be just like them. Just as big. And Eva Rae Thomas could definitely help him achieve that goal.

Yes, her coming to the island did speak to his advantage. To be honest, he couldn't have scripted it better himself. It would be like in those cartoons where the cat chased the mouse, but never got him. She would force him to be the best — or worst, depending on how you looked at it — version of himself that he could be. She would force him to push himself to new heights, to go where no one else dared to go.

He was in the big leagues now.

Chapter Twenty-Two

"IT DOES SOUND like crazy talk to me, to be honest, Eva Rae."

Matt stared at his screen. He was sitting at his desk in an almost empty room at the station. He was only halfway done with his report while everyone else had left for the day.

He had been on call last night when a drunk tourist had decided he had enough and beat up his wife right outside of Coconuts on the Beach. Other tourists had taken photos as evidence and called for CBPD. They had arrived just in time as the perpetrator decided to make a run for it, and they had chased him down. He had spent the night in a cell, and Matt and his colleagues had spent the entire day interviewing witnesses and the man himself. The wife was in the hospital and would have to stay there for a few days, they said, to recover from her bruises and a concussion. Her eyes were swollen, and her lips cracked. She was visibly shaken up and scared when Matt spoke to her earlier.

Of course, it wasn't the first time her husband had done this. Hopefully, it would be the last.

Matt felt good about taking him in and nailing him for what he did. There was nothing worse in this world than a wife-beater in

Matt's opinion. They were the scum of the earth. No, worse. They were the parasites that lived on the scum.

As he was in the middle of writing his report on the incident, Eva Rae had called him. Hearing her voice was just what he needed right now, and he had listened carefully as she had told him all about her day and how she had looked into her brother's case and how she believed her father might be right after all, that maybe Adam was innocent. Maybe something else was going on.

"Hey, you were the one who told me to look at it," she said. "Don't you tell me it sounds crazy. I know perfectly well how it sounds, but that's not gonna stop me from taking a closer look."

"I know," he answered. "I know that very well, indeed. So, how are you going to approach it?"

"I don't know yet, or … well … that's not entirely true. I do have one idea," she said, then stopped.

He imagined her biting her lip like she often did when she was pensive.

Gosh, I miss you, Eva Rae. Why are we always apart?

"Of course, you do."

"But it involves you," she said cautiously. "It involves you doing something for me. Do you think you can do that?"

He leaned back in his office chair with an exhale. Was that the only reason she had called him? Because she needed his help? It had been like this a lot lately, that he felt like she was always too busy for him or always too occupied with some case to be with him, to have time for him. Every time he went to her house, there were always so many people that she barely had time for him. There was always a kid who needed something or her mother or her sister who needed her. Or Chad would be there because of the kids, always butting into their conversation or getting in Matt's way.

When was there going to be time for them to be a couple?

I need you too, Eva Rae.

"All right," he said. "You know I can't say no to you. What is it?"

Chapter Twenty-Three

THEY WERE SCREAMING in the hotel lobby.

"We did it. I can't believe we did it!"

George Reed put his arms around Liam Bell, his partner through the past fifteen years. When he let go, he had tears in his eyes ... tears of happiness.

"Can you believe it, old buddy? We finally did it. We've dreamed about this for how long? Five years? Ten years? Heck, I don't even remember anymore. But now, we've finally done it."

"It is truly amazing," Liam said. "I can hardly believe it. I mean, is this really happening? Did we just do this? Am I dreaming?"

"If you are, my friend, then please don't wake me up," George laughed.

George kept his arms around Liam's neck as he looked at the others in their group. They had all been with the company for years; they too, had fought to make this happen. They too were smiling, their eyes moist, while patting each other's backs.

"This calls for some champagne," George said and looked around him to spot a waiter.

The ground floor of the Ritz-Carlton Hotel had spectacular views over the Atlantic Ocean from all sides. There was a bar and lots of small sitting areas where you could enjoy a drink and maybe a snack. George's hands were still shaking. They had been like that since he woke up this same morning on the eighth floor, but most of all when he had to hold the pen and sign the contract, selling the company he and Liam had spent the past fifteen years building.

Now it was done. And they were billionaires.

He never had to work a day in his life again. He could buy a house in Aruba and stay there, drinking, partying, and hooking up with beautiful, well-shaped women who would only want him for his money. He could buy anything he wanted in this world, anything. The thought was beyond intoxicating.

George had given up everything for this company and lost a lot along the way. After seven years, his wife had taken the kids and left, unable to take it anymore. His long work hours, often never coming home even to sleep, the partying when something succeeded, the gloomy mood when it didn't … Fact was, George was never home; even when he was, he was never really there. He was still at the office, still working on new ways to solve this problem or that. Never participating in the daily routines of his family, never enough.

It had broken his heart when she left. But by then, it was too late. He couldn't fix it, even though he tried with promises they both knew he couldn't keep. It was a shock for him the day she packed her bags and took the kids to her mother's. He had somehow believed he could make it up to her in time, once it was all over, on the day when they finally made it, and he would be a billionaire. Then, everything would be good, and he would have all the time in the world for her and the children.

But she couldn't wait that long.

"Life is more than money, George," were her last words to him when she left.

George sighed deeply and felt a pinch in his stomach. If only Emily could have been there now to see him triumph, to celebrate with him.

"Waiter, six bottles of your most expensive champagne!"

Three waiters rushed to them with glasses and bottles. They

handed George one of the bottles, and he got to open it. When the cork hit the ceiling, they all yelled with excitement.

"Twenty-four billion dollars!"

The champagne was poured, and they clinked glasses while yelling with excitement and laughter. When the six bottles were empty, they bought six more, and then six more. They paid the waiters to keep people out of the bar area downstairs of the hotel and partied all night, cranking up the music and drowning themselves in the delicious and dangerously alluring bubbles.

At first, when they saw Liam sitting in the soft chair in the corner, his head slumped, white foam dripping onto his suit, they naturally thought he was just sleeping, that he'd drunk too much like they all had. After all, Liam had always had a harder time holding his liquor than the rest of them. But when someone touched him and he fell forward, his body thudding onto the tiles, lifeless, they knew something was awfully wrong. Especially George, who felt his heart rate go up so rapidly it soon made him dizzy. He reached over to grab for something to hold onto, a chair or a table but missed it by an inch. Soon, he too tumbled to the tiles, his heart beating so fast it felt like it would never stop.

Until it did.

Chapter Twenty-Four

THEN:

"What we're trying to do next is to establish what part you played in the abuse," Rivers said after clearing his throat. Someone had brought water into the interrogation room, and Marlene had drunk greedily like she was trying to wash this nightmare away.

"Abuse? What are you talking about abuse? What are you basing this on? Because our son said those things to his teacher? Because he said his dad would beat him? So what if she said that; he never did. Bruce never touched him. I don't even know why you'd think that just because of what he told some teacher. He might have been joking or maybe looking for attention. Kids do that."

"We'll be the judge of that. You're here to answer our questions, and we ask that you do just that."

This can't be happening. This can't be true. What am I going to do? How am I going to convince them that this isn't true?

Marlene's eyes met Rivers'. She'd have to be careful in choosing her words; anything could be used against her right now. She'd have to make sure that what she said couldn't be misinterpreted. Apparently, she was under accusation as well. It was all so ridiculous that she felt like laughing. Except it wasn't funny. Nothing about this was remotely amusing. How dare they accuse her and her husband of this? Where did they come off?

"Did you see the bruises? Did you notice the signs? Did you close your eyes, or did you participate?" Waltman said.

"Participate?" Marlene spat. "What are you saying with this? Now, wait a minute; I'm a good mother. I'll have you know ..."

"Most mothers would say that," Waltman said, interrupting her.

Marlene tightened her lips. It really didn't matter what she said, did it? They had already determined that she was guilty.

"But I am," she said with a snort. "I am a good mother. And Bruce is a good father who would never lay a hand on our son. Ask anyone who knows us. They'll testify that we are the most devoted parents in the neighborhood. No one does more for their kid than us."

"Okay, so if you're such a good mother, then you must have noticed the bruises," Rivers said, fiddling with the papers next to him. He pulled a sheet out, then looked up at her above his glasses, lifting both eyebrows.

"What bruises?" Marlene asked, confused.

Then, she remembered. There had been bruises in the fall, but it wasn't what they thought it was. She felt a sudden relief. Was that what this was all about? Now, she understood. This was all just a misunderstanding.

"You mean the ones on his back? Yes, I remember those. He got them when he was climbing the tree in the backyard. We have a big magnolia tree that he's always climbing around in, and yes, he fell from it in the fall and had a very bad bruise on his back. He's had a couple of falls like that, and yes it gives him bruises from time to time. Besides, he bruises easily. I know it sounds like a dumb excuse, but he really does."

Rivers placed the sheet in front of her. It was a very close-up photo of a deep purple bruise.

"Like these?" he asked, then placed another photo in front of her and pushed it closer. "Or these?"

Marlene stared at the photos, her heart pounding in her chest. "Where did you get these? Listen, I know what this looks like, but

I'm telling you, it's just from playing in the backyard. This one was the one on his back, the one I told you about. He fell from the tree; I specifically remember that happening."

"Did you see him fall?" Waltman asked.

"Excuse me?"

"Did you see him fall from the tree?" he repeated.

Marlene felt the blood drain from her face. "I ... I ... no. I was in the kitchen when it happened. He was outside playing."

"And where was his dad at the time?" Rivers asked. "When it happened?"

"I ... I ... I don't know, probably doing yard work."

Rivers gave her a serious look, then wrote something on his notepad. Marlene felt like she couldn't breathe.

"What are you scribbling there? Please don't assume that just because he was out there at the same time, that ... oh, no, please, that's rich."

Waltman pointed at the second photo, ignoring Marlene's protests. "And this one, how did he get that on his thigh?"

Marlene sighed. "That's from his bike; I'm pretty sure. Yes. I remember now; he fell on his bike."

"And did you see him fall?"

Marlene looked at him, her lips quivering. She was searching for words, for anything she could say to make them change their minds, but there really weren't any. She could hardly lie to them. But telling them the truth would only make matters worse. She knew what it looked like. She knew what they were thinking, and every time she spoke, she seemed to make matters worse.

"Please, answer the question," Rivers said. "Did you see your son fall on his bike?"

She shook her head in desperation. "No. No, I didn't. I didn't see him fall from the tree or on the bike since I'm not outside with him usually when he's playing. I have to cook and clean and ... there's also the laundry ..."

"But your husband was there, am I correct?" Waltman asked. "He was with Jack when he got that bruise as well."

"I ... I ... yes, he usually looks after Jack when he plays outside.

He gets some yard work done, or they build stuff together sometimes while I take care of the house."

"And how often would you think that Jack comes in with bruises after being left alone with his father?" Rivers asked.

Marlene's eyes grew wide. How could she possibly answer such a question?

"I ... I don't know," she said. "They're boys; they get wild."

"So often, is that your answer?" Rivers said.

"I ... I guess."

Marlene felt her shoulders slump as she watched Rivers scribble more on his notepad. Her stomach was in knots, and she felt like crying, but she knew it wouldn't do her any good. She was stuck here, and there was nothing she could say or do to make them understand that they had the wrong parents. They weren't that kind of parents, and her husband most certainly wasn't that kind of a man.

Right?

Chapter Twenty-Five

"I've DECIDED to help you out. Well, not you, but Adam. I think you might have been right when you said that he would never hurt anyone."

I stared at David, who was lying on the couch back at my grandmother's house. His eyes were red-rimmed; he had been crying. He sat up straight.

"But I'm not doing it for your sake," I repeated, making sure he got that part down. "Just so we make that clear."

David swallowed, then nodded, his nervous eyes looking up at me. He spoke in nearly a whisper.

"Thank you."

"And just so you know, I'm risking a lot by doing this. I could get in a lot of trouble for what I did today, just so you know."

I bit my lip, trying hard to swallow my anger and not show it. Just looking at him made me want to scream.

Did he even know how much damage he had caused; how much he had hurt me by what he had done? Did he even realize that?

"Okay," he said. "Thank you, sweetheart."

I shook my head. "Uh-uh. You don't get to call me that."

He shook his head. "I'm sorry. I keep doing it. I'm so sorry."

I swallowed the knot forming in my throat. "Okay, then."

I was about to walk away when he stopped me.

"How are you?"

I turned on my heel and stared at him, clenching both my fists so hard my nails dug into my palms.

"You don't get to ask me how I feel; do you understand? You left me when I was a child and took my sister from me. You don't get to pretend to be a father; do you read me?" I hissed, my blood boiling.

"But I am your father," he said.

I felt like I was standing in front of one of my children, talking back to me or misbehaving terribly. It was the same kind of anger that welled up in me.

And then some.

"No, you're not. You never will be. You left, remember? You left me. You didn't even try to contact me."

"Is that what your mom has told you?" he asked.

I was fighting my tears now. I wasn't going to give him the plea-sure of seeing me cry, and I pushed them back with all the strength I could muster.

"Because it's not true," he continued. "I wrote to you. In the beginning, I wrote every month, but when I didn't hear anything back, it became less and less until it was only on your birthdays. But I take it she never gave them to you. I figured as much."

I stared at him, my blood still boiling, but now feeling slightly calmer. A deep confusion was beginning to take over. Had my mother really hidden those letters from me? It did sound like some-thing she would do, but still.

"That doesn't change anything," I said. "You still came here fifteen years ago and didn't even try to find me."

David shook his head with a sniffle. "When I came back to the States, I looked for you and found you up in Washington. I followed your career closely and told myself I'd contact you, but I was scared. I knew your mother had poisoned you against me, just like I did to Sydney because I didn't want her to want to go back. I changed her name and gave her an entirely new life in London, thinking she'd forget about her mother and sister, but she never did. I'm not proud of it, but once she started to talk about going back after she had grown up and moved out and begun her career, I refused to tell her where to find you and your mother. It's not my proudest moment, but I was scared. I was scared of losing her, and then I did just that. I know now that it was a mistake."

This was all a little too much for me. I was fighting to breathe. I felt dizzy and had to lean against the back of the couch so I wouldn't fall.

"Are you okay?" he asked and got up.

I lifted my hand to stop him. "Don't come near me; you hear? Don't you dare touch me. I don't need anything from you. I've done fine without you in my life so far. I am not going to change that, no matter what excuses you might come up with. It's too late, David. That ship has sailed."

And with that, I turned around and stormed out of the living room. I ran out to the porch and stood for a few seconds, catching my breath when about ten police cruisers from the sheriff's office rushed past, sirens blaring.

Chapter Twenty-Six

E.T. STARED at the three dead bodies in the sitting area of the bar. The area was crawling with uniforms and serious faces, and he was secretly filming it with his phone without anyone noticing.

For his fans. His devoted fans.

The ones that were still alive when the paramedics came had been sent away in ambulances, while the ones that were dead were still on the tiles. A crime scene photographer took pictures and video of the scene and the bodies while a detective took the witnesses' statements.

Three dead wasn't half bad, but he still hoped more would join them. Hopefully, they'd die in the ambulance or maybe at the hospital. If E.T. were ever to make it to the heights of Eva Rae Thomas's former targets, or any of the really big ones in history, then he needed the numbers to be significant.

Ted Bundy killed thirty women ... that he confessed to. It might even be more, they say. But the most prolific modern serial killer, Harold Shipman, killed two hundred and eighteen that they know of. They assume the number goes as high as two hundred and fifty.

E.T. could only hope he'd get anywhere near those numbers.

But that didn't mean he wasn't going to try. He wanted to be the biggest. He wanted to be the best. And this was only the beginning.

E.T. slipped out of the room and found a bathroom. He closed the door behind him, then looked at his face in the mirror. He was sweating heavily with excitement. The saggy skin underneath his chin dangled when he splashed water on his face and reminded him that his time here on Earth was limited.

He then pulled out his pocketknife and opened the blade. He opened the camera on his phone, then rolled up the sleeve on his other arm and started to carve. Blood dripped from his skin into the sink as the letters were shaped and a word emerged.

JOY

Chapter Twenty-Seven

"WHAT'S GOING ON?"

Sydney had come down from the room we shared upstairs where she had been reading most of the evening. I was still out on the porch when she came out into the damp, hot night. I was staring in the direction where all the fire trucks, ambulances, and police cars had gone. I could see their lights in the distance, illuminating the palm trees with red and blue colors.

"I don't know," I said, "but with this many police cars, it can't be good."

"It looks like it's up by the beach by all the big condominiums and hotels. Do you want to go check it out?" she asked.

She didn't have to say that twice. We got into my minivan and drove up the long road toward the beach, where the trees with their Spanish moss dangling from the branches covered the roads, making it feel like we were driving in a tunnel. During the daytime, I found it charming, but I had to admit that at night, when it was dark, it became a little spooky, especially when we were going toward the blinking lights.

"It looks like it's at the Ritz-Carlton," Sydney said and pointed as we neared the big hotel's entrance.

I continued up toward the huge building, then stopped when we reached the police barrier. I parked, and we both got out, joining the crowd of people who were standing there, watching.

"What's going on?" I asked the valet parking guy. His name tag said, Phil. He looked pale and shaken up.

"Ten guys were celebrating some big deal they had made in the bar downstairs when suddenly they got sick, and several of them died, right there on the spot. They say they're still in there, on the floor.

"Oh, my," Sydney said.

"A lot of them were taken away in ambulances," he said. "I saw one of them. He was completely lifeless. He just lay there on the stretcher while they rushed him into the back of the ambulance."

"Do they know what happened?" I asked.

Phil shook his head while biting his nails. "Who knows? Food poisoning, maybe?"

I looked at the entrance where I spotted Detective McMillen coming out, flanked by a uniformed police officer. They chatted seriously before McMillen walked away.

"McMillen?" I yelled and waved.

He stopped when hearing his name, then gave me an indifferent chuckle. "Miss Thomas. What are you doing here? Snooping around?"

I shrugged. "Maybe. What's going on?"

"Food poisoning," he said.

"But several are dead?" I asked. "What kind of food poisoning kills people instantly?"

"The dangerous kind," he said. "Now, I have to go. Kind of busy around here."

"You're bleeding, Detective," I said and pointed at his sleeve.

He looked down. "Oh, that, no, that's not mine. One of the victims threw up blood on me."

"What are their chances of making it?" I asked.

"I don't know yet, little Miss Nosy; I'm not a doctor. Now, if you'll excuse me, I should be going. And by the way, please stop going around pretending to be an FBI agent when you aren't. You quit, remember?"

Chapter Twenty-Eight

"*WHAT WAS SUPPOSED to be a joyous occasion ended tragically last night when at least five people died after celebrating here at the Ritz-Carlton Hotel on Amelia Island behind me. The group was celebrating after finalizing a deal selling their company for twenty-four billion dollars when they became suddenly ill and started to drop like flies. The police still don't quite know what killed the five people and sent five more to the hospital, where they are still in critical condition. Food poisoning, they suspect, I was told when I spoke to Sheriff Evans earlier. He also added that it needs further investigating before they can say anything for certain. Back to you, John.*"

I stared at the TV screen in my grandmother's kitchen while she was making bacon and scrambled eggs for me. I had just gotten off the phone with the kids who were — once again — fighting about who should take care of the bunnies, and I had ended up telling them they'd have to figure out a schedule with their dad, and then stick to it. I was getting sick of this discussion, to put it mildly. It was ruining every chat I had with them on the phone, and I hated that. It wasn't like I got to talk to them a lot these days. I missed them like crazy.

"Awful story," Eileen said and served me a plate. "All those people getting sick from some food, was it?"

"Maybe," I said pensively and drank my coffee, holding the cup tightly between my hands. Sydney was still upstairs in the shower. It always took her forever to get ready, and I had to wait to take my shower until she was done. She wasn't used to living in an ordinary house and having to share a shower with others; it was obvious. And she always believed she had to look so perfect, even just for coming down to breakfast with her family. I told her she didn't need to wear impeccable makeup or have her hair completely straightened or in perfect curls. I never did any of that, and my hair was fine. It was a little bit of both … curly and straight at the same time … and it worked great for me.

At least, I thought so.

When are we going home from this place? I miss my children and my love.

David had left early for the hospital, and Eileen was going out there soon too. Adam's condition was status quo they said. There was still swelling, and that was why he wouldn't wake up. I prayed that he would soon. Then he could tell us what really happened on that day when he was shot.

But of course, it wasn't going to be that easy. Nothing ever was. At least, not in my experience.

My phone vibrated in my pocket, and I picked it up. It was Matt. I smiled, then rushed to the living room, holding it against my ear, then sat down by my laptop.

"Just the guy I was hoping to hear from," I said and tapped my keyboard to wake it up.

"Hi there beautiful. Nice to hear that I'm wanted."

I exhaled. "You're always wanted, baby; you know that. And missed. I miss you like crazy. I just want to get to the bottom of this strange case and then get back home to you. I can't wait to be with you again."

He sighed. "I miss you too. A lot."

"Did you get me what I need?"

"Yes. Check your email. It should all be there. Now remember, no one can know that I shared these documents with you, or I'll be in trouble too."

"What do you mean too? I'm not in trouble," I said. "At least not yet."

He chuckled, but it sounded a little strained. I knew that this brought back some terrible memories from this summer when I was in Miami. It had to be unpleasant for him. I was gone for three months, and he didn't hear anything from me. I know he worried, and it was unbearable. Was I asking him to do the same thing again? Had this become some sort of pattern in my life?

"It's not gonna be Miami all over again," I said. "I promise it won't."

"I sure hope not," he said.

"I just ... well, I can't just leave this alone. Not when I know something is going on that no one else sees."

"What do you mean?"

"Well ... did you hear what happened at the Ritz-Carlton?" I asked. "Last night?"

"Vaguely. Chief Annie briefed us on it this morning. Said we should look out for similar symptoms and react fast if we hear of something that looks like it. Food poisoning, they said it was?"

"That's what they're calling it, yes, but I'm not so sure. I mean something seems off with that too. Don't you think?"

"How so?"

"Usually, you get sick from food poisoning and throw up or something like that. You don't suffer instant heart failure."

"If you have a weak heart, maybe, or another previous condi- tion," he said.

"True, but three of them died instantly. Three, Matt. That's a lot of people. Two died in the hospital, and they fear more will follow. It's just ..."

"What?" he asked. "What is it?"

"Coincidental."

"So?"

"You know I don't believe in coincidences. It feels fishy."

"Oh, well, by all means, we should stop the presses. Eva Rae thinks it feels fishy," he said. He tried to sound like he was joking, but I heard the seriousness in his voice. A joke wasn't always just that. Especially not when it contained sarcasm. And Matt usually never used sarcasm. It hurt me slightly.

"I mean it, Matt. Five people don't just die like that. Something is going on. Just like something is off with Allyson's murder and my brother's case."

"So, now you think that someone murdered them? The five men at the hotel?" Matt asked. He sounded like it was the most preposterous thing he had ever heard. This wasn't how Matt usually talked to me. Had I made him mad somehow?

Maybe, but I didn't have time to deal with him right now.

"Listen, thanks for the email. I'll go check it out now, and then we'll talk later, okay?"

I hung up before he could protest. I simply didn't want to talk to him anymore. I was afraid of saying something I might regret later. I was sick of continually hurting everyone around me. It was like it was all I could do lately.

Chapter Twenty-Nine

"You're such an idiot, Matt!"

Matt slammed his hand onto his desk in frustration, then pinched the bridge of his nose and closed his eyes.

Why had he acted that way when talking to Eva Rae? Now that she finally called and wanted to chat, he had hurt her by not believing her?

Not smart, Matt. Not very smart.

It wasn't that he didn't believe her; it was just that he had gotten so annoyed with her and was resenting her priorities. The past couple of days, he had been so angry at her for leaving him again, feeling like it was Miami all over again. But it wasn't. This time, she was actually calling him, and she had only been gone a few days. It wasn't going to last three months this time, and she wasn't going to put herself in that type of danger again.

Still, he couldn't help himself. He worried about her and what she was up to now. If there was a killer on Amelia Island, then he was a clever one, and going up against him would be a huge risk.

Still, you can't just close your eyes and not do anything when suspecting a crime has been committed. That's how Eva Rae thinks, and you do too, remember?

"You have a visitor."

Matt looked up and spotted Sgt. Mason.

"Excuse me?"

"At the front desk. Some guy was asking for you."

"Really?" Matt asked as he rose to his feet and walked to the front desk. When he saw Chad waiting out there, he almost turned around and went back, but then decided against it. What if it was important? What if it had to do with Eva Rae?

"Chad, to what do I owe the pleasure?" Matt said and reached out his hand toward him.

Chad took it, and they shook, holding each other a little too tight, flexing their muscles.

Gosh, we are such clichés. It's a wonder any woman can ever love us.

"Hi, buddy," Chad said as their hands parted.

"What can I do for you?"

"I wanted to ask for your help with something," he said.

"Me? Like what?"

"Well, the thing is, the kids miss their mother terribly, and so I … well, I want to take them up there this weekend. To Amelia Island. They have Monday off, so it's a long weekend, and I thought we could surprise their mother with a visit since it doesn't seem like she'll be coming home anytime soon. And I was just wondering since Eva Rae's mother is going to be out of town too, if you could feed the children's bunnies for them?"

Matt stared at the man in front of him, blinking.

Feed the bunnies? Feed the bunnies while you go and be with my girlfriend? Feed the bunnies, while you're off to do the one thing I want to do?

Oh, no, you don't.

"I would," he said, rubbing his forehead, "but I've kind of planned to go up there myself. I have a few days off and wanted to spend them with Eva Rae. Maybe explore Amelia Island with her, if you know what I mean."

Chad looked surprised. "Oh, really? Oh, I didn't know. Eva Rae didn't mention it when I spoke to her this morning."

"Yeah, well, I wanted to surprise her too. You know, be a little romantic. So sorry, *buddy*. You'll have to find someone else to feed those bunnies."

Matt patted Chad amicably on the shoulder, then turned around and left, the rush of victory running through him. At least until he realized he'd have to start begging Chief Annie for the weekend off.

Chapter Thirty

I HAD ASKED Matt to help me get access to the police report from Nassau County Sheriff's Office from the day when my brother walked into Fernandina Beach High School with a gun in his hand.

I clicked the email, still feeling frustrated with Matt and battling with my own nagging sense of guilt. I hated being away from him like this again. It wasn't fair to him or to us. But then again, he was the one who told me to look into the case; he was the one who encouraged me to do something about it, to try and help my brother if I could. Why was he suddenly angry that I actually did it?

He misses you, and you miss him.

I guess I could understand him. It just felt it so frustrating that he took it out on me. What was I supposed to do? Not go see my brother when my dad called? Not listen to my gut instinct and take a closer look at his case when they begged me to? Of course, he knew that I had no other choice, and that was why he was so frustrated. Because he had no right to be angry about it. Because he had encouraged me, and now, he couldn't be the one to tell me it was a bad idea just because he felt it was harming our relationship.

Why did everything have to be so complicated?

I sighed and clicked to open the report. I opened a document and read through it, skimmed the areas that I already knew, then read a couple of eye-witness reports. I read Lauren's and Chris's testimonies and felt my heart drop for them both. It had to be tough to go through, seeing your best friend do something so awful. Both of them kept saying that they didn't understand, and it was noted in a side remark on Lauren's file that she was visibly in shock.

"Poor kids," I mumbled, then looked at my brother's picture on the shelf above the fireplace. He was posing with our dad, David, by a lake, holding up a big fish that he had caught, smiling from ear to ear.

"You had everything," I said to the photo. "A father who loved you, a girlfriend, good grades, friends who adored you. You were doing so well. Why would you destroy that? What on this Earth, what evil, could make you ruin everything?"

I turned my eyes back to the screen, then opened the pictures taken at the scene. I scrolled through most of them. But then I spotted something that made me stop. I stared at the picture for a few minutes while my mind kept spinning.

Was this important? Somehow, it seemed to be.

"What are you looking at?"

It was Sydney. She had made herself a green smoothie and was holding it in her hand. Her hair was still wet from the shower. I stared at the drink in her hand, then pulled my face into a smile.

"Back on the wagon, huh?"

"Yeah, well, laugh all you want to. I'm gonna try and get back in shape. I have to do something. I'll start running again tomorrow as well. They have great beaches here for just that. It'll be good for me. Plus, my agent called. He has a part for me that they think I'll be perfect for. It's been a while, you know, since my last big movie. I fear that I'm getting too old for them, and they're starting to bypass me for the younger girls out there. Younger and prettier. It's a tough competition, you know. Especially when you're past forty-five like me. I gotta be in better shape than the younger girls, or they won't cast me. We start shooting three weeks from now, so I'll have time to get healthy, at least a little bit. The thing is, she's at least ten years younger than me, the character I'm playing and well … I have to look younger than I am. Fun." She lifted the glass to salute me, then drank.

I chuckled and shook my head. "I don't know how you put up with it. I couldn't do it. I wouldn't last two days in that industry." I said the last part while pulling my belly fat on the sides.

"You could get in shape with me. It would be fun; we could do it together like a sisterhood thing," Sydney said.

I gave her a look, lifting my eyebrows. "Just when I thought you knew me so well. But to answer your first question, I'm looking through pictures from the evidence found on the day that Adam was shot."

She took another sip of her drink and grimaced. "Gosh, I hate this stuff. Who loves kale? Seriously?"

"Look at this," I said and pointed at the screen. "I want you to see this. I have a feeling it's important."

"What is it?"

"According to the report, it was found clutched in Adam's hand when he was shot."

Sydney came closer, squinting her eyes. "It's Allyson, right? I recognize the long brown hair and the eyes."

I nodded. "It's a picture of Allyson when she was a little younger, I think. But you can tell he's been squeezing it tightly in his hand. I want to know why he did that. Why did he carry that picture with him on the day he was shot?"

Sydney pointed at the next photo. "And what is that then?"

"It says here that it is something that was written on the back of the photo. You know on the backside."

"What does it say?" she asked and put her drink down on the table. I had a feeling she wasn't going to finish it.

"SYLM."

Sydney wrinkled her forehead. "That's an odd thing, isn't it? Why was that written on the back of it? What does it mean?"

I shrugged. "Who knows? But I'm thinking it must be important since he was holding it clutched in the palm of his hand. And I kind of want to know what it means. Now, the police think he was carrying the picture because she broke up with him. They believe that is why he killed her and then went berserk at the school afterward."

Sydney shrugged. "That is the logical conclusion."

"Exactly," I said and grabbed my phone. "Let's go."

"But ... where are we going?"

"You'll see. Come."

Chapter Thirty-One

I DROVE the minivan up to the front office and got out. Sydney was wearing her disguise, the wig and sunglasses, as always, and walked inside with me. At the front desk, I spoke to the same woman I had the last time I was there.

"I need to speak to Lauren Simmons," I said.

The woman stared at me like I had told her I was visiting from the moon. "I'm sorry," she said. "I can't let you ..."

That was when Principal Green came up behind her. "Oh, no, you don't. You are not allowed to be on school property anymore. You lied to us. We had a visit yesterday from Detective McMillen from the sheriff's office. He told us everything. We know who you are, and we can't let you be on school grounds anymore. I'm sorry, but you have to leave."

I exhaled. "I just need to talk to Lauren about something. Or Chris. I have one little question to ask them; that's all. It'll take all of five minutes."

"If you don't leave right now, we'll have to call our SRO-officer to escort you off the premises," Principal Green said. "Detective McMillen was very clear that we shouldn't let you in again. He told us to call him if you came back."

"Oh, come on," I said.

Principal Green lifted her Walkie Talkie, then called in it. "Officer Conroy to the front office, please."

I lifted both my hands in resignation. "All right. All right. I'll leave."

Sydney and I walked outside and got back into the minivan. I grumbled loudly when we closed the doors. I started the engine up, then took off. I made it out of the parking lot when Sydney spotted someone on a bike, driving up toward the school.

"Guess who's coming in late today, huh?"

I looked at the girl and realized it was Lauren. "Thank God for the snooze button."

I drove onto the side of the road, making sure I wasn't on school grounds, then got out and approached her. She spotted me and stopped the bike, then took off her earbuds.

"Lauren," I said. "Could I take five minutes of your time?"

She looked at her watch, then nodded. "Sure. I'm late anyway. It doesn't matter. They've cut us a lot of slack these days, after the … well, you know *that* day. They don't even give us tardy slips anymore. It's been hard for us all to get out of bed these days. It's also hard on our parents. This morning, my mom kept crying; I just couldn't … I couldn't leave her like that. She's so worried something is going to happen to me. I keep telling her that the chance of something like that happening twice is really small, but she's just … so worried. I can't blame her. I'm terrified too. I can't stand being in a crowd of people anymore, you know? I keep looking around me and checking every face and hand, thinking I can spot it on them if they're about to pull out a gun and start to shoot. I've looked into the eyes of a school shooter once, and I keep thinking I now can see it in them as if there's some sign to look for, some tell. But there isn't."

"I'm sorry you have to deal with this, and your mom too," I said, thinking about my own daughter, Olivia. She had been through her share of tough stuff to deal with this year, and it broke my heart. All you want to do is protect them, but no matter how protective you are as a parent, you just can't control everything. It was a hard lesson for me to learn. I wanted to wrap my poor babies in the softest cotton and keep them safe from anything this world might expose them to, but I couldn't. Some things were just out of your control. You had to send them off every day and pray that they'd make it home, that some guardian angel watched over them, helping them get through the school day alive.

"And I'm not going to take up much of your time. I just need you to take a look at a picture."

I pulled out my phone and showed her the picture that was found in Adam's hand.

"That's Allyson," she said.

"That's what I thought," I said. "But what about this? It was written on the back of the picture. These letters here. SYLM? Do you know what that means?"

I showed her the text, and she read it. Her lips pulled into a sad smile. "It's an abbreviation for something they used to say to one another. One would say: *Say you love me*, and then the other would repeat back: *you love me*. It was a thing between Adam and Allyson. It was kind of cute."

Chapter Thirty-Two

THE HOSPITAL WAS SO QUIET. At least in the small room he was in. E.T. stood bent over the boy, filming him with his phone. The machines were breathing for him, making sweet music, as his chest heaved rhythmically up and down. The smell in the room was of decay. The boy was half-dead already.

E.T. reached out and stroked the boy gently across the cheek, then whispered in his ear.

"It won't hurt, not even a bit."

E.T. filmed the entire body and looked at the numbers on his phone. So far, only fifty had tuned in. There weren't as many as last time when he had filmed the men dying at the Ritz-Carlton. That one attracted almost a thousand viewers and hundreds of comments. Today, there weren't even close to one hundred people watching, but it would have to do. The few that checked in certainly shouldn't have done so in vain. They came to watch a show, and he'd give them just that. Besides, more might check in as he went along.

E.T. smiled deeply before he reached over and pulled out the tube from the boy's mouth and throat, making sure he filmed every part of it as it slid out. The sound it made when coming out made him think of a slithering snake. He stood for a few seconds and looked at the sleeping boy, while the boy gurgled, then gasped for air, and his body began to spasm.

E.T. felt his heart rate go up as he watched him, filming the entire thing. He noticed that the numbers were going up rapidly. Word that he was at it again was spreading among his followers, his fans. He reached a hundred and fifty; then it bumped up to almost five hundred. That wasn't half bad.

E.T. felt that the seconds went by like years. The monitor next to him finally flatlined, and an alarm went off. E.T. kept filming as he could hear voices coming from outside the door. He put the tube back in the boy's mouth, stuffing it forcefully down his throat as far as he could get it with the little time he had, then turned around and left. He got out of the door and filmed just as nurses rushed in, fixated on the boy, not noticing him at all.

He then gave his viewers a thumbs up before he rushed down the hallway, looking forward to seeing her face when Eva Rae found out, once she realized what had happened.

He wanted her to know he was in charge. That was his message for her today.

Chapter Thirty-Three

I DROVE BACK to the house, feeling disappointed. No, it was more than that. I was discouraged. I really wanted those letters on the back of the photograph to be something else. I wanted it to be something that would break open the case for me, giving me a lead of some kind, but it wasn't. It just confirmed to me that they loved one another and that Allyson had something to do with why Adam decided to go into the school and shoot.

I just wasn't sure it was the reason that everyone else believed.

"Maybe there's something else in the report that can help us," Sydney said as I drove the car up in front of our grandmother's house. Her car was gone; she had gone to visit Adam like she told us she would this morning.

I exhaled, feeling flustered. Was I just grasping onto a string that wasn't there? Was I trying too desperately to prove that my brother was innocent?

And if yes, then why?

Because I wanted to prove myself to my dad? Because I wanted to prove something to myself? Was that it? And was it blinding me completely to the truth, a truth I refused to face?

No, something is wrong. You saw it. You saw the bullet holes under the ceil-

ing. You heard that he closed his eyes. Nothing about this boy adds up to the picture that the police are painting. He doesn't fit the profile, not even a little bit.

"Maybe you're right," I said and killed the engine. "I'll have to go back and look again. There's got to be something that can help us."

"I'll go read the script for my movie," she said. "I need to get into this character if I want to nail this one."

Once inside, I sat down at my laptop, staring at the screen in front of me, not knowing how to go about this. I felt so certain that my brother was innocent, and somehow, I had this notion that it all had something to do with the many deaths at the Ritz-Carlton the night before. I don't know why I was so obsessed with that thought, but I kept going back to it. It was just so unusual for so many people to die on this island at almost the same time.

I ran a search and began reading what the media was saying about the incident. There were many speculations, but most seemed convinced that it was food poisoning, which I found to be odd. According to the journalists, they had all been eating dinner with the men that had bought their company after signing the contracts. They had eaten at the restaurant Le Clos, an upscale restaurant in downtown Fernandina Beach. But they hadn't eaten the same thing, and the two men who had bought the company weren't sick, nor were any of the other guests who had visited the restaurant that night.

Why was it only those ten men?

I heard Sydney's phone ring upstairs and heard her pick it up, then go quiet. There was nothing but silence from upstairs for a few minutes; then she came rushing down the stairs and into the living room, where I was sitting.

Her eyes were wide, and she looked pale.

"We need to go to the hospital."

I gave her a frightened look. "Why? Did something happen?"

"Adam just went into cardiac arrest."

Chapter Thirty-Four

WE MET David and Eileen in the hallway at the hospital. He looked like he was sick, while Eileen stared into the air, an empty look in her eyes. Adam wasn't in his room.

"What happened?" I asked.

"He went into sudden cardiac arrest," Eileen said. "They took him down the hallway. We haven't heard anything since."

David was biting his nails. He looked like he was about to break down any second now, and part of me wanted to put my arm around him and comfort him. He suddenly seemed so fragile ... and nothing like the man I had been so angry at. He didn't look like he could steal a kid or make someone's life miserable. He didn't look like the monster I had made him out to be.

He still did it, Eva Rae. No matter how innocent he looks, no matter how sad he appears, he is still guilty. It doesn't change the fact that he took Sydney and destroyed everything. Everything.

"How could he suddenly go into cardiac arrest?" I asked.

David shrugged. "It happens, they said. I think ... I think I need to sit down."

David looked like he was losing his balance and staggered toward me. I grabbed him in my arms and suddenly stood there, hugging the man I refused to call my dad, the man I loathed. And suddenly, I couldn't feel angry at him anymore.

"Help me, Syd," I said, and she rushed to grab his other arm. Together, we helped David to a row of chairs and sat him down in one of them.

"I'm sorry," he said, eyes filling. "You must think I'm such a fool. Can't even stand on my own two feet anymore … I'm just …" He looked directly into my eyes, and my heart sank.

"I can't lose him too."

Don't give me that. You're the one who left.

"Adam was my second chance; you know? The chance for me to do it right this time. Somehow, having him around made it easier for me to accept that …" He shook his head. "Listen to me. I sound like an old fool. Old and weak."

I swallowed the knot growing in my throat. I didn't know how I was feeling anymore. It was all in a whirlwind of emotions, and I hardly knew what was up and what was down anymore. Did I feel bad for him? Was I letting go of my anger? Was I ready to?

I stood up straight, biting back my tears.

"I'll go see if I can find a doctor," I said.

My grandmother put a hand on my shoulder, and I got a brief look of sympathy from her, then I rushed down the hallway, tears piling up in my eyes.

Please, don't let Adam die. Please, don't let him die before I even get to know my own brother.

I sniffled, then tried to stop a doctor who rushed toward me, but he didn't have time and just continued past me. A nurse did the same, and I ended up just standing there, all my emotions swirling inside of me, wanting to cry, but not really able to one second, then fighting to hold it back the next. It was the strangest thing.

I turned to face Adam's room, then rushed inside and closed the door behind me. I slid to the ground with my back rubbing against the door and finally let the tears roll freely.

Chapter Thirty-Five

I SAT BY THE DOOR, tears rolling down my cheeks. I was feeling hopeless and sorry for myself when I spotted it. I stared at it for a few seconds, then rose to my feet and walked closer. The bed had been rolled out of the room, with Adam in it, and there was an empty spot where it had been. But on the floor, I found something that made my heart drop.

What the ...?

I got up and walked closer, then bent down and picked the nail up from the dusty floor. I turned it in the light while my heart began pounding in my chest. The nail was long, and it was coated with light pink nail polish.

This is a girl's nail.

I stared at the nail in my hand, and I could hardly breathe. The room was spinning around me as I tried to make sense of it all. Then I turned around — still with the nail in my hand — and rushed outside. I found Deputy Corel standing outside with my grandmother.

"Hey," I said and approached him.

He turned to look at me, startled at my sudden approach.

"Where were you?" I asked.

"Excuse me?"

"When Adam went into cardiac arrest, where were you?" I asked. "Were you on your post outside, guarding his room?"

"I was just down the hall, why?" he answered, visibly offended by the question.

"Down the hall? So, anyone could have walked into my brother's room?" I asked. "Aren't you supposed to be guarding him?"

"I need you to calm down, ma'am. Not that I need to justify myself to you, but my job is to keep the kid from running away if he wakes up."

"Someone recently threatened to kill him right in front of you, and you don't think it's a good idea to guard his door, to make sure this person doesn't actually try to make good on his threats?" I asked.

"Now, ma'am …"

"Is everyone on this forsaken island completely incompetent?" I yelled louder than I wanted to.

"What's going on here?" David said and approached us. He pulled me aside. "Why are you attacking the deputy, Eva Rae?"

I tried to calm myself down. It was easier said than done, especially with David standing right in front of me. Sydney came up behind him.

"You think someone tried to hurt Adam?" she asked.

"Yes," I said.

"And you think it might be Ryan, Allyson's father?" David asked. "You think that Ryan tried to kill Adam?"

I shrugged. "I don't know who it was, but he did threaten him the other day, remember?"

"And why do you think someone tried to kill Adam? The doctor said it was cardiac arrest; it's not uncommon in comatose patients," David said.

"I know. But I … well, I found this in his room."

I opened my hand and showed them both the nail. David stared at it, then up at me, a look of concern in his eyes.

"A nail? I don't understand … what does that mean?"

102

"It's a girl's nail," I said.

"And?"

"It's been pulled out by the root, look."

"I … I'm still not quite following you," he said.

"I think it might be Allyson's. The detective at the sheriff's office told me she had her nails pulled out when still alive. I think the killer is sending me a message by placing the nail there and trying to kill Adam. He wants me to know that he knows I'm trying to stop him, and he wants to tell me that he can get to me anywhere. He probably also wants to get rid of Adam since, if he ever wakes up, he can tell us who made him walk into the school with that gun. When Adam wakes up, the killer will be exposed."

David bit his lip in the same manner I always did, and it made me want to scream. I hated how much I looked like him, whereas Sydney looked like our mother, always gracious and flawless.

Why did I have to be the one who took after him?

"I don't know, Eva Rae," Sydney said, her head slightly tilted. "It sounds a little out there, even for you."

"Maybe," I said pensively. "But my instinct is telling me to pursue this. He is showing me he's ready to play games. I've been down this road before. If he wants a war, then he's got it."

"The doctor is here," our grandmother said coming up to us, a serious look on her face. "He has news about Adam's condition."

We all turned to face the doctor, who came walking toward us. He took in a deep breath before he spoke, then looked at David first. In a moment of despair, David reached over and grabbed my hand in his. I gasped and looked down at our clutched hands. He was squeezing it hard, and I let him, while the doctor spoke.

"We were able to resuscitate your boy. The next few hours will show if his heart is strong enough to keep him alive."

A sigh of relief went through us all.

"But he's alive for now?" David asked, tears springing to his eyes once again, but this time of joy.

The doctor nodded with half a smile. "Yes. He is. His status is the same as before, but his heart is beating again."

"Oh, thank God," Eileen said, clasping her chest.

As the doctor left, I realized David's hand was still in mine. I pulled my hand away before things got awkward. Secretly, I couldn't help noticing that he had grabbed my hand when he needed someone to hold onto.

Not Sydney's and not his mother's, but mine.

Chapter Thirty-Six

DAVID AND SYDNEY stayed at the hospital to spend the night there, keeping an eye on Adam. Meanwhile, Eileen took me back to the house. I needed to get some research done, and Eileen needed to feed the neighbor's cats that she was taking care of while they were away.

It felt strange to be in the car with the woman that was my grandmother. I had never had one, so I wasn't really sure what to make of it, if I wanted her in my life or not. I guess a big part of me did. She seemed pretty cool with her silver mane under the bandana and Harley Davidson T-shirt. I couldn't help picturing her as young. She must have been one hot chick.

"The thing you said the other day in the garage," she said as we reached a red light and she stopped. "About us, that the least we could do was to try and reach out to you?"

I fiddled with the corner of my shirt while looking out the window. "Yeah, well …"

"The thing is," she said. "We tried."

"Excuse me?"

"Well, I tried. Your dad went to London with Sydney, and I never heard much from him during that time. I went there a couple of years later to visit and especially to see Syd, but I never got to know her really well either. I didn't have much contact with my son for those years, not till he came back, suddenly with a son, asking for my help to raise him properly. But the thing is, when he left for London, I reached out to your mother and asked if I could see you. But she wouldn't let me. I can't blame her. She was angry with David, of course, she was. And probably me as well because I didn't stop him from doing what he did. But how was I supposed to know that he would kidnap her and take her out of the country? It's not like he came to me and told me his plans. I would have told him he had lost his mind; of course, I would. But the thing is … well, it wasn't just your mother who lost someone. I did too. I lost my son and both of my granddaughters. I was robbed of the chance to see you both grow up. I have been so angry at my son for what he did, but at some point, I had to forgive him, you know? Not because he deserves it, but because it was eating me up. A life lived in anger and bitterness is hardly a life worth living, if you ask me."

I exhaled. "So now, you're telling me to forgive him as well? Is that it? Or my life will be miserable?"

"Heavens, no. What you do to him is none of my concern. That's between you and him, dear. No, I want you to forgive me," she said with a grin as we drove onto her street. "I want to make sure you know that I tried. I really did. But you also know your own mother. There was no way I could make her budge. In the end, she simply refused to speak to me. If I called, she'd hang up; if I wrote letters, she never answered … if she even read them. If I sent you a present, she'd return it unopened."

I smiled. That did sound like mommy dearest.

"What I'm trying to say is that people do crazy things sometimes out of a desperate need or maybe even out of spite because they think there's no other way out and maybe, well maybe they regret it later on, and maybe they don't know how to tell you that."

"And now we're back to talking about David again," I said.

"Yeah, well, I guess so."

"And maybe Adam, too," I mumbled, then repeated: "Because there was no other way out."

SAY YOU LOVE ME

Eileen drove up into the driveway and parked her Jeep.

"What was that?"

I shook my head and opened the door. "Nothing. Just a thought."

"Oh. Okay."

"Who is that on your porch?" I asked, then answered the question myself once I saw his face. "What does he want?"

Chapter Thirty-Seven

THEN:

"Listen, I know what it looks like."

Marlene looked from Rivers to Waltman. She was getting tired now and wasn't sure she could take much more.

"But you're wrong. My husband, Bruce would never touch Jack. I can assure you he wouldn't. Jack must be lying, maybe to get attention or something. You know how kids are. Kids say stuff and never think about the consequences. But I assure you; it's all lies. Maybe the product of a child's wild imagination. Kids lie from time to time. You must know this?"

"Do they?" Rivers say. "Do they lie about things like this? About abuse?"

"Well, naturally, they must from time to time, right? Like they lie about other kinds of stuff."

"Okay," Waltman said and leaned forward, folding his hands. "Let us recap what your son has told our social workers so far, in just the few hours they have been interviewing him, and then you tell me if he's lying."

Marlene leaned back in her chair, a big knot in her throat making it hard for her to swallow properly.

There was more?

"When I'm bad, he locks me in the shed in our backyard," Rivers read from the file. "It's very hot in there, and I can't breathe. I don't get food or water, and I am very hungry and thirsty."

Marlene wrinkled her forehead. "Excuse me? I have never ..."

"He beats me with his fists, or he kicks me. Sometimes, he uses a tool from the shed, and that hurts," Rivers continued reading.

Marlene shook her head. What was this? It seemed so foolish when knowing Bruce. Sweet and caring Bruce. Bruce who adored his son more than anything in this world. Who loved to hang out with him in the yard or put up a kite?

There was the time when he slapped him, remember? When he slapped Jack for talking back. But that was because he had a bad day at the office. He promised he'd never do it again.

"He punches me in my private parts when I'm not tough enough," Rivers continued. "Like if I cry after falling on the bike. He once punched me in the stomach because I cried after scraping my knee. But mostly, he hits me in the back. Kicks me in the back if I fall down when we play baseball. He tells me that's how it is in real life. That I need to be tough for real life."

Rivers looked up from the paper. "Do you want me to continue?"

Marlene didn't know what to say. She shook her head, feeling terrified. If her son really had said those things, then they had to be true, didn't they? They were awfully detailed to be made up by a seven-year-old, weren't they?

But what did that mean? Did that mean that Bruce was, in fact, abusing their son? And had she been a part of it by not seeing it? Could they accuse her of closing her eyes and being an accomplice in that sense? Would they take Jack away from her because of this? Because she hadn't noticed? Did she deserve that?

Maybe.

What kind of a mother doesn't know that her own son is being abused?

Chapter Thirty-Eight

I TRIED to pretend like I wasn't annoyed by seeing him on my grandmother's porch. To be honest, he was the last person on Earth I wanted to see right now, and yet there he was, sitting on the porch swing. As he spotted us, McMillen rose to his feet and pulled at his tie as he approached me. His blue shirt had sweaty patches under the arms and on the chest. I wondered how long he had been sitting there waiting for us to come home.

"Detective McMillen," I said and walked up the five steps leading to the wooden wrap-around porch of my grandmother's Victorian style home.

He nodded, tipping his hat at my grandmother, who continued inside. "Mrs. Clarke, Miss Thomas."

The screened door slammed shut behind my grandmother after she said an absentminded and indifferent *hello* to the detective.

"So ... what can I do for you, Detective?" I asked, hoping he'd make this quick. "It's been quite a long day."

"I know," he said with an exhale. He wiped sweat from his upper lip with the back of his hand. I debated whether or not to invite him inside in the AC, then decided against it. He wasn't here on a social call; that much was certain. "I heard what happened at the hospital. That must have been awful for your family."

Yeah, well, you don't know the half of it. It would probably have been easier on you if he had just died. Save you a lot of time and trouble, wouldn't it?

"It was," I said.

I thought briefly about the nail. I had put it in my purse in a plastic bag. I knew in my heart that someone tried to kill my brother today, and I was determined to find out who. But I had a feeling it was going to be without help from the local law enforcement.

"Listen, I came to talk to you because there's something you should know," he said, "about your brother and the case."

"Yeah? And what is that?"

"I know you think everything was wonderful and innocent between Allyson and Adam," he said. "But the thing is ... well, we found out that Allyson was seeing someone else."

"And just how do you know this?" I asked.

"We found a series of texts in her phone records."

"Okay. And who is he?"

"We don't know that yet."

"How can you not know? This guy might be a suspect?" I asked.

"He had no name in her phone; she used an emoji instead of a name. A happy face."

"But surely you traced the number?" I said.

"We did. But it belongs to a burner phone. Bought with cash at a Wal-Mart three months ago."

"So, it could be anyone," I said pensively.

"But that's not the point," he continued.

"Why is that not the point? To me, the point here is very clear. You have another suspect, another person of interest that you need to look into before you close the case on my brother."

"He knew," McMillen said. "That's the point I'm trying to make. Adam knew that Allyson was seeing someone else behind his back."

"How do you know this?"

"From his phone records. They were fighting about it. He confronted her a few days before they went to the beach party and asked her about it. He had seen her texts with this other guy. Furthermore, we have statements from friends at the party saying that they were fighting on the night she disappeared. At one point, Adam grabbed her by the arm and tried to force her to kiss him, but she left angrily, and he ran after her. That's the last time she was seen. Paints quite the picture, don't you think? But it also makes a lot of sense. He got angry, jealous, and she refused him. So he snapped. He killed her, then decided to kill himself by shooting up the school because he was angry at the world and the other students. Maybe some of them knew about it and didn't tell him, so he was angry at them; maybe Allyson's secret boyfriend was among them. Who knows? But it gives your boy a motive for doing what he did. Now, I know he's your long-lost brother and all that, but the fact is, you don't know him at all."

I bit my lip, realizing he was right, but not wanting to admit it.

"I think you have it all wrong, Detective," I said. "He didn't want to kill anyone at the school. He didn't even try to. He closed his eyes and shot for the ceiling. And today, someone tried to kill him. Because when he wakes up, he can tell the truth. He can explain that someone else murdered Allyson and made him walk into the school with the gun. Adam did it because there was no other way out. He was holding the picture of the one he loved in his hand because this killer, whoever is behind it, used her to pressure him, telling him that Allyson would die if he didn't do it. That's my theory. I also believe this killer murdered five people at the Ritz-Carlton, and if you look closely at the champagne they drank, you'll find that it was poisoned. There was nothing random about this; it was no coincidence. My only question is, where and how will he strike next? That's what we need to focus on."

McMillen stared at me, his eyes growing wide, his mouth gaping slightly. His lips then pulled into a smile.

"You're even madder than I thought," he said. "That has got to be the craziest story I have ever heard."

"Yeah, well, I had a feeling you might say that. But nonetheless, I feel like I have to warn you. You have a very clever killer on your peaceful little island, and he won't stop until someone makes him.

Believe me. I've faced killers like him before, and the more they succeed in their affairs, the more they think themselves invincible. Last time, he killed five people in one strike. There's no telling how many he'll go for next. The question is, how many deaths you can have sitting on your conscience before you start to listen?" I stopped to take a deep breath before continuing. "Now, if you'll excuse me, I have to go call my children. The ones I am neglecting because I have to stay here and solve this case since no one else seems to care enough to. Goodnight, Detective. I can't say it has been a pleasure."

I turned around on my heel and walked to the screened door, then pulled it open. McMillen put on his hat and took a couple of steps across the wood, then stopped.

"You're seeing ghosts here, Miss Thomas. But I understand where it's coming from. It's your brother. You want to think the best about him, of course, you do. And I don't think he was bad. I think he was heartbroken. I agree that he believed it was the only way out, but not for the reasons you do. I'm going to ask you respectfully to stop interfering with our work and let us do our job."

And with that, he left while I stood on the threshold to the house, my hand still on the door handle, fighting to suppress my desire to scream.

Chapter Thirty-Nine

I ASKED my grandmother for his address and was told that Chris lived just down the road. Chris and Adam had been friends since early childhood and used to hang out all the time, she added. I noticed she drifted away for a second while telling me this, and I sensed she missed those days. I couldn't blame her.

Chris came to the door immediately when I knocked, then used his crutches to hump out on the porch.

"Miss Thomas? What are you doing here? Is everything okay? Is Adam all right? Did something happen?"

He closed the door behind him.

"I'm sorry. I didn't mean to scare you. Adam is fine after the scare we had yesterday; his heart is back to beating again, and he's okay for now."

Chris looked relieved. "You had me scared there for a second. I heard about what happened yesterday and worried he hadn't survived the night."

"Oh, no, Adam is okay, as far as I know."

"Oh, good. I was planning on paying him a visit later in the day if they'll allow me."

"That is very sweet of you. Listen, I hope I didn't come too early and wake up the whole house," I said. "I wasn't able to sleep much last night and frankly didn't think about it being Saturday and all."

"That's okay," Chris said. "I don't like to sleep in anyway. Too much of the day is wasted that way, and who wants to waste time you have off, right?"

"True. Better get something out of your day."

"What can I help you with?"

"Well, it's a little delicate, so you'll have to excuse me if I'm being blunt, but I wanted to ask you if you knew that Allyson was seeing someone else. According to the police, Adam knew and was angry with Allyson because of it. They see this as a motive, while I still have my doubts."

Chris went serious, then he nodded. "Yeah, I knew about it. Adam told me he suspected she was seeing someone else and that he had seen texts on her phone from him. He was terrified of losing her. It would break him if he did. Everyone knew that, no one more than me."

I nodded pensively. "Do you know who he was? Was he a student at the high school?"

Chris shook his head. "No, that I could understand. I mean a lot of guys liked her at the school."

"So, he wasn't from the school. Was he a student somewhere else?" I asked.

Chris swallowed and shook his head again. "No. It was all a little odd if you ask me. And gross too."

I wrinkled my forehead, puzzled. "Gross? What do you mean by that? How was it gross?"

Chris's eyes avoided mine. "He was kind of an older guy. You know, older than us. An adult."

"Older?" I said, thinking it was beginning to get interesting. If he was an adult, then he could very well be the guy we were looking for. My heart started to race in my chest when thinking about this. This was a real lead, one that could crack the case wide open. This could be exactly what I was searching for.

"Do you know him?"

"Not really. I only know of him, like I know who he is and all that."

I nodded. "Okay, but do you know his name?"

He nodded. "Sure."

Chapter Forty

Mr. Jenkins lived in a brand-new house on Robert Oliver Court at the end of a cul-de-sac. The street was all brand-new houses, and the neighborhood seemed a little more high-end than the rest of the island. It was within walking distance of the beach.

I pulled up and parked my car on the street outside, then looked at the gray house in front of me and its columns in front of the entrance.

I got out and walked up, then spotted a girl's bike in the front yard, and my heart sank.

This guy had children.

I knocked. A young girl no more than five or six opened the door. I smiled. "Hi there. Is your dad home?"

"Daaad?" she called.

I heard a voice coming from behind her. It belonged to a woman. A face peeked out, and a woman soon stood in the doorway.

"Yes? How can we help you?"

I felt my heart beat fast. Not only did this guy have a child, but he also had a wife. What was he doing seeing a fifteen-year-old girl? Was she his mistress? The thought made me sick to my stomach. I kept picturing Olivia with an older guy and what it would make me do if I found out.

"I was just ..."

Another voice came from behind them, and a man's face appeared. Looking into his eyes made me forget what I was trying to say. I couldn't come here and destroy a family like this. I had to make something up.

"I'm doing a survey," I said. "I'm sorry to be knocking at your door so early, but we're trying to research whether or not ..."

"Let me just stop you right there," Mr. Jenkins said. "We're not interested, no matter what it is. We're trying to have a nice Saturday morning as a family, and frankly, we don't care much. You have a nice day."

With that, he closed the door, sending me a sly smile as his face disappeared. I stood back, my heart still racing in my chest.

Was that the guy I was looking for? Was he my killer?

I walked back to the minivan and got in, then took in a deep breath. Somehow, I had to know more about this Mr. Jenkins, but how? I didn't exactly have back-up from law enforcement.

I started up the minivan, then drove down the street. I drove up along the coastline and past the Ritz-Carlton Hotel, my heart sinking when thinking about all the families that had been destroyed that night, then stopped at a grill called Salt Life Food Shack and went inside. I was starving since I had left the house without anything to eat, and it was lunchtime now. I ordered fried grouper and key lime pie for dessert, then ate it all while wondering about this strange case and the recent turn of events, feeling the anger rise up inside of me.

What kind of a man had an affair with a fifteen-year-old girl? There had to be something wrong with someone who did that. Terribly wrong.

Chapter Forty-One

HE HAD GOTTEN up early and started driving. He wanted to beat Chad to it and make sure he made it to Amelia Island before he did. It was childish, yes, but he couldn't bear the thought of Chad arriving first and then acting like he was the owner of the place. And of Eva Rae. Matt needed to make sure his position was secure and that Chad knew his place.

Now, as he drove over the bridge to Amelia Island, he felt a tingling sensation in his stomach. What if she didn't want him to come? What if she didn't seem surprised and happy to see him?

What if she told him to go back home?

That would just about break his heart.

Of course, she'll be happy to see you. Why on Earth wouldn't she? She loves you. You worry too much, Matt. You need to relax.

Matt took a deep breath as the wheels landed on the island, and he continued. He had never been to Amelia Island before, but so far, it had been a beautiful drive. Lots of water, marshland, and low-lying roads, and he wondered how they coped when a hurricane rushed through with the flooding and all. It had to be hard to evacuate the island quickly with all the bridges you had to drive over, and all the marshland that risked getting flooded. Matt had been to

Jacksonville before and thought this would be more like that, but it was very far from the big city he had known. This reminded him a lot of home.

Chief Annie hadn't even blinked when he asked her for a couple of days off. She had told him to say hello to Eva Rae for her — even though he hadn't told her that he was going up there — and to make sure he didn't do any police work while there.

"Time off is meant to be taken seriously," she said. "You work way too hard these days, and you need to rest too, or you won't last in the long run."

So, that was his plan. His mother had taken Elijah for the weekend so he could go to Eva Rae and spend time with her, hope-fully resting and relaxing a little bit. All he wanted was to be near her; the rest would have to wait.

He just hoped that Chad wasn't going to be in their way. Or everyone else for that matter. Well the kids, of course, they needed her more than he did. But he could live with her attention going to them. It was their father that he didn't want in the way of things.

Oh, dear lord, Matt. You're jealous.

Matt couldn't remember ever feeling this stirred up inside over a girl. Not since high school when Eva Rae dated Tim Spencer for three weeks. That was awful for Matt, and he remembered feeling like he was going to die. That's how bad it was.

But he wasn't fifteen anymore. He was forty-one, and he needed to get a grip.

Matt chuckled at himself and his stupidity, then let the GPS guide him across the island toward Eva Rae's grandmother's house. As he found it and drove up into the driveway, he was content to see that no other cars were parked outside of the garage. There were no kids running around outside.

And no Chad in sight.

Chapter Forty-Two

Is THAT ... Is that ... no, it can't be, can it?

I couldn't believe my own eyes as I drove up the driveway and spotted the red Toyota in the driveway. I killed the engine, sprang out of my minivan, and slammed the door shut behind me.

"Matt?"

He was standing on the porch, talking to my grandmother. My heart was beating so fast in my chest; I could hardly contain it.

There was no person in this world I'd rather see right now.

"Matt?"

He smiled nervously, then threw out his arms. "Surprise!"

"I ... I can't believe it," I said and ran up the stairs toward him. I smiled and pulled him into a hug, then kissed his soft lips, closing my eyes. As our lips parted, he looked deep into my eyes. It melted my heart.

"What are you doing here?" I asked. "I didn't expect you at all."

He shrugged. "I had a few days off and thought I'd surprise you."

My grandmother smiled. "I told him he'll have to stay here at my house. Lord knows I have plenty of room. Especially since your grandfather died. I have to tell you that Matt here reminds me of him. When I saw him at first when opening the door, I thought it was him. Almost gave me a heart attack. To be honest, I thought the good Lord had sent him to come and take me home, but I ain't ready for that just yet. Still got lots of good years in me."

"I sure hope so," I said, putting my arms around Matt's waist and pulling him close.

"Come on in," Eileen said. "Sydney and David just got back from the hospital and are eating in the kitchen."

"How's Adam?" I asked.

She shrugged. "Same, they say. But at least he's alive, am I right?"

I nodded. She sure was, even though I desperately wanted the boy to wake up soon.

"Don't just stand there and sweat," Eileen said. "Come on in."

Matt and I were just about to walk inside when another car drove up the street. It was honking loudly while I heard voices yelling. I turned to look, and my heart dropped for the second time this morning.

"MOOOOOM!"

"Alex?" I said.

The black Lincoln Navigator drove up and parked behind my old minivan. Alex was hanging his head out the window, screaming. As the SUV stopped, he jumped out of the door and ran toward me, arms stretched out.

"Alex!" I shrieked, then grabbed him in my arms and spun him around in the air. I closed my eyes and smelled his hair, then kissed him excessively until he got tired of it and wanted to be put down. I had tears in my eyes as I saw Christine and Olivia get out as well and walk up to me. I pulled them both into a deep hug, fighting my tears. I hadn't realized just how badly I had missed them till this moment. I knew I did, but I had pushed it back, forced myself to not think about it since it hurt so bad. Now, they were here, and I could hardly believe it.

"What are you guys doing here?" I asked with a sniffle.

Chad came up behind them. "We missed you." He spotted

Matt, who stood a few steps behind me, then looked disappointed. "Ah, I see you've already been surprised. Guess he beat us here."

I gave Chad a quick, friendly hug, then grabbed my girls in my arms again. "I can't believe you're really here. Gosh, I missed you."

Then I paused. "Wait, what about the bunnies? If you're all here, who is taking care of them?"

Chad leaned into the car, then pulled out a big cage. The children's three angora bunnies were sitting inside, nibbling their hay.

"Ta-da."

Chapter Forty-Three

IT WAS GOING to take some time to get used to living there. Billie's daughter, Robyn, had told her this over and over again; still, Billie wasn't sure the move was such a good idea. She missed her home. She longed to be among her own things, her furniture, her paintings, and especially her yard that she loved to tend to on a nice day like today. What she wouldn't give to be out there again, even if it was just for a few fleeting yet precious moments.

Life at the nursing home wasn't what she had wanted it to be. It was good in case you had an accident and needed help, but it took so darn long for the nurses to get to you once you rang for help, it almost seemed like it was useless.

"Did you know I survived the fire in thirty-six?" Olivia, sitting next to Billie in the commons room, said. She suffered from short-term memory loss, and Billie had heard this story over and over again. It was okay, though. Olivia was sweet and always happy, and one day, Billie might miss listening to her stories over and over again.

It was the third stroke that had made Robyn start talking about the home. Billie wasn't herself, she said. Billie couldn't do a lot of simple tasks like go to the bathroom on her own anymore. She struggled to get dressed alone, and even eating was hard.

Still, being in a nursing home at the age of only sixty felt devastating. Was this what was left for her in this life?

Was this all there was?

Billie looked at the cup in front of her. She reached over and grabbed it between her hands. Shaking and spilling half of the liquid on the table in front of her, she lifted it toward her mouth, but she had to stop halfway since her hands wouldn't obey. They wouldn't be able to reach her mouth.

Come on, Billie. You can do this!

Billie exhaled tiredly. She couldn't believe this was what it had come to. Her living among all these old people, most of them who already had one foot in the grave. Was there really nothing more in this life left for her?

Reduced to a vegetable.

They had taken Billie into the commons room because her daughter was coming to visit today. It was Sunday. Usually, Billie preferred to stay in her room and not socialize a lot with the other *inmates*, as she liked to call them. Just like she called the home her prison, much to her daughter's chagrin.

"I'd take care of you myself if I could," she had said over and over again to relieve her own guilt. "You know I would, right, Mom? But I can't."

Because your work makes you travel all the time, I know. But maybe if you got another job? One that didn't require you to travel? There must be plenty of nice jobs around here? Maybe one that required you to work from home? I took care of you when you needed me. When you couldn't do anything on your own. Life is fragile; don't you realize this? I know I did way too late. Don't you make the same mistake. At least learn from what happened to me. We only have this time together. We don't know when it'll suddenly all be over.

Those were the things she wanted to tell her daughter but never did. Simply because words could barely leave her lips anymore after the third stroke. Still, there was so much she wanted to say to her daughter, so much it felt like she would explode from time to time when she tried but didn't succeed. She wanted to urge Robyn to have some children, or at least to get married and settle down. All the good stuff. Not climbing the corporate ladder. Not constantly striving to impress her bosses and get by in what to Billie was a man's world.

It's not worth it. Take my word for it. None of that matters in the end. You need to focus on what's really important.

A nurse approached Billie, then grabbed a tissue and wiped drool from her chin, then sent her a smile of pity. Billie felt embarrassed. She hadn't even felt the drool. Just like she could no longer feel it if she had to go to the bathroom.

It was beyond embarrassing. Not being able to perform even the simplest task on your own was humiliating.

They had gathered all the inmates in the commons this morning. Some were just sitting by the big windows, staring at the road outside and the cars driving by. There was a group of inmates that were playing cards in the couch area. Others were playing chess or other board games. Some were just walking around, pacing, with nowhere to go, pushing their walkers in front of them. All of it was to pass time. Billie didn't want to pass time; she didn't want not to have anything to do. She didn't want just to wait here till she had no other choice but to die, just to get out of there.

"Billie? Your daughter is here," a nurse said, approaching her.

A figure came up behind her.

"Hi, Mom, how are you today?"

Billie lifted her eyes and met those of her daughter's, then recognized the pity in them that she probably mistook for sympathy.

Robyn sat down in a chair across from her with a deep sigh. "Ah, it's good to be here again," she said and crossed her legs, a task so simple you would never think that someone would envy you the ability to do that.

"You won't believe the stressful week I've had. Going from one airport to another, talking to people, riding in taxis, all the cars honking and sirens blaring when in the big city, you know? It feels good to be back and in here ... in this place ... it's so, well ... it's so nice and quiet. Peaceful even."

I don't want peace and quiet. I want to be able to live my life and tend my garden.

Billie noticed a shape out of the corner of her eye that didn't drive past the nursing home, nor seemed to stop at the entrance. She noticed it, and also that it didn't stop. But she couldn't say anything. All that came out of her were grunts. Seeing her struggle to find words, her daughter grabbed her hand in hers, then gave her that same pitying look as earlier.

"It's all right, Mom. The words will come."

The truck rammed through the front doors and splintered the glass, then accelerated directly toward the inmates where they were sitting in a cluster. Some screamed, others — the ones who weren't in wheelchairs — tried to get up and run. But most of them were too slow, and only a few — the ones closest to the back — made it out. Those who were tied to a chair, like Billie, didn't stand a chance.

Chapter Forty-Four

"DON'T TAKE ALL THE STRAWBERRIES."

Alex looked up at his sister, then reached over and grabbed the last of the strawberries and put them in his mouth, grinning at Christine.

"Oh, my God, you're such an idiot!"

Christine yelled the words out so loud I almost choked on my pancake that Eileen had made for us. Alex whined next to her.

"Mo-om! She called me stupid."

"No, she didn't, you doofus. She called you an idiot," Olivia butted in.

I sent her a look; saying *was that really necessary?* She answered with a smile and a shrug.

"Mooom?" Alex said.

I looked at Matt, and our eyes met. We had spent the night together in my room, while Sydney had moved in with our grandmother so we could be together, something I'd have to make up to her somehow in the future. I could tell Matt wanted to go back up there and close the door just as much as I did. I could have stayed there all day, in his arms, but the children needed me too. They had missed me terribly, and for some unexplainable reason, that always made them completely whiny, grumpy, and impossible. It was like they wanted to punish me for having been away, for forcing them to miss me.

I knew that they just wanted things to go back to normal, and for me to be there for them. But that just wasn't possible right now.

"What a gorgeous morning," Chad said as he stepped into the kitchen. He had been out running and was shirtless. It was obvious he had been working out since we were married, and I couldn't help staring at his sweaty abs. Not because I thought it was hot, but because he had never had them before, and it made him look so different. He had also lost a lot of weight, and to tell you the truth, he looked great.

Matt saw me staring, and I let my eyes glide toward my food. Chad grabbed an orange and started to peel it, bouncing it off his arm a few times, and juggling with three of them first, making Alex laugh loudly.

Eileen had given him his own room, whereas all three children shared one. It didn't make things easier.

To say that having all of them in the house was chaotic would be putting it mildly. I was happy they had come; don't get me wrong, I really was, but it was just … a lot. Especially since I sensed this weird rivalry going on between Chad and Matt, and it was getting on my nerves.

After breakfast, I told Alex to go into the yard and play, to blow off some steam. Christine and Olivia went on their phones while I took my coffee and sat on the back porch swing, looking at Alex as he went on the old swing set that I guessed was there for Adam when he was younger. The yard had everything a young boy could desire, and Alex was occupied enough for me to get a break. Matt came out to me, holding a cup of his own, and sat next to me. I smiled and kissed him gently, then took in a deep breath, enjoying this rare moment with the man I loved.

I put my head on his shoulder, wanting it to last forever.

A sigh from Matt broke the calm.

"Can we talk about what's in your room, please? On the walls and the desk? It's plastered with articles and pictures. The back of the wall is filled with your notes in your handwriting, with bullet points noting ways to force someone to kill others and motives for doing it. I saw a list of the victim's characteristics, race, gender, and age, but also marital status, job, education, criminal history, social media presence, pets, hair color, and weight and height? Can we talk about the fact that you were up last night on your computer when you thought I was sleeping and snuck back into bed before I opened my eyes, pretending like you'd been there all the time? I woke up at two and found you sitting there in the light from your screen. So, don't tell me it didn't happen."

I shrugged and sipped my coffee, then pulled my legs up under me on the swing.

"It seems a little obsessive; don't you think?" Matt said.

I gave him a look. "What do you mean, *obsessive?*"

He exhaled. "I know I was the one who told you to try and help your family, but I didn't know it would come to this. I didn't realize you'd take it this far. You told me last night that the police think you're seeing ghosts, that you've gone mad. Did you ever stop to think that they might be right?"

I scoffed. "Did you come all this way just to tell me to stop? Because then you've wasted your time, my friend."

He sighed, and I looked at Alex, who had found a bat and a baseball and tried to hit it. I suddenly feared for the windows in my grandmother's house.

"Of course, that's not why I came."

"Then why did you come here?"

"I missed you," he said. "Don't you get that? Can't you accept the fact that I love you and want to be with you? Does there have to be another reason? Isn't that enough for you?"

I sipped my coffee, looking into the black substance, then up at him again. "I don't know. It's just that … well, it feels like there's more to it than that. You don't usually do stuff like this, Matt."

"Well, now I do," he said as he rose to his feet and walked toward the door. "I don't usually love someone either. You're my first."

"Matt …"

He walked inside before I could say what I wanted to.

Shoot. I hurt him.

"Look at me, Mom!" Alex yelled, then threw the ball into the air and slammed the bat into it, forcing it to dart through the air toward the neighbor's house. I held my breath, waiting for the big crash as the ball went through glass, but it never came. Instead, it ended up somewhere in the yard, and Alex looked up at me.

"Moom? Can I go get it?"

I nodded. "Sure. Go ahead."

I sat back with my cup, then wondered if I should go up and make sure Matt was okay once Alex got back. As I did, I felt my phone vibrate in my pocket, and I picked it up. I had received a text from a number I didn't know. It was a video. I played it, then froze to ice.

At first, I couldn't really figure out what I was looking at. It was a video filmed from inside of a car, through the windshield. The car — or truck, I realized — soon rammed through glass doors and continued inside the building. I heard screams and saw people jump for their lives. Some disappeared, while others, most of them, were knocked down by the truck. Wheelchairs were hit, and people who had sat in them were slung into the air. At one point, the truck got stuck, and the driver backed up, then put it back in drive and slammed into a woman standing against a wall.

That was when I stopped the video and threw the phone into the air till it landed on the wooden porch. I felt physically ill and hugged myself when Chad came out the door.

"Hey, hey, what's going on?"

I threw myself in his arms, then cried, my stomach feeling like it would explode.

Chapter Forty-Five

DEPUTY GRIFFINS COULDN'T GET the pictures out of his mind. He had been the first at the scene after they got the report about the nursing home, Waterfall Hills this same morning. Now, he was one of the many patrols on the lookout for a black MACK dump truck. The truck was stolen from a construction site; they found out when they called in what the witnesses — the few that had survived — had seen.

Now, Deputy Griffins was staring at a black dump truck parked on the side of the road in a rest area on A1A. The dump truck was smoking from the front and was visibly damaged on the bumper. There was no doubt it was the one they were looking for, the one that had rammed through the front doors, killed a bunch of people, and then left, driving away.

Griffins had stopped his patrol car behind it, then called for backup.

"I have eyes on the vehicle. Someone is sitting inside of it," he said over the radio. "I repeat; I have visual on the possible nursing home killer."

Seconds later, another patrol car drove up to assist him, and he got out, hands shaking, gun pulled.

"Hands where I can see them," he yelled as they approached from both sides. More patrol cars were arriving now, and colleagues were jumping out to assist. Griffins feared it would only agitate the driver of the car further, and he was a desperate man at this point.

Killing all those poor old people.

He was a sick man, no doubt about it. A very sick man. The question remained if he was also armed.

"I said, hands where I can see them."

Griffins came closer, but the man still had his hands where he couldn't see them. It made him nervous, even more so than he already was.

"Hands where I can see them!"

No movement. The man in the truck sat completely still, almost eerily so.

"Roll the window down, sir," Griffins said, the gun between his hands shaking. As he came really close, Griffins realized the man was, in fact, moving. He was trembling. He turned his head and looked at Griffins, and that made his heart rate go up even further.

"Show me your hands," he yelled.

The man's lips quivered as he lifted both his hands in the air. It looked like he was mouthing *Please* and then added *Don't shoot*, but Griffins could be mistaken.

He had lost a colleague two years ago in a similar situation. A pick-up truck ran a red light, and he set after it. The guy pulled out a shotgun and killed him. He was never found. Griffins' colleague left three children and a wife, who had no idea what to do next.

Remembering this, Griffins wasn't taking any chances. He'd rather shoot first than being the one going down. That was just the way it was in his line of duty. Things could get ugly real fast.

"Is he armed? Does anyone see a gun?" someone yelled.

Griffins stared at the man inside the car, who was shaking and crying. Griffins felt like his heart was about to explode. So far, he hadn't seen a weapon of any sort, but that didn't mean he couldn't have one in his lap or maybe down between his legs.

"Now, step out of the vehicle, sir," he said. "Keep your hands where I can see them."

The man did as he was told. He opened the door and stepped out, hands high above his head.

"Please," he said between sobs. "Please, don't shoot me."

Griffins scanned his hands, then his pants to see if he could spot a gun anywhere. That was when he noticed the blood — blood on his pants, and blood running from his fingers down his stretched-up arms.

Panic emerged inside of Griffins. Where did all that blood come from? The man was weeping, his torso shaking. It made Griffins nervous. His colleagues were looking in the back, searching for weapons. Two of them had their weapons pointed at the driver, who now sank to his knees, arms still behind his head. As he did this, one of his arms fell down to the side, and one of the deputies yelled.

"He's going for a gun!"

In that instant, all three of them fired at the man. His body spasmed back and forth as the bullets went through his torso, piercing through him until his body fell forward, nose digging into the gravel.

As he laid there, Griffins approached him, hands still shaking, sweat springing from his forehead. As they waited for the ambulance to arrive, for some reason, he couldn't stop staring at the alligator-shaped scar on the side of the man's cheek.

Chapter Forty-Six

"Who would send a video like this?"

Chad stared at Deputy Williams from the sheriff's office who had finally come out to the house. At first, when Chad called them, they had said that all cars were occupied today due to an incident, but they'd get to us as soon as possible. It took them a few hours to come. I had handed over my phone to him, so he could see the nasty video. He had asked to take the phone with him for examination but promised I'd have it back as soon as possible.

"I'm sure we'll be able to answer that question soon," Deputy Williams said.

"But it happened, didn't it?" I asked. "This was a real video, not something that had been created, right?"

Deputy Williams nodded. "This happened this morning, I'm afraid."

"Oh, Lord. Those poor people," I said, clasping my mouth in shock. The images from the video still flickered through my mind, making me feel sick.

"We have apprehended the driver, though."

"You got him?" I asked. "What happened?"

"He's dead, ma'am. They approached him, and when they did, he went for a gun, so they shot him on the spot. He died immediately. They didn't dare to take any chances with a guy like that."

"Of course not, Deputy," Chad said. "Sounds like a very sick person."

"I'm afraid so. Even small towns like this harbor some strange existences every now and then, unfortunately. Even though it is rare, but this guy messed with the wrong people; that's for sure."

"And they're certain it was the same man who drove the truck in the video?" I asked.

He nodded. "Yes."

"You're absolutely certain?" I asked, even though I knew it was provocative. "Like no doubt whatsoever in your mind?"

"Yes, ma'am. No doubt whatsoever. He's gone now. You don't have to worry about a thing. He won't be sending any more of these."

Deputy Williams lifted my phone inside of the evidence bag to indicate he meant the video.

"At least you can use this as evidence," Chad said. "If it came from his phone, then you'll be able to prove it was him, right?"

"Indeed, we will. You have been of great help."

Chad and the deputy shook hands. I stood with my arms crossed, wondering why this — once again — rubbed me the wrong way.

"Have a nice day, ma'am."

As the deputy left, Chad put his arm around my shoulder and pulled me into a hug. "That was a bad experience, huh? Awful, what happened. I can't blame you for being upset."

As I let him hold me, I looked at Matt, who was standing behind us, looking like a child who had lost his toy. Seeing him, I pulled out of Chad's grip.

"I'll be fine. I just need to rest a little. I'll go lie down for a while."

I walked to the door, then turned my head and my eyes locked with Matt's the second before I disappeared inside, wondering why I once again had hurt the man I loved. Why couldn't I just get it right this time? What we shared was special, yet I didn't seem to be able to hold onto it. It was like trying to hold onto water with your bare hands. I felt he was slipping away, and there was nothing I could do to stop it.

Chapter Forty-Seven

I SLEPT for about half an hour, getting some much-needed rest. When I woke up, Matt was sitting on the bed next to me, watching me sleep. I smiled when I saw him, but he didn't smile back.

"Maybe I shouldn't have come," he said. "I feel like it was a mistake."

I sat up straight. "Are you kidding me? I love that you came. I missed you like crazy. You have no idea."

He exhaled. "I just feel like … I feel like an outsider, between you and Chad. Like you have this bond between you two, and there's no room for me."

"Where is this coming from? Was it because I was hugging him when I received that video? Because that was just because he was there. It could have been anyone."

"But it wasn't just anyone," he said. "It was your ex. Besides, it's not just the hug and the fact that he took care of you when you needed it; it's also when I see you two together. You're always chatting and laughing. I don't know what it is; it just feels like you have something together that I can't compete with."

I looked down at what was on the floor next to him and realized he had packed his bag.

"You're leaving already? But we were supposed to spend the day together, and then you'd leave tomorrow."

Matt nodded. He leaned over and kissed me on the cheek. "I'll head back. You don't need me here."

"Matt … please … I … don't say that. I love having you here. Please, give me a second chance to make it up to you …"

He rose to his feet, suitcase in hand. "It's okay, Eva Rae. Don't worry about it. You have your family here. These are the people you should be with. I won't stand between you and your family. I won't blame you if you want to get back together again. I mean you should at least try, for the kids. It's what's best for them. And Chad isn't as bad once you get to know him a little. He's really good with the kids."

"Matt, please, I …"

He sent me a look that told me it didn't matter what I said or did. He had made his decision, and it wasn't going to change. I watched him walk to the door and leave, taking a painfully big chunk of my heart with him as he did.

I ran to the window and watched as he got into the car, then said his goodbyes to the children. Alex hugged him tightly, and I felt tears welling up in my eyes. Chad stood with the children and waved as Matt left, while I couldn't stop crying. I looked down at my children, who went back to playing in the front yard with their dad. Well, Alex and Christine did, whereas Olivia sat on the swing, looking at her phone.

Was Matt right? Did I owe it to my children to give it a second chance? Chad left me for another woman, yes, and he did cheat on me for a very long time. That, in itself, was inexcusable, but was it something I could forgive? Weren't we all entitled to make a mistake? Didn't I play as big a part in it as well? I hadn't exactly been home to take care of my marriage. I had been busy with my career in the FBI, thinking I could mend the broken pieces later.

I had to admit; I did enjoy hanging out all five of us again. And I did like how happy it made my children to have both their parents together again. We wouldn't be the first family to go through a thing like this. It could be done.

I sighed while biting my lip, watching Chad playing baseball with Alex and Christine. Chad threw the ball to Alex, and he hit it perfectly. The ball soared into the air and disappeared into the neighbor's yard, and Alex screamed loudly.

"Did you see that shot, Dad? Did you?"

I chuckled as all three of them went on a search for the ball next door, then wiped the tears from my cheeks.

Was this, in fact, what I really needed? To mend the broken pieces and be a family again?

Chapter Forty-Eight

SUNDAY NIGHTS at the Green Turtle Tavern were always among the most crowded for some reason. Maybe it was because most other places were closed on a night like this; maybe it was just the music and the company that continued to make it the most visited bar in downtown Fernandina Beach.

"Can I have a beer, please?" E.T. asked the bartender after having elbowed his way through the crowd. Outside on the porch, a guy with a guitar had set up and was playing songs per request from the audience. People were getting rowdy and loud now as the alcohol was setting in. The singer wasn't very good and struggled with hitting the high notes. But the audience loved him, and the interaction between them was fun and something you wouldn't see anywhere else.

"Play *Waltzing Matilda*," someone yelled as E.T. went outside with his beer in hand. His eyes scanned the area for a place to sit, and he found a spot on a bench next to a couple that was sitting with their arms and legs tangled up in one another, kissing between sipping their drinks.

People hollered at the suggestion. A dog dressed in a shark

costume walked by, its owner holding a beer and a cigarette in her hand.

"Play *Bobby McGee*," someone else suggested. That seemed to please the man with the guitar, and he began to play.

Two women in denim miniskirts with cigarettes in one hand and beers in the other started to dance. It was hot out, and the fans were turned on under the ceiling, yet still not giving E.T. much relief. On the wooden walls, people had written messages or carved in their names. Like BETH and MIKE inside of a heart. A couple was playing table tennis in the back.

E.T. looked at the people present, thinking with great satisfaction about this morning's events. Everything had gone the way he wanted it to. And Eva Rae had received the video. He needed her to see what he had done, and the satisfaction of knowing that she had was intoxicating.

E.T. touched his thigh gently. The skin underneath his jeans was throbbing where he had carved the word earlier.

PEACE

E.T. had watched the news all afternoon and knew they had found Jeff in the car and that he had been killed before he could talk. Everything was as it should be. Fourteen people had been killed at the nursing home, one still in critical condition. Not bad, but still, it wasn't good enough. One of the guys in the Philippines had just walked into a church this same morning and killed fifty-six people while broadcasting it live on the website. It had gotten more views than his from the nursing home, and it angered him.

He knew he could do better than this. And he intended to prove it.

Just as he thought about his next plan, that to him was a stroke of pure genius and a masterpiece, the girl he had appointed to be the center of his next accomplishments walked out from inside the bar, beer clutched in her hand. She heard the music and started to swing her hips while her friend smiled at some guy across the porch.

E.T. stared at her until she noticed and finally gave him a smile back, then scratched herself gently on the cheek with her long, painted nails.

Chapter Forty-Nine

MELANIE KAGAN SWUNG her hips from side to side. She felt like dancing, but she didn't want to do it in front of all these people. Not like her friend Ella, who was standing a few steps in front of her, dancing with two other women, holding their beers high in the air, while the men surrounding them hollered and whistled. Ella kept signaling for Melanie to join them, but she shook her head.

It just wasn't Melanie's thing. She was too shy. Even if she had something to drink, she still didn't dance. Not like they did.

There was a guy who kept eyeing her, sitting right behind her. She felt flattered that he was looking at her and not at the sexy girls dancing. Melanie wasn't used to that. Usually, all the men looked at Ella and not Melanie when they went out. But this guy seemed only to be interested in her, and no one else. He kept staring at her, and when she turned her head and smiled back, he lifted his beer and saluted her. She saluted him back, then turned away, blushing, then put the beer down on the table behind her and lit a cigarette. The guy was pretty old, maybe in his forties, whereas Melanie was only twenty-five, but still. She liked the way he looked at her. His hungry look, the way he smiled at her. It was all very flattering.

It wasn't like she'd go all the way with an old guy like that, but maybe she'd indulge him a little. After all, he was the type that probably had a wife and family somewhere and was just looking for some fun. Melanie wasn't one to sleep with guys she didn't know, especially when she didn't think it would lead to anything afterward. Her sister had been pregnant at eighteen because she made that mistake. The guy, who had been thirty at the time, and who had been some tourist passing through the island, hadn't been heard from since.

No, Melanie knew how to take proper care of herself and to be careful, but she also knew how to have fun. And she might have a little fun with this guy, just a little.

When the song ended, Ella came back, sweating and groaning. A guy she had been dancing with pulled her arm, and she winked at Melanie.

"You don't mind, do you?"

Melanie shook her head. "Not at all. Have fun."

"Thanks, hon," Ella said, then disappeared giggling with the guy.

Melanie stood alone for a few minutes, pondering what to do … whether she should go sit with that guy who kept staring at her, but when she turned to look, he was gone. Disappointed, Melanie put down her beer, then looked at her watch and decided she might as well go home.

She walked down the stairs from the porch in front of the Green Turtle Tavern, then staggered across the gravel, realizing she might be a little drunker than she thought.

How can I be this drunk from just one beer? I didn't even drink the entire thing?

Melanie tried to focus on the trail ahead of her, taking a shortcut to where she lived through a small bushy area. It felt like the Earth was moving beneath her, and her vision grew blurry.

As she spun around, tripping in her high heels and fell toward the ground, a set of strong arms grabbed her before she hit the gravel below.

Chapter Fifty

THEN:

They had let her go. For now, they said. But she'd have to go back in for more questioning in two days. Meanwhile, Jack was in the care of the DCF, and they had found a temporary home for him, where they weren't allowed to visit until the case was fully investigated.

Marlene cried all the way home in the car, wondering about her poor son and whether she'd ever be allowed to see him again.

They can't keep him away from me forever, can they?

She feared they might. And maybe it was the right thing. If her husband really had abused the boy and she hadn't seen it, then she could hardly call herself a suitable mother, could she? She just couldn't — for the life of her — understand how this could have happened without her at least suspecting it?

How could she have been so blind?

Or maybe she wasn't blind at all. Had she, in fact, seen the signs and chosen to ignore them? Did she know it was happening somewhere deep down? Had she maybe just closed her eyes because it was too painful? Because she didn't want to see it?

It didn't seem possible. Yet, here they were.

As Marlene drove up the driveway, she took a deep breath when she saw Bruce's car parked there.

He was home.

Bruce waited for her in the kitchen. He was sitting on a stool at the breakfast counter, his face hidden in his hands, and as she opened the door and walked in, he lifted his head and saw her, his eyes red-rimmed.

"Marlene, thank God."

He rushed to her and held her in his arms. She didn't hug him back. When he let go of her, she put her purse down on the small table by the door, then walked past him to the fridge where she pulled out a bottle of leftover white wine and pulled out the cork. She poured herself a glass, then downed it in one long sip. After that, she poured herself another glass while staring at the chicken on the counter. It was still there, and the dog hadn't eaten it. But she didn't want to cook at all. She just wanted to drink her wine. Marlene had never been much of a drinker since she didn't like to lose control, but now she craved the drops that would numb her and every fiber of her body.

Anything to drown out the screaming voices in her head.

Seeing this, Bruce looked at her with his sad eyes. "They took me in too. Questioned me about my relationship with Jack. Went on and on about how I played with him in the yard and the things we did, and what I did when I got angry at him, how often I beat him, and if I ever used a tool to hit him. Crazy stuff like that. It was like they had decided that I was abusing our son beforehand, and there was nothing I could say or do to stop it. What did you tell them?"

Marlene exhaled and rubbed her forehead. "I couldn't really tell them much since I never saw any of it. I was never around when it happened."

"Wait ... you believe them?"

Marlene stared at the man she had loved so dearly up until this point. Now, she felt nothing but resentment toward him. She kept seeing him in the yard with Jack, hitting him, kicking him, and locking him up in the shed where he knew she would never go. Just like he knew she would never come into the yard because she was so busy with housework and because she trusted him. She even thought that the two of them spending time together outside, playing, had been good for the boy. She thought she was being a good mother by letting them play, by encouraging them to go out there and bond. She had been proud of her husband because he spent time with his son. Because he actually did what most men didn't. He prioritized his family and especially his son. Jack was going to grow up with a strong father figure in his life. He was the fortunate one compared to all those who didn't have a father around. All the media talked about was how boys these days were neglected and grew up to be mass murders or school shooters because they were so angry at the world and because they didn't have fathers.

Jack had been the lucky one. That's what she had thought. Boy, what a fool she had been.

"I ... I have to say, I don't know what to believe, to be honest."

His shoulders slumped, and it was like all air left him, along with every ounce of hope.

"You ... you can't be serious?" he said, his voice shivering. "Are you telling me that you believe that I could have abused our son? Our ... my son, Jack? The boy I love more than anything in this world?"

A tear escaped her eyes, and she wiped it away, then sipped her wine again. "The things they said, the things Jack told them; how am I supposed ..."

Bruce grabbed her by the shoulders. The gesture frightened her slightly. He looked into her eyes.

"Can't you see that it's what they want? They want to turn us against one another. Don't let them win. We have to be there for one another through this, Marlene. I won't survive it if we don't. Neither of us will. We need to be a united front. Don't believe them, Marlene, please. I never laid a hand on the boy. You have my word for it. You must believe me."

She sighed again. "I don't know, Bruce. I don't know what to believe anymore. I feel so confused. You won't believe the way they looked at me. Like I was the worst mother in the entire world. But

I'm not, Bruce. I'm a good mother. I have always been a good mother."

"Yes, you are," he said. "And I am a good father. We are good parents. No, we're more than that. We're excellent parents."

"But ... how ... why do they say those things?" she asked, now crying. "Those awful, awful things?"

He pulled her into a deep hug. She felt like he was squeezing her a little too tight. It made her feel uncomfortable.

"I don't know, honey. But we'll get to the bottom of this. I've called my lawyer, and he'll help us. We'll figure things out. We always do. We just can't turn on one another; do you hear me? We just can't."

Chapter Fifty-One

"IT'S HIM AGAIN. I just know it is."

It was late Monday afternoon when I sat down across from Detective McMillen at the sheriff's office on the mainland. I had barely put my behind in the seat before I started to talk.

McMillen sighed and leaned back in his chair. "And just why on Earth do you think that?"

"It has him written all over it."

"So, because a young girl disappears after a night out, you think it's your killer — whom we have no proof actually exists — that has kidnapped her?"

I nodded seriously. I knew he didn't believe me, but I felt like I had to warn them, or at least tell someone. As soon as I heard about the young girl, Melanie Kagan that had disappeared the night before, I knew it was him again.

"Yes."

"And let's just say this guy actually exists. I'll indulge you a little here. Could you please explain to me why he has kidnapped this young girl? It doesn't exactly fit his former pattern, does it? Assuming again that he exists and that he isn't just a product of your very vivid imagination."

"He kidnapped Allyson," I said. "Besides, I don't know his exact pattern yet, but I'm working very hard on finding it, and then I'll let you know."

"You know, not everything that happens on this island is connected to some greater plot schemed by some sick killer."

I exhaled, annoyed. I had the same discussion with my sister earlier the same morning. She too thought I was getting a little crazy in my assumptions when I said I believed Melanie was kidnapped by my killer. She too meant that I didn't have to think everything was related to what happened to Allyson and our brother.

Much to my surprise, I had received backup from our father. I didn't like that he was supporting me much since I didn't want anything from him, but he had told my sister that there could be no harm in looking into it if that was what I wanted.

"Come on, Dad," Sydney had said. "You really believe all this?"

My dad had nodded and looked at me. Our eyes had locked for a few seconds, and I felt something I hadn't before, something I didn't really want to feel, so I looked away, trying to avoid it.

"I do," he said. "If I believe my son is innocent, then I must also believe Eva Rae is right. And I do believe he's innocent. Make no mistake. He never meant to hurt anyone. Not my son, not Adam."

I tilted my head and looked at McMillen. "The nursing home was part of it. I am certain of it. Just like the people at the hotel were his doing."

He sighed. "Of course, you are."

"He sent me the video. Did you have time to look at it?"

McMillen nodded. "Yes. We saw it. It was nasty. Can't blame you for wanting to see things that aren't exactly there."

"So, what is your explanation for me receiving that video?" I asked.

He shrugged. "The guy who did this had heard about you … heard that you were on the island. He wanted to make sure you saw it. Anyway, it doesn't really matter; we'll never know for sure since he's dead."

"What if I tell you I don't believe you got the right guy?" I said.

McMillen laughed. It was expected. It didn't surprise me or

even make me angry. I was way past that now. This wasn't about me anymore.

"I'd say you're imagining things again. Besides, the video was recorded and sent to you from the phone we recovered on the scene from inside the truck. It was Jeff Facer's phone."

"How do you know?" I asked. "Was it registered in his name or was it a burner phone and you just assumed it was his since it was in the truck with him?"

McMillen went quiet, and I had my answer.

I rose to my feet and gave him a victorious smile.

"That's what I thought."

Chapter Fifty-Two

I DIDN'T LEAVE RIGHT AWAY. I walked out of McMillen's office and turned right down the hallway, toward forensics, the evidence unit. I had been told they were done with my phone, and I could get it back. They had copied its contents and didn't need the physical phone anymore.

I signed the paper to retrieve it, and the woman behind the counter went to find it. While I waited, I looked out the window next to me, then spotted something that piqued my interest.

A big black MACK dump truck was parked out back.

The woman returned with my phone in a plastic bag that she handed to me. I grabbed it, then left, rushing out the doors, and hurried toward the truck. A tech, dressed in a bodysuit and gloves, was dusting for fingerprints inside of it as I approached the front.

I glared inside the truck, then the tech noticed me.

"Yes? Can I help you, ma'am?"

"Was the front seat in that same position when you found the truck?"

The tech looked confused. "What do you mean?"

"Did you change the position of the front seat at any point?" I asked.

He looked puzzled. "No. The truck is exactly the way it was found."

"And you haven't pulled the seat forward to be better able to get in behind it or anything?" I asked.

He shook his head. "No. Everything is left the way we found it."

I nodded, feeling content with the answer. "And that goes for the positioning of the mirrors and the steering wheel too, I assume?"

"Yes. All of it."

"Great. Thank you so much."

"No problem, ma'am."

I left, almost rushing out the doors, holding my phone in my hand. I was about to call Matt, out of habit, as I got into my car, but then stopped myself, feeling heavy at heart. I stared at the display and his name.

Was it over between us? Or was he waiting for me to make a move? Did I want to, or did I want to try and mend things with Chad? Was I just running from having to deal with it by chasing ghosts? Was me trying to solve this case really just a way to escape? Because I didn't want to have to make a decision?

I started the engine and backed out of the parking lot, then left. I drove across the marshland while the thoughts rushed through my mind. The more I got to know this guy, the more I realized he truly believed he'd get away with this, that he could keep himself under the radar, and even put his actions right in my face, laughing at me, yet still get away with it.

The question that remained was why? Why was he doing this? And what would it take to stop him?

I had alienated most of my family and my boyfriend by now. Was I going to lose everything while trying to catch him? Was it worth it?

Of course, it's worth it. This is a killer that thinks he is too smart to be caught. But that only shows you one thing:

He doesn't know you very well.

Chapter Fifty-Three

"HEY, buddy, how about we take a dip in the pool, huh? Do you want to go with me?"

Matt stared at Elijah. He was sitting on the couch in the living room, legs pulled up, an iPad planted in his lap. He didn't even look up as Matt spoke to him.

"Elijah?"

Matt stared at his son, then sighed deeply. The boy kept pretending like he didn't exist. Meanwhile, Elijah loved being with Matt's mother, and to be honest, Matt was fed up with it. He wanted to have with Elijah what he saw Chad have with Alex.

The thought of Chad made Matt's blood boil. Truly, he had come to loathe the guy. He couldn't believe he had actually walked out on Eva Rae and left her in the arms of that idiot.

It had been the right thing to do. He still believed it was since they were a real family, and they could be one again if Matt weren't in the way.

It was the only right and noble thing to do.

Now, Matt had an entire day off since Chief Annie had told him to get some rest, but the boy, his own son, didn't even want to hang out with him, let alone talk to him. Not even if Matt begged him.

It was pathetic. Matt felt like such a fool. Maybe he just wasn't cut out to be a father.

"Well, I'll just go alone then," Matt said and turned around and walked to the sliding doors. He paused for a second before opening them, hoping that Elijah would stop him, that he would tell him to wait because he wanted to go with him after all.

But he didn't. He remained still on the couch, engaged in some silly useless game on the iPad. It was all he ever did once he came home from school, and when he was off from school on the weekends or a teachers' workday like today.

"He's been through so much," Matt's mother would say when Matt complained that the boy didn't talk to him, and when he talked about taking the iPad away from him. "Give it time."

But he had given it time, hadn't he? It had been almost a year now, and the boy still wasn't the least bit interested in his dad. Maybe he never would be. What if he never talked to him again?

Was Matt going about it the wrong way? Did he need another approach?

He often thought about being stricter, maybe grounding the boy or yelling at him for not answering, but that just wasn't Matt's way of doing things. He didn't have a temper, and he seldom yelled at anyone.

It just wasn't who Matt was. He wasn't an angry person. It wasn't in his nature, and it never had been. Maybe that made him a doormat from time to time, but he just didn't believe in yelling at or hurting kids. After all, yelling was just a way to hit children with words, wasn't it? He had always believed it was. His own dad had yelled every chance he got, and that just made Matt lose all respect for him. He loved him, yes, and he missed him every day since he died from lung cancer, but he hadn't been a very good father, in Matt's opinion. With Elijah, he had always believed that the boy would eventually come around if he treated him nicely and just talked to him. Why was the kid being so stubborn?

He blames you for the death of his mother. You know this, Matt.

Matt walked outside and closed the sliding doors behind him, then felt tears well up in his eyes as he plunged into the water.

I need you, Eva Rae. I'm not sure I can do this life without you.

Chapter Fifty-Four

"HOW DID IT GO?"

My sister looked up from her manuscript as I entered our grand-mother's house. She was sitting in the living room, rehearsing her lines. It seemed like it was all she did lately.

"At the sheriff's office?"

I exhaled. "Great! They think I'm a raving lunatic, but hey, nothing new there, right? It seems to be the general opinion around here lately. But I got my phone back. At least that's something."

"I'm sorry," Syd said. "That they don't believe you."

"Why? You don't believe me either."

"I never said that."

"You said something like that, and you meant it."

She wrinkled her forehead. "I did not. Of course, I believe you."

I chuckled. "You need to practice your acting a little more there, dear sis. Not quite convincing."

She exhaled. "I was just trying to say that maybe not everything that happens around here has to do with your case. Maybe some things are coincidental."

Now, it was my turn to wrinkle my nose. "See, that's the word I don't like. I don't believe in ..."

"Coincidences, I know that now," she said. "But what I meant to say was that I still believe that Adam's story has more to it than what the police are saying. That part I am still in on. So, don't give me that *I-am-all-alone-in-the-world* attitude. You're not."

"You just don't believe the rest. That's great."

I walked to the stairs and was almost up the first step when she spoke again:

"Chad took the kids to the beach, by the way. He said you could join them if you liked."

I looked at my watch. It was late, and I didn't really want to go to the beach. Still, I felt that I had to for my family's sake, so I did. I found my swimsuit and packed a bag, then drove down there and found them, playing in the sand with their father. I stopped a couple of feet away and stood for a few seconds, staring at them. Alex was being covered up, and both girls helped out by pouring sand on top of him. They were probably getting a kick out of making sure their little brother couldn't move and annoy them. Even Olivia looked like she was enjoying herself. Alex was shrieking with joy until Christine shoveled a big portion of sand in his face, and he began to cry. Chad told her to stop.

"Sorry," Christine said.

I felt my heart drop. Having Chad in the children's lives was such a blessing. He knew exactly how to handle them, and not carrying the full responsibility for them was a major relief for me. It was like a huge weight was lifted off my shoulders.

I wasn't alone anymore.

Olivia spotted me as I walked closer to them.

"Mom!"

I came up to them and put down my bag. Chad looked up and smiled widely. "Yay, Mommy's here."

"Mommy. Mommy! Look at me," Alex said.

"Oh, my Lord," I said. "You have no body! We must call the police. Someone stole your body."

That made him laugh. And me too. Not because it was funny, but because I felt happy. Being with my family again made me feel happy.

We spent a couple of hours on the beach until the sun went down, then drove back to the house, a newfound feeling of completion settling inside of me, a sense of belonging. It had been years since I had seen my children this happy.

Once I got back in my room, I put my bag on the floor, then saw my dad sitting on a chair in the darkness, staring at the wall with all my pictures and notes.

"David?" I nearly gasped. "You scared me. What are you doing in here?"

Chapter Fifty-Five

DAVID DIDN'T MOVE AN INCH. He didn't even turn to look at me as I approached him. He sat with his hands put together in front of his face, looking pensive. When I finally caught his gaze, his eyes were ablaze.

"David? Are you okay?"

His tightened his lips. "Seeing him like this, Eva Rae. It's like … It's torture."

I nodded. "When it comes to our children, there …"

I stopped myself as I teared up, thinking about my own children and if it had been any of them that were lying out there.

"He was the one I did right, you know? He was my second chance at getting this right. I was the best father; I was everything that I could never be to you or even your sister. With Sydney, it was like … well, I guess I messed both of you up pretty bad, huh? But with Adam, it was different. I had a clean slate with him, and we were doing well. He was doing so well. He was a good student, most of the time, getting mostly As and Bs and an occasional C, but he was doing well for himself. He never got himself in trouble. He had friends. He had a sweet girlfriend that he adored. He was running track and had just been accepted on the varsity team. I just know in my heart that there is no evil in him; I know my kid. And now he's lying out there, completely lifeless, and even if he wakes up, they'll take him away. He'll spend most of his life in prison for something he didn't do. He didn't kill Allyson; he didn't."

"Hey, I believe you. You know I do," I said with a sigh. "But I can't seem to convince anyone else."

"I want to catch him," he said. "I want to catch whoever did this to my son so badly. I might be able to help you. Fill me in on what you've got. I want to help. I can't stand to sit out there at the hospital and wait for even one more second. I can't stand it anymore. I want to do something."

I looked at David. Did I want his help? Could I put my anger aside enough to act civilly around him? Could I stand being around him?

I exhaled. I could hardly deny a father's desire to save his son. If anyone knew what that was like, it was me.

"All right," I said and walked to the wall with all my sticky notes plastered all over it. I grabbed one and showed it to him. "I call him the Leech. Because I believe he uses others to take the fall for his murders. Just like a leech, he uses others for personal gain, without giving anything in return, exhausting the other's resources, finally killing them. He's a bloodsucking worm."

My dad sent me a faint smile. I wasn't trying to make him laugh or even cheer him up; I was just explaining how this guy worked … how I believed he managed to stay under the radar and not be discovered.

"That's the only pattern for him that I've come up with so far," I said. "The way he arranges his kills, he manages to make it look like others are doing it. And no matter what he does, no one believes it. Nobody would go that far is the reaction I get when trying to point it out. It seems impossible, just my speculations, or crazy even. That's how clever he is. That's his talent if you'll call it that."

My dad nodded heavily. "Sounds just about right to me. Now, do you have any suspects so far?"

"That's the hard part." I walked to my desk and picked up a photo I had printed from Facebook. "This is Mr. Jenkins. He's forty-five, lives here on the island with his wife and child, and works at the Ritz-Carlton as a bartender. He's my main suspect."

David stared at the photo, then up at me. "Why him?"

"Because he was seeing Allyson behind Adam's back. Adam found out, and the police believe that's why he lost it. According to them, that was his motive for killing her and shooting up the school. Jenkins is connected both to Allyson and the deaths at the Ritz-Carlton since he works there."

"I see," David said and stared at the Facebook photo intently. "And so, you believe that what happened at the nursing home was his work too? Why?"

"First of all, there was the video he sent me. No one in their right mind would record something like that and send it to me if it wasn't to taunt me, to tell me *see what I am doing. No one will ever believe you*. He's getting cocky because he can tell that he's getting away with it all, and no one even suspects that it's all connected."

"Except for you," he said.

"Exactly, but no one will believe me, and he's getting a kick out of that. Makes him want to do more and to accelerate, to kill more and more people because he feels invincible, untouchable. It's very dangerous because we don't know what he might do next. There's no real MO, so I can't guess it. But there's something else that made me certain that he was behind what happened at the nursing home. I went to see the truck when I was at the sheriff's office," I said. "To get my phone. That's where I saw the truck. I got to look inside, and there was no way Jeff Facer could have driven it. Look."

I showed him the picture I had taken with my phone when the tech guy didn't see it.

"Look at the positioning of the driver's seat and the mirrors. I've been teaching my oldest daughter, Olivia, to drive, and she has way longer legs than me and is taller than I am, so she has to adjust the seat every time or her knees knock into the steering wheel. Jeff Facer was a tall guy with long legs. Look at this photo from the online article about him. He was six-foot-four. There is no way a guy that is six feet four could sit in that seat and drive. No way."

"So, you're thinking that whoever drove that truck — and

placed Jeff Facer in it when dumping it for the police to find — had shorter legs?"

"Yes, like Mr. Jenkins. He's only five-foot-seven, so he could easily have fit there. Someone his size drove that truck through the nursing home and killed all those people. Not Jeff. But the Leech knew that once they found the truck with the person inside of it, the police would be so terrified, they'd end up killing him, or at least he hoped they would."

"Just like in Adam's case," David said, his face lighting up. "This is exactly like his story. The Leech knew that there was an officer at the school because all schools have that now since the Parkland shooting. He knew Adam would be shot, and then he would be to blame for Allyson's death and for whoever was killed at the school."

"But luckily, Adam was smart. He didn't aim for anyone. He closed his eyes and shot the wall right under the ceiling, hitting no one."

"But why?" David said. "That's what I don't understand. Why did he do it?"

I exhaled. "My theory is that the Leech had kidnapped Allyson on the night after the party and that he was threatening Adam, saying if he didn't, Allyson would be killed. That was why he had her picture clutched in his hand when he walked inside the cafeteria. He didn't want to do it, but he saw no other way out. He believed it was the only way to save her life. But of course, the Leech would kill her anyway."

David nodded. "It makes sense. That would be the only reason why my boy would do such an atrocity. For love."

I sat down with an exhale. "That also explains why Allyson was found in the dumpster. She wasn't useful anymore. She had served her purpose, and he just tossed her. If only I could get to talk to the deputies who tried to arrest Jeff Facer and ended up shooting him. But the sheriff's office isn't exactly cooperative. They really hate me out there by now."

David lifted his head, a surprised look on his face. "Actually, I might be able to help with that."

Chapter Fifty-Six

THE PALACE SALOON was located in downtown Fernandina Beach. It boasted of being the oldest bar in Florida, and it was said that ghosts from ten decades would join in drinking to your health.

I didn't know about ghosts, but there sure were people being haunted in there by their pasts. Like Deputy Griffins. We found him sitting alone at the counter. In front of him stood a tall glass of half-finished beer. He stared at the TV screen at the end of the bar that showed some game being played, but he didn't seem to be following it closely.

David was the one who approached him, putting a hand on his shoulder. David had told me he had known Deputy Griffins for years, that their kids had grown up together and were the same age.

"Mark?"

The deputy smiled. He seemed like he'd had more than enough to drink. His eyes were swimming.

"David, my man."

They shook hands, and David introduced me. "This is my daughter."

It was strange being introduced like that, and it was going to take some time getting used to. I reached out my hand, and he shook it.

"Nice to meet you."

"Can I get you something to drink?" he asked, his speech slurred.

My dad ordered beers for us all. I would usually prefer a glass of wine, but I didn't say anything. I wasn't there to drink.

"So, how are you holding up?" David asked. "After what happened?"

David made sure I sat in between them, so I could hear everything.

Deputy Griffins shook his head and sipped his beer. "They gave me a week of paid leave."

"Well, maybe that wasn't the worst," David said. "To take some time off, after seeing those things."

"You were the one who got Jeff Facer, right?" I asked. "I read about it."

He nodded, looking proud, yet heavyhearted.

"He pulled a gun on you?" I asked.

Griffins looked away. He downed the rest of his beer, then ordered a new one. I could tell he was getting pretty hammered by now, as he could barely sit still on the stool. He kept sliding to the side. A long pause followed where he watched the television before he finally whispered.

"There was no gun."

"There wasn't?" I said, feeling my heart rate going up.

"We just thought there was. But don't tell anyone," he said and put a finger to his lips, barely reaching them. "They told us to keep it to ourselves."

"She's a cop too," David said. "You can trust her."

He looked at me, then smiled. "You're a colleague, huh? Who would have known? A small thing like you?"

"Small but lethal," David said.

"Can I ask you something?" I said.

His beer arrived, and he took a deep sip, then nodded. "S-sure."

"Did you notice his nails?"

165

"His nails?"

"Yes, Jeff Facer's nails."

Griffins drank again. "What about 'em?"

I leaned closer, so no one would hear what I asked. "Were they pulled out?"

Griffins went quiet again. He drank, then put the beer down. He almost fell off the stool, then nodded.

"There was ... blood. Running down his arms. They said he did it to himself before ... you know, getting into the truck and driving through ... Maybe he just lost it, huh? I just still ... well, I kept thinking, who does that? Who pulls out his own nails? It must have hurt like hell, you know?"

"Well, maybe he didn't exactly do it himself," I mumbled, trying to hide my enthusiasm. I had finally found an MO. Pulling out their nails was the Leech's trademark. He knew it was dangerous, yet he still did it because he needed to put his mark on them; he needed them to carry his brand.

It was the first time the Leech had shown weakness.

I stared at Griffins, who finally lost his grip on the counter and fell backward. David grabbed him before he could fall and tipped him back into place.

"I think we should get him home," I said. "You know where he lives, right?"

David nodded, then put Griffins' arm around his neck and supported him while they walked. I had seen my share of law enforcement losing the battle with alcohol when the job got to them. It was a terrible thing, and it haunted me. Often, I wondered if it could ever happen to me. With the things I had seen, it was a wonder it hadn't happened already.

Chapter Fifty-Seven

AFTER DROPPING OFF THE DEPUTY, we drove home where Chad and the kids had prepared a wonderful steak dinner with mashed potatoes and Caesar salad for us all. We ate together in Eileen's dining room, and I realized I was actually able to finally let go of some of the anger I had felt toward David and just enjoy all of us being together. It felt so incredible, like a dream come true, and I could tell the kids enjoyed it just as much as I did.

I couldn't help thinking about my mom, though. She had tried to stop me from going to see my father and told me nothing good would come of it, that I would only end up getting hurt.

"It's what he does," she said. "He hurts the people he loves."

It had almost made me stay home, but now I was glad I had decided to go anyway.

After having cleaned up after dinner and put Alex to bed, I walked out on the porch and sat down on the swing with a glass of wine. I enjoyed the sound of the ocean roaring far away, mixed with the noise from the cicadas in the trees next to me. The warm moist air felt wonderful on my face. It was hard to believe that somewhere out in the Atlantic Ocean roared a tropical storm, ready to cause havoc and damage should it decide to make landfall. They had been talking about it all afternoon on TV. Damian was its name. So far, the computer models all said it would stay out to sea, but it was coming awfully close to the coast as it became a hurricane. It happened every year at this time when living in Florida. It wasn't a part that I had missed while living in Washington. You never really knew what would happen, if you had to pack your bags with nothing but a few hours to get out of there, or if it would — like it did for the most part — just pass by without even causing rain. You had to remain prepared for both scenarios, yet you still had to continue your life as usual until you knew for certain what it was going to do. It was maddening at times.

I sipped my wine, then Chad came out to me and sat down, also holding a glass in his hand.

"This is nice," he said. "Out here."

I smiled. "It sure is."

He drank, then exhaled. He turned to look at me. "So, the kids and I will be going back tomorrow. You think you can get by without us?"

I chuckled. "I think I can, but it has been so great to have you all here. Thank you for surprising me like this. It was very sweet of you."

"It was nothing, really."

"No, it was, Chad. It was extremely thoughtful of you. The children have really enjoyed having all of us together. And, frankly, so have I."

"Well, maybe we should do more of that," he said, sounding suddenly very serious. "Being together."

"Yeah, we can totally do that. Once I get back."

"No, I mean for real, Eva Rae," he said and looked into my eyes. His expression was different, and he touched my hand. "I'm serious."

"Chad, I ..."

He kissed the top of my hand. "I miss you, Eva Rae."

I was about to speak when he leaned over and kissed me. At first, I was so surprised, I didn't know what to do, but then I found out that I actually enjoyed it and let him. His lips felt soft against mine, and he smelled and tasted like beach and saltwater. I closed my eyes and kissed him back.

As our lips finally parted, he took my face between his hands and looked deep into my eyes.

"I mean it, Eva Rae. I want you back. I want us to be a family again. I realized I can't live without you and the kids in my life. What I did was stupid. It was ridiculous. It was my mid-life crisis, and I have to say, I regret it desperately. It was the stupidest thing ever, and I want to tell you how sorry I am."

I stared at my ex-husband, wondering what he had eaten. Why was he suddenly saying all the right things, saying everything I had wanted him to tell me a year ago?

I exhaled.

"I don't know what to say, Chad."

"Say you want it too because I know you do. I can see it in your eyes. We were good together. We were a good family. Yes, we drifted apart over the past several years because you worked so much, and maybe I didn't do anything to make things better either, especially not when I decided to punish you by having an affair. But we can get past all that. I know we can. We're better than this, Eva Rae. We are so much more."

I swallowed, not knowing what to say to him. I felt so confused. I thought about Matt, then about what he had told me on this same porch, how he believed he was in the way of a family getting back together again, and he didn't want that. I didn't want that either. I enjoyed having a family.

Could the solution really be that simple?

"Say you'll try again with me," Chad said. "I promise I'm over that mid-life crisis. Kimmie is history, and I've realized what I fool I was for throwing away what I had. I'm ready to beg you to come back to me if that's what it takes."

"Please, don't," I said.

"Then tell me what it will take. Because I see it in your eyes; heck, I felt it in that kiss we just shared. You want it as much as I do."

Maybe I do. Maybe I really do. But do I dare trust him again?

"No, don't answer me now," he said. "Give it some thought. I was thinking that the kids and I could come back next weekend. Then you can give me your answer. Until then, think about it. Think about how wonderful it could be."

He gave me another kiss, then rose to his feet and walked to the door. He sent me one last glance, then sighed before he opened the door and walked back inside. I stayed on the porch, hugging myself, feeling like I had just betrayed Matt.

He left, remember? He told you to get back with Chad. He doesn't want to be in the way of your happiness. It's not fair to him either. If you're not done with Chad, you can never be in a relationship with Matt.

I finished my glass of wine while pushing all the questions aside. I forced myself to think about something else, and soon I was wondering about Melanie Kagan, the kidnapped girl. Where was she now and what was the Leech planning for her? Whatever it was, I just knew it was going to be nasty. For the Leech, there really was no slowing down. Every act had to be ghastlier than the one before it.

Chapter Fifty-Eight

THEN:

There was no way she could sleep. The many thoughts kept rushing through her mind, and she couldn't keep them quiet long enough to doze off. Marlene kept going over every memory she had of Jack's childhood when he was with Bruce. She searched desperately through her recollection of events they had been through together.

The time they went to his grandmother's funeral. Bruce yelled at Jack in the car on the way home because he hadn't stayed quiet in the church. Had he hurt him then? Maybe after they came home and she wasn't looking?

Is it really possible that it could have taken place without my knowledge? For several years?

Marlene finally had enough of lying there and got up. She walked downstairs to grab a glass of water, then looked at her own reflection in the window as she drank. She had gotten old to look at. It wasn't a pretty sight what was staring back at her. In this moment, she despised herself.

Have I just been a fool all this time? Have I been betrayed for all these years? Deceived into thinking we were a happy family?

She put the glass down, then walked into the living room where she looked at the many pictures on the walls. She stopped by the ones that were taken of them when they went on their neighbor's boat once when Jack was just four years old. Marlene remembered the dolphin that jumped out behind it when they were going at full speed. It was the first time Jack had seen a dolphin, and he had been ecstatic. Bruce had put him on his shoulders so he could see better, and Marlene had been terrified that he'd drop him somehow. The two of them had laughed at her for always being so anxious. They did that a lot — the boys ganging up on her.

Was it all just a lie, Bruce?

Marlene turned around with a deep exhale. She felt the tears welling up in her eyes as she thought more and more about what had happened. She missed Jack so terribly and couldn't stand the thought of him not being home with her.

What if he never came back?

She wouldn't survive it.

Still, she didn't know what to think anymore. She had loved Bruce so deeply for all these years, and they had shared so much together. Was she just supposed to throw all that away? Just like that? Wasn't she supposed to stand by her husband through *thick or thin*? Of course, but how did you do that if that meant your son was being hurt? When it meant she was being betrayed?

No, you must trust him. They got it all wrong. It can't be true. It simply can't be the truth.

Marlene sat at the dining table, staring at Bruce's laptop next to her. She thought it over for a few minutes, contemplating back and forth what to do, then finally succumbed to her own suspicion.

She opened the lid and logged herself in, using the password that he used for everything, the old fool.

She opened his browser, then looked at what he had been looking at last. It was a site selling refrigerators. Nothing strange about that since they were in desperate need of a new one, and she had asked him multiple times to replace it soon.

Feeling silly and guilty, Marlene closed the browser again. She wasn't even sure what it was exactly that she was looking for. She stared at the desktop for a few minutes, especially at a small icon that she didn't recognize. Then curiosity got the better of her, and she clicked it.

Probably just something work-related.

As she watched what it contained, fighting the urge to throw up, Marlene realized that life would never be the same again.

She would never be the same again.

Chapter Fifty-Nine

WE WERE STALKING HIM. David and I sat in my minivan and watched as Mr. Jenkins left his house and got into his white van. I had said goodbye to the children and Chad as they went back to Cocoa Beach that same morning. It was David who had suggested we kept a close eye on Jenkins today, and I didn't object. I didn't have a good feeling about this guy at all. If he had taken Melanie Kagan, then we were the only ones able to save her.

"He's in the register," David had told me the same morning. He pulled me aside before breakfast and told me. "I checked him, and he's a sex offender."

"That's usually not a good sign," I said. "But it fits well with him being our main suspect."

So, now we were following him as he drove to the local Winn Dixie and went inside. David and I walked in as well and did a little shopping while keeping a close eye on Jenkins. He filled his cart, then paid and left. We also paid for the few items I had found, then rushed back to my minivan in the parking lot just in time to see him take off. We followed him closely as he went back to the house and carried all his stuff inside. We ate the snacks I had bought while the house remained silent, and he didn't make his next move until late in the afternoon. As his daughter and wife came home, he left, rushing to his white van.

We followed him as he drove to an old house down by the beach and drove into the garage.

"What do you think he's doing in there?" David asked, crunching sour cream and onion chips. They were my favorite too, and I hoped he wouldn't eat them all. As soon as his hand was out of the bag and he put it down to get a sip of his soda, I reached for the bag and dug in.

"Who lives here?" I asked.

David shrugged.

A second or so later, the garage door opened, and he backed the van out again.

"He's leaving," I said and wiped my greasy hands on my pants like my mother always told me not to. I noticed David did the same.

I stayed a good distance behind Jenkins, then followed him through town until he reached an old wooden building in the center. Jenkins drove into the back and we lost sight of him.

"What is this place?" I asked.

"It's the local theater," David said. "They have a performance tonight. Opening night. It's usually a big deal around here. Lots of people come, both locals and tourists. The whole town's gonna be here. It's usually pretty good."

"So, you think he's part of the show?" I asked, thinking we might be wasting our time. "That he's helping out?"

He shrugged. "I guess he could be. Let's just stay and wait and see what happens. He might leave in a few minutes."

Thinking we might as well, and that we didn't have anything better to do, I nodded in agreement. Of course, the guy didn't leave, and after a few hours, people started to swarm the place. Cars parked in the parking lot and people flocked indoors.

"Do you think he might have left if there's another exit in the back?" I asked.

"Maybe," David said.

"I'm gonna go check."

Pretending to be one of the crowd, I got out of the car and

walked up to the theater building. I then ran around it and spotted Jenkin's white van still parked in the back.

He was still there. If he were part of the show, then he would be there for the entire evening.

And apparently, so would we.

Chapter Sixty

IT WAS pitch dark when she opened her eyes. Melanie blinked, but it didn't help much. She was so confused, it was almost overpowering, and she wanted to cry. Yet she managed to hold it back while a million thoughts flashed through her mind at once, mostly asking questions.

Where am I? What happened?

Desperately, she tried to recollect what had taken place before this moment, but she couldn't. No matter how hard she tried, it was all just a black hole, just as black as the view she was staring at right now.

What is going on?

Panic began to rise inside of her as she felt pain in the tips of her fingers and reached out her hand. The tips scraped against something like a wall, and she kept touching it, then reached out to the sides next to her and felt the wall behind her.

Am I trapped somewhere?

As the realization sank in, she felt anxious. Crying out in fear, Melanie reached out both hands and knocked them both on the wall in front of her, forcing it to slam open with a loud bang. A sea of light overwhelmed her. With a loud gasp, she closed her eyes and stepped out, then looked back at what was behind her, still covering her eyes halfway because of the bright light.

What is this place?

A type of closet was behind her. An old-fashioned wooden armoire with no clothes inside of it. Had she been kept in there? Why? And who put her there? Or did she go in there voluntarily? Had she slept in there?

Had she really been that drunk?

She remembered going out with her friend, and she remembered music and drinking beer, but that was about all she could recollect. It was like everything was just this big dark gap.

It'll come back to you. Once you figure out everything else. Take it one step at a time. It'll come.

Melanie touched her head and tried to figure out where she was. There was a lot of light shining directly at her, making it impossible for her to see properly. She heard someone cough and tried to look past the lights, wondering if someone was out there. That was when someone suddenly yelled or almost screamed.

"It's a bomb! She's got a bomb!"

"Who?" Melanie asked, scanning the area around her before she looked down at her own chest. She lifted a hand to touch the vest while the reality sank in.

"It's probably part of the show," someone yelled back. "Sit back down."

What were they talking about?

The crowd in front of her went quiet while Melanie stared at them, her pulse beginning to quicken as her fingers touched the wires. Sweat sprang to her forehead, and she felt her hands begin to tremble.

Her. They were talking about her.

Chapter Sixty-One

I COULDN'T BELIEVE my eyes. David and I had walked inside to watch the show and hopefully keep an eye on Jenkins. I had spotted him standing by the stage, a camera in his hand, filming.

Now, I was looking at the girl on the stage.

She was standing in the center of it, touching the vest she was wearing, visibly weeping in distress. The crowd was murmuring, unable to figure out what was going on. Someone had yelled it was a bomb, while others said it was just a part of the show.

I had my doubts. It didn't take me long to recognize Melanie from the pictures in the local online newspaper. And the vest she was wearing was a real bomb. I had no doubt about it.

"We need to get these people out of here," I said to David in a low voice. "Preferably without anyone get trampled in the panic."

He rose from his seat, and I followed, trying to do so calmly, but by then, it was too late. The woman in the front who had yelled that it was a bomb was still whimpering, and now as Melanie stepped forward and they could see her distress, a wave of shock went through the crowd.

"Help me," Melanie said through tears, her voice quivering. "Please, someone help me."

That set them off. The woman from earlier grabbed her child in her arms, turned away from the stage, and set off toward the doors. It didn't take many seconds before about fifty others followed, stumbling for the doors, tripping over one another, screaming.

But as the first woman reached the doors and she tried to open them, they didn't budge. It was then that my blood froze.

"Try the other door," I said to David, and he ran to the one behind us, but it was also locked. Someone tried the emergency exits too, but they were locked as well.

We were trapped. Trapped inside a small room with a bomb.

Screams filled the air as people panicked and hammered on the doors. David grabbed his phone and called nine-one-one while I tried to calm people down around me and prevent them from panicking. But it was no use. They were screaming and yelling and knocking on the doors hysterically. There was no way I could calm them down. I felt the panic spread inside of me as well. I had never been good with claustrophobic situations and being trapped inside a room with hundreds of people and a bomb wasn't exactly *not* claustrophobic.

I took a few deep breaths and calmed my poor beating heart, focusing not on the danger or the fact that we couldn't get out, but on what to do about it, what I could possibly do to make sure we made it out alive.

Instead, I turned to look at Melanie on the stage. She was still weeping and had fallen to her knees.

Heart in my throat, I elbowed my way through the crowd, going against the traffic toward the stage, where I climbed up to her. She was pulling at the sides of the vest, her face strained in fear.

"Melanie?" I said.

She looked up, and our eyes met. I cleared my throat to make sure I didn't sound shrill or like I was about to freak out, which I was.

"Hi there, Melanie. My name is Eva Rae Thomas. I'm with the FBI, and I'm going to try and help you, okay?"

"Please," she said and pulled at the vest. "Please, just get this thing off of me!"

Chapter Sixty-Two

"IT SEEMS to be connected to some sort of measuring device," I said as I examined the vest. David had come up to us on the stage and knelt next to Melanie.

"I don't know much about these things," he said. "But my guess is it is very real. I can't take the chance and say it isn't. I know we first need to find the switch, a trigger, or a timer. It could be operated remotely in case the carrier of the vest has a change of heart; then it'll go off anyway."

I was sweating in the heat from the lamps and because of the tense situation. My fingers were also trembling as I examined the vest closely.

David took a closer look at something, a small monitor that was also attached to Melanie's arm, then wrinkled his forehead.

"Please," Melanie pleaded. "Please, just get this thing off of me. I can't breathe properly; I'm so scared."

"We're doing what we can," I said. "But it's easier said than done. You can't pull at it, though; you risk setting it off. Now, it seems that the detonator is attached to something, and we need to find out what makes it set off the bomb."

"It can't be," David mumbled.

"What can't be?" I asked. "What's going on?"

David gave me a puzzled look. "It's … it's … I think it's a sphygmomanometer."

"What are you saying? What's going on?" Melanie shrieked. "Please. Can't you help me, please?"

"English, please," I said, "what's that?"

"A … a blood pressure monitor."

"What's going on?" Melanie asked, sobbing loudly. "Please. I'm about to burst into a panic!"

"I don't understand," I said.

He pulled me aside. "It's connected to a blood pressure monitor, keeping an eye on Melanie's blood pressure."

"What? Why?"

"I have no way of knowing this for sure, but let me tell you what it looks like to me. My guess is, the more agitated she gets, the higher her blood pressure will go, right? And when it reaches a certain level, it'll go off."

I stared at him, eyes wide. Melanie was whimpering behind us, making strange nervous sounds.

"Well … can't we just take it off of her? So it won't monitor her blood pressure?" I asked. "Rip the thing off her arm?"

"That will most likely set the bomb off too," he said.

"You think?"

"Do you want to take the risk?" he asked. "Now, I called for help, and they're on their way. The only thing we can do right now is to make sure the bomb doesn't go off before they get here."

"But how?"

"We keep her calm," he said. "We prevent her from going into a panic, whatever it takes."

Chapter Sixty-Three

IT WAS EASIER SAID than done. Melanie was out of reach, panicking, and her blood pressure was through the roof. I took Melanie's hand in mine and stroked it gently. I could feel her rapid pulse underneath her skin, and it made mine soar as well. I still couldn't hear the sirens yet but prayed they weren't far away. Problem was, they had to find someone to be able to defuse the bomb first and then bring that person here. I desperately wondered how long that was going to take.

Meanwhile, everything was chaos in the small theater. People were still hammering on the doors, screaming for help. Others were on their phones, calling their loved ones, some saying goodbye, telling them how much they loved them, crying.

"What did he say? What did he tell you?" Melanie said, her voice shrill.

I swallowed the knot growing in my throat. I tried hard to not think about my own children and the fact that I might never see them again if this bomb went off before the help arrived.

It was difficult not to.

"He said that you need to remain calm."

"Calm? Calm?" she almost screamed. "How am I supposed to remain calm with a bomb strapped to my body?"

David, who was keeping a close eye on the blood pressure monitor, sent me a concerned look. I had to calm her down. We didn't know how far up her blood pressure had to go for the bomb to go off, but my guess was that she was walking a thin line. The Leech wanted the bomb to go off, so he'd have set it at a reachable level, to make sure it went off as soon as she got agitated enough when realizing what was going on.

"There's a blood pressure monitor keeping an eye on you, and once it reaches a certain level, we think it'll set the bomb off," I said, using the calmest voice possible.

In reality, I wanted to slap her and shake her, but that wouldn't be the best way to do things. If I wasn't calm, she wouldn't be either. Yet my heart beat so fast in my chest it was maddening. I focused hard on breathing calmly and speaking in a low and pleasant voice.

"It WHAT?" she almost screamed.

"Please," I said, reaching out for her arm. I really didn't want to touch her out of fear of setting off the bomb, but I still did it. "Please. You must calm down. Your blood produces a surge of hormones when you're in a stressful situation. These hormones temporarily increase your blood pressure by causing your heart to beat faster, okay? But the problem is that the faster it beats, the higher the blood pressure gets, the bigger the chance that the bomb goes off. So, we must try and keep you calm. And you need to do your best to remain tranquil. Can you do that for me, Melanie? Please?"

I looked deeply into her eyes, making sure she had heard me even with the panic going on inside of her, blocking all sense from entering her mind. I couldn't blame her. There was no escaping this for her. She couldn't just run away, even if that was her instinct. It was all any of us wanted to do right now. Remaining calm had to take all of her strength. I know it did for me.

I stroked her hair gently, hoping it would have a calming effect. "We've called for help, and hopefully they'll be here soon," I said.

"Then they can defuse the bomb, and we'll all get to go home. But it won't happen if you don't remain calm, you hear me?"

Melanie was hyperventilating, and David sent me another concerned look. I grabbed her by the shoulders. "Now, I want you to do as I tell you, okay? I want you to take in a deep breath. Come. Do it like me. Take a deep breath; see how much air you can get in your lungs. Close your eyes and think about something that makes you happy. Imagine yourself lying in a quiet field of grass somewhere. Or in the mountains or maybe the beach? Do you like the beach?"

She nodded, her eyes still closed.

"Okay. Imagine you're there. You're lying on the sand, breathing in the fresh salty air; you're reading a book, and you have all the time in the world, okay? Everything is peaceful."

It took a few seconds, but then she nodded.

"All right," I continued. "Then breathe it all out again, remaining in this same spot of quiet. Peace and quiet."

Melanie did as she was told, and my eyes caught David's. He gave me a faint smile and nodded with a thumbs up. It was working. She was relaxing. In the distance, I could hear sirens, and my own blood pressure seemed to drop a little, while sweat still sprang from my forehead. They were here. It was only a matter of minutes before they'd get the doors open and people out of here.

"You're doing really well," I said. "Really well. Just keep breathing. Just keep breathing. We are so close now. So close."

Chapter Sixty-Four

THE SOUND of the doors being unlocked and then opened was the most soothing sound I could remember hearing. The panicking crowd almost stumbled on top of one another to make it outside, and it didn't take long before they were all gone. Only David and I remained on the stage with Melanie. I was constantly touching her arm, making her feel calm.

Then the soldiers entered. Men in thick protective suits, carrying guns, entered the theater. They started to yell at us, and suddenly everything became beyond chaotic again.

"Get down from there!" they yelled while pointing their guns at us.

"No, please," I said.

"Step away from the bomb NOW!"

I felt Melanie's hands begin to shake in mine as she opened her eyes and looked at them approaching us.

"They're gonna shoot me," she mumbled under her breath. Her breathing was getting ragged again, and David got that concerned look back on his face.

"You don't understand," I said addressed to the uniformed soldiers.

"NOW!"

I rose to my feet and placed both of my hands above my head to make sure they understood I wasn't armed.

"The bomb is attached to …"

"Get down from the stage, ma'am," he interrupted me. "We need to clear the room now, so we can defuse the bomb."

I glanced at the monitor. It was reaching a new spike. The systolic blood pressure reached a hundred and fifty and counting. This wasn't good.

"Please, sir, you need to listen to me …"

The yelling intensified. Several of the soldiers yelled at us at once, and I could barely hear myself think. All I could hear was my own heartbeat thumping in my ears. I could only imagine what this was doing to Melanie's heart rate.

"I'm not gonna say it again; step away from the stage," the soldier yelled, pointing his gun close to me.

David grabbed my hand and began to pull at me. I stared at Melanie, who looked at me with pleading eyes.

"No, don't go. Please, don't leave me. Please, I need you …"

I didn't want to move. I figured they'd have to shoot me if they wanted me to leave, but David grabbed me by the arm hard and yanked me away from Melanie. She whimpered and reached out her hand for mine. I touched it gently before David pulled me away, and our hands slipped out of one another's. I was crying heavily as David pulled me away and dragged me out an emergency door. I was crying heavily as first responders approached us.

"You did what you could," David said and put his arm around me. I wanted to protest and push him away, but I didn't do it. Behind us, we heard Melanie scream in distress, and I just waited for that blast, preparing myself for it.

Chapter Sixty-Five

THE THEATER BUILDING remained eerily silent while we waited outside in the parking lot at a safe distance, behind the police barrier. My hands were still shaking as I sat down on the ground. I was worried sick about Melanie, my stomach churning.

Was she going to survive this?

We heard her scream again and feared the worst. I closed my eyes and folded my hands while praying.

Please, let her live. Please, don't let him have this victory.

I waited and listened, fighting to calm my nerves and remain at ease.

The blast never came.

After a few minutes that felt like hours, one of the soldiers in suits came out of there and told us that the bomb had been defused.

We were all safe.

The soldier received a round of applause, even though it probably hadn't been him who defused it. It didn't matter. People were relieved. They had survived a situation that they didn't think they would, and they needed someone to thank. I breathed a deep sigh of relief. David grabbed my arm and helped me get up. He pulled me into a hug, and I didn't protest. It actually felt kind of nice, and I needed it.

"I thought we were going to die," he said, half chuckling, half crying. "I thought this was it for us."

"Me too," I said with a deep raspy sigh. "I thought I wasn't going to see my kids ever again."

I still didn't feel as relieved as the rest of them. I watched as a couple of deputies from the sheriff's office took Melanie away in handcuffs. What worried me was that most people thought this meant it was all over, while I knew it wasn't. We had disarmed the bomb, and no one had died.

This time.

We still hadn't found the Leech. We had won this round, yes, but he'd be back for more, with even greater strength. He wasn't the type to let himself get knocked down by a little resistance. On the contrary. If I had him figured out just a little bit — and I truly believed I had with my many years of profiling experience — then he would only grow stronger; he would only grow nastier.

"Did you see where Jenkins went?" I asked, wiping away a tear that had escaped my eye.

David shook his head. "I lost track of him when we got up on stage. But I saw that he was filming before it all went down. After that, I don't know."

"Could he have put Melanie on that stage? Inside the armoire?" I asked. "Was that what he had in his van? Was it her that he picked up at that house by the beach?"

David shrugged with a deep sigh. "It's certainly possible."

"Did you notice her nails?" I asked.

He nodded. "They had been pulled out."

"The Leech's trademark."

I took a few steps to the side and looked at the small area behind the theater. The white van was gone, and I guessed so was Jenkins. I smiled when thinking that at least now we had Melanie. She would be able to help us find him. Once she told her story, McMillen was bound to start listening to me.

Chapter Sixty-Six

"I AM GONNA KILL HER!"

E.T. grabbed a glass from the counter and threw it against the wall. It shattered, and glass scattered all over the tiles of his kitchen. E.T. growled angrily and removed a pile of papers from the dresser, swiping them to the floor, bringing down pens and a picture frame with it. All of it scattered on the floor, while E.T. raged on.

In front of him ran the video from inside of the theater on his computer screen. The live broadcast had been a failure. Many had tuned in, expecting great things, but as soon as they realized it wasn't going to happen, they had been angry. Some had left spiteful comments, and a lot had even unsubscribed.

She had messed it all up. She was the one to blame.

The theater seated three hundred people, and he had wanted to take them all in one strike, or at least he hoped for half of them. And now he had ended up with no kills at all — not even the girl.

"Gosh, I hate you!" he said to the screen as he played it all back and saw her go onto the stage and sit with the girl, calming her down.

E.T. had saved the live-feed to his computer, and now he was replaying the video over and over again, frustrated, raging about the woman who was supposed to make him look better and not stop him.

She can't stop you. She never will. You can't let her get to you like this.

But he was far from done yet; that was for sure. She was going to realize that soon, very soon.

E.T. ran a hand through his hair to remove it from his face. He grabbed the knife, then placed it on the skin of his stomach and began to carve. As the letters were carved into the skin, blood trickled down his abdomen. E.T. closed his eyes, then pressed down on the knife. But he pressed too hard, and the knife slipped.

E.T. let out a roar that echoed in the old house. He looked down at the skin and realized he had messed it up. He panted agitatedly and bit back the pain, then wiped the blood away and looked at the letters, shaping the word:

PATIENCE.

He winced in pain, then bandaged it up and put his shirt back on. Grunting in anger, he approached the man he had tied to his chair in the kitchen. He was panting heavily behind the gag, fighting to breathe. E.T. smiled, grabbed the camera, and began filming. There was no time for him to rest now and lick his wounds. He had to get back up on the horse, right?

The show must go on.

"Hello, fans," he yelled, putting on his most exciting smile to hide his disappointment and anger. There was no need for them to know he had messed up. He'd just have to make the next one count even more. Besides, he'd get back at Eva Rae Thomas soon enough. It was all going to come together soon.

In due time.

E.T. clasped his hands happily, then filmed the man in the chair, going real close in on his face to make sure everyone who was tuning in could get a proper look at him.

"Yes, dear fans. As you've guessed, I've got something GREAT in store for you."

Chapter Sixty-Seven

MATT STARED at the TV in his kitchen and turned up the sound. He listened to the weatherman explain about the tropical storm Damian that was now approaching Puerto Rico and expected to make landfall later that same day. The experts had it forecasted to intensify afterward as it came back out on the warm water and then headed for Florida's East Coast. Exactly where in Florida it would make landfall was still very uncertain, but chances were, it would hit them as a hurricane, maybe even a CAT3.

"You think it's gonna hit us?" his mom asked as she came out to him. She had just taken Elijah to school.

Matt sipped his coffee, then shrugged. "It's too soon to tell. You know how it is at this time of year."

She scoffed. "Yeah, well a Cat3 isn't too bad. I think we'll just ride it out, as usual, right?"

Matt nodded. He had ridden out both Cat4 and Cat5s. He'd been there for Andrew, Charley, and Irma just two years ago. This storm wasn't big, at least not yet. Still, he couldn't help worrying more this time than usual.

"You should have seen them at Publix yesterday," she said. "They're already stocking up on water and sodas like there's no tomorrow. Batteries were completely sold out, and there was just flavored water left once I got there."

"And I bet you stocked up on that, then."

"Well, I had to; didn't I? We have to be prepared. You never know."

Matt chuckled faintly. He stared out at the Intracoastal canal and his mother's boat in the backyard. He'd have to secure that later today just in case.

"What about Eva Rae?" his mother said.

"What about her?"

"Is she coming back before the storm hits?" she asked.

Matt sighed. He had no idea. He hadn't spoken to her since he left her on Amelia Island. But he worried. He was concerned that she was so immersed in catching this imaginary killer that she wasn't preparing for the storm, should it come. He knew that Chad and the kids were back in town, and he felt that she should at least be with them if she decided to ride it out.

"She's staying with her dad and grandmother. I'm sure she'll be fine," he said, then finished his cup and put it down. The weather guy was still talking about spaghetti models, possible scenarios, and the *cone of uncertainty*.

"What happened with you two?" his mom asked. "Did you have a fight or something?"

Matt stared at her, then suddenly had a strange flashback to when he was a teenager in high school, and he had been in some fight with Eva Rae, as they were from time to time. Here he was, forty-one years old, and still living with his mom. So she could help take care of his son, yes, but still. Fact was, he was still living with her. Nothing had changed. Was this all there would ever be to his life? More than twenty years later, he was still living in the same house, mourning over the same girl. Was he never going to move on?

Matt leaned over and pecked his mom on the cheek.

"I have to go; I'm late. See you tonight."

"I'm making lasagna, your favorite," she said with a smile, that same smile she used to send him when he was off to school. It made the hairs stand up on his neck.

"Sounds good, Mom," he yelled back, then rushed as fast as he could out to his cruiser in the driveway and got in, his chest suddenly feeling so tight he was almost unable to breathe.

Chapter Sixty-Eight

I WAS SITTING at my laptop when David entered my room the next morning. I had gotten half an hour of sleep, just about. Sydney was still asleep when the knock sounded.

David peeked inside. He saw the laptop, then looked at me.

"What are you doing? Have you been up all night?"

"I slept … a little," I said and signaled for him to be quiet so Sydney could get her beauty sleep. She was going to do that movie soon, and she had been going on and on about how important it was that she looked young and rested. She was using all these creams that made her green in the face while she slept. She had barely eaten anything the past couple of days, just to stay slim, and she was working out, running on the beach every day now. It was self-torture, in my opinion. Yet I still respected her for wanting to give it all she had and for the career she had managed to build for herself without any help. She was a hard worker like me, and for that, I had the deepest admiration.

David sat down on the chair next to me. "They're not talking much about what happened last night at the theater. I watched the news on TV this morning, and they didn't even mention it. The newspaper had just a small note on page three."

"Because no one was hurt," I said. "And they don't want to scare the tourists away. Since there is no danger anymore — or at least that's what they believe — they tone it down. Make it into a small thing. They'd much rather focus on the danger that is still out there like the storm that will most likely never even come close to Florida's coast."

"They are talking an awful lot about that," he said.

"And I bet people are hoarding canned food and bottled water," I said. "Like always at this time of year."

"It's not a bad idea to have a plan prepared," he said.

"Of course not. But when you've been around a while, you get tired of being all riled up again and again, and then it never comes, or if it does, it turns out to be nothing."

"So, what have you been looking at?" he asked, nodding toward my laptop.

"I'm trying to find out what his next move will be. I know that he will be angry now. We messed up his plans, and he'll try to retaliate somehow. And probably pretty soon to make sure we don't think that he's defeated. He won't let a small setback like the one yesterday get in his way. He'll be angry, yes, but he'll get back on track as fast as possible. My guess is he has already kidnapped his next victim and laid out the plan. But I can't seem to find any recent kidnappings on the island. I've looked through all the police reports and Internet searches, Facebook, Instagram, and so on. I'm searching for anyone who wrote anything about a loved one who didn't come home or someone who is worried about one of their drunk friends who hasn't been seen in a while, stuff like that, which usually doesn't make the police reports because they'll never go to the police and report them missing. Like prostitutes that someone says is missing, or homeless people, or maybe a runaway teenager that they believe will come back, or maybe they don't care, but the sister does. Stuff like that. I have this terrible feeling that we'll hear from the Leech very soon. And that has me worried. He'll strike back even harder, and I have no idea how. Since I still don't understand his pattern, I have no way of telling what his direction is, what he wants to accomplish. It's very frustrating. I'm usually always able to figure them out. But I can't seem to see the connection between his victims and the way he kills them. I have this system where I run all their similarities and their differences, but it still doesn't create a usable pattern. I can't seem to …"

I tapped on the laptop aggressively with a groan. "See? Nothing!"

David placed a hand on top of mine. "Maybe I can help? Let's try together. Show me what you've got so far."

Chapter Sixty-Nine

WE WOKE up Sydney with our talking. The more I talked, the more agitated I became, and then I forgot all about her sleeping next to us. She sat up in the bed and stared at us from behind the green facial mask.

The sight made both David and me laugh out loud. Sydney sent me a look.

"I'm sorry we woke you up," I said. "I know it's early, but ..."

"It's okay," she said and put her feet on the floor. "I have to get up anyway. I'm behind on my reading and need to get the first few scenes down by today. I'm going off-script tomorrow. I also have to go for a run and lose at least two more pounds before the audition."

I exhaled. "Syd, you're working yourself too hard. If they want you for this part, if you're perfect for it, they'll take you no matter what. Two pounds won't change anything, will it? I can hardly imagine it would."

She scoffed. "Then you don't know the business."

I nodded. I didn't. She was right about that. Sydney got up and walked to the bathroom while I returned to my notes.

"So, as you can see here, what I have so far is just the fact that he uses others to hide what he's doing, and I believe he thinks no one will know. But why he is killing them and why he is doing the things he does in that way is odd to me. But it's not strange that someone like him emerges at a time like this. That's no surprise to me."

"Why not?" David asked.

"A guy like him has one goal. To punish society for his misfortunes. And mass murderers like him are on the rise. We see them as shooters at musical festivals like the one in Vegas; we see it in the shooter who killed people at a Wal-Mart in El Paso, or the garlic festival in California. Their mindset is what we often refer to as an 'injustice collector.' These men — overwhelmingly, they are men — often feel that they have been personally wronged, mistreated, or overlooked. Sometimes they see broader injustices they perceive against their gender or race or religion. They're latching onto some anger that is bigger than them."

"And you think the Leech is like them?"

"Yes. That is my firm belief. I also think he's very, very clever, and that he — unlike most of the others — isn't planning on dying while doing his killing. He's no martyr, which is a tendency we see more and more too. He's not planning on getting caught either. He sees himself as way too important for that. That's why he's covering himself behind others, using them, like he did to Adam. He's making others do the dirty work for him, so to speak. In that way, he can continue for way longer than others we have seen and know of. He'll go down in history as the one who made it, the one who succeeded. He idolizes those other killers, but he wants to up the game. He wants to do even better."

"But if he hides behind others, then chances are no one will ever know it was really him who was behind it; how does that fit with his profile?" David asked.

"That's the thing that has me mystified as well," I said.

"So, you think that he might have an outlet for those desires somewhere that we don't know about?" David asked. "That there is somewhere he's showing the world what he's doing? Like in the video he sent you?"

I stared at him, puzzled. "Yes, that's exactly what I was thinking."

Chapter Seventy

THEN:

Marlene's heart was beating fast as they showed her back into the interrogation room. Rivers and Waltman were both there, looking seriously at her as she sat down across from them.

She hadn't told Bruce about what she had seen on his computer and did her best not to let him know as she sent him off to work. He too was going to be interrogated, but not until later in the week; he had been instructed. Marlene gathered that they first needed to have enough ammunition against him.

"I need you to know that I have always done what was best for my son," she started. "I am a good mother. I have read every book there is about children and parenting, well almost that is, and I have found *Triple P Positive Parenting* to be among the most effective techniques."

"Ma'am, we're here to establish how much you knew about the abuse," Rivers said. "I don't think your parenting technique makes much of a difference."

Marlene swallowed. She had thought about this all night, lying awake in her bed, eyes wide open, staring into the ceiling, thinking about how she was going to tell them that she had no part in this. She had prepared an entire speech that was to show them how terrific a parent she really was.

But now she wondered who the speech was really for. Was it, in fact, for herself? For her own sake? Because she felt so devastated to know that this could have taken place under her nose, on her watch?

"I didn't," she said with a sniffle. "I didn't know anything."

Waltman leaned forward and folded his hands on the table. "Now, we want to believe you; we really do, ma'am. But you can see how we're having trouble, right? You've spent the entire time in here defending your husband, even with the evidence we presented to you. You haven't been very cooperative, nor have you tried to defend your son, who is the victim here. Add to that the fact that you haven't wondered about the bruises or anything else, and then you'll see why we have a hard time believing in your innocence."

Marlene nodded. She understood. "What does Jack say?"

"Excuse me?"

"About me. What does my son say about me and my part in this?"

They looked at one another like they didn't know how to answer that.

"Please. I have a right to know."

Rivers exhaled deeply, then leaned forward. "He says you haven't seen his dad hurt him, that he can't recall you seeing it happen or being there when it did. We don't know if he is just protecting you yet, as small children often do with their mothers."

Marlene bit her lip. This was the answer she was hoping for. It didn't acquit her, but it did help her case.

"There is something that I have come to know since yesterday," she said, feeling heavy. She was going to betray her husband, but she had to do it. To save herself. Besides, with what she had seen on the computer, she knew she would never want him in her life or her son's life ever again.

"Yes?" Rivers said.

Marlene handed him a USB port. "I put it all on this. It's from his laptop. Now, before you see what's on it, I want to make one thing clear. I had no knowledge of this until last night. It is something he has kept completely hidden from me. You have my permission to prosecute him for this. I will even testify if needed. I am done defending him for what he has done. I am done with him completely."

Chapter Seventy-One

IT WASN'T A VERY good day. Six-year-old Owen Brown glared after his mother as she drove off from the drop-off line at school. A teacher guided him inside, and he sat down at his desk. No one noticed the tears running down his cheeks all morning as they went through their classes, just as no one noticed how he didn't want to talk to anyone.

Why not?

Because it was his birthday and his momma had forgotten. It wasn't unusual for Owen's mother to forget things, but it was the first time she had forgotten his birthday.

"She's not well."

The words had fallen from his aunt's mouth the night before when she came to visit and cook for them. Owen had overheard her speaking on the phone with their mother, Owen's grandmother.

"We need to do something."

Owen had known for a long time that things weren't as they were supposed to be with his mother. It had started with her forgetting to pick him up after school. Then she had forgotten his name while speaking to him, or things she was about to say. She also forgot to grocery shop, and he had to eat cereal with bad tasting lumpy milk or sometimes just eat it dry. He didn't like to complain about these things because his mother got so confused and often so very sad when he did. Once, when he told her she had forgotten to wash his PJs, she went to the bathroom and cried for half an hour. Later, when she came out, she seemed to have forgotten why she went in there in the first place, and his PJs weren't washed until he did it himself.

Owen had taught himself to do a lot of stuff, like toast his own bagels and even fry an egg for dinner when his mother forgot what time of day it was. He could make simple meals for himself and wash his own clothes. He even remembered to make sure he got to bed at bedtime, and he set the alarm to get up and get ready in the morning.

"It's too much for the boy. He's so young," his aunt had said on the phone. "I'm afraid she might burn the house down with both of them in it, forgetting she was cooking or something. It's getting serious."

It was just Owen and his mother in the house. His aunt had recently begun to come over and cook for them every now and then. She wasn't a very good cook, and Owen didn't like having her there much. She was so harsh on his mother, he thought. Always telling her what to do and what not to do.

Owen didn't like that. He liked it better when it was just him and his momma, alone against the world. He missed the old days when she still remembered things.

Like his birthday.

At recess, they were all sent outdoors to play on the playground, and Owen was the first one to storm out of the doors. He ran to the swings to be the first to get one when he spotted something on the bench in front of him, something that made him smile for the first time that day because it could only mean one thing:

His momma hadn't forgotten about his birthday after all. She had just pretended to while planning this big surprise for him.

Only Momma knew how much Owen liked clowns, and right

now, there was one sitting on the bench in front of him, and in his lap, he had a big basket filled to the brim with Pixie Sticks.

Owen's favorite candy.

Chapter Seventy-Two

I CALLED the sheriff's office, but McMillen hadn't come in yet, his secretary said. Instead, she sent me to one of the other detectives on duty, a guy named Detective Foster, who seemed like an even bigger prick than McMillen.

I asked about Melanie Kagan.

"She doesn't remember a thing," he said, sounding annoyed. "That's all we know for now."

"So, she was drugged?" I asked. "Have you checked her blood-work for roofies or any other drugs? Did you get a blood sample when you took her in last night?"

"Listen, Miss …"

"Thomas."

"We're swamped down here today. I don't have time for this. Was there anything I could help you with?"

"How far are you in the case? Do you know why she did it?" I asked.

"We're working to get to the bottom of this," he answered. "But as I said, the last thing she remembers is going out to a bar with her friend. She doesn't remember anything else."

"What if I tell you I believe someone did this to her? Someone roofied her at that bar, then placed the vest and the blood pressure measurer on her body and left her in the armoire?"

He went quiet on the other end. "Then I'd say you have a very vivid imagination, Miss ..."

"Thomas. Listen, I know it can be hard to believe, but you need to realize that this isn't her doing. There's someone on the island who ..."

"Listen, Miss Thomas. I really don't have the time for this. Thank you for calling. Please, don't do it again."

The line went dead, and I stared at my phone, raging. I hadn't even been able to tell him about the nails yet. I had hoped that this guy might believe me since I knew McMillen wouldn't give me the time of day. All I needed was a few minutes of his time, a few minutes to explain. Then I was certain he would see it the way I did. But I wasn't even going to get that. They wouldn't give me a chance.

I was just about to lose my patience with this place and especially the law enforcement.

I looked up abruptly from the phone and at the wall next to me. My heart began to race in my chest as I clenched the phone hard in my hand. A sensation rushed through me and caused me to tremble. It was a feeling I was very familiar with and that I welcomed whole-heartedly. One I had longed for in this case.

The feeling of a piece of the puzzle falling into place.

"David?" I said as I dropped the phone and ran for the door. I rushed into the hallway and to the top of the stairs, then yelled at the top of my lungs:

"DAVID?"

Chapter Seventy-Three

"WHAT IS THIS?"

Owen looked at Bryan, who had come up next to him. The clown in front of them hadn't moved.

"Is that candy?"

Owen nodded and grabbed another stick, unwrapped it, and poured its sugary contents into his mouth and felt it melt on his tongue. It was his third one, and he knew he might get a tummy ache, but since it was his birthday, he felt like he deserved it.

"It's my birthday," Owen said. "My mom sent the clown here to surprise me with the candy."

"Cool. Can I have some?"

Owen nodded. "Sure."

Bryan dug in and took a stick. He opened it, poured the sugar into his mouth, then went for a second one. He dug in his hands and grabbed an entire handful. Bryan then turned around to face the other kids on the playground and yelled:

"Hey, guys! Free candy over here!"

Seconds later, they were surrounded by all the children in the entire playground. They were digging their small fingers into the basket in the clown's lap, stuffing their little faces with the sugary powder, eyes glistening in excitement.

Owen felt especially proud that his mom had managed to pull off something like this for him, and it gave him extra hope for her and for their future. Maybe she was getting better? Maybe everything would soon go back to normal? Maybe his aunt didn't have to come and cook anymore?

Maybe everything was going to be fine, after all?

The thought felt intoxicating, and Owen couldn't stop smiling. It wasn't until Bryan collapsed next to him and fell to the ground, ragdoll limp, that Owen realized nothing would ever be fine again.

Chapter Seventy-Four

"WHAT'S GOING ON? Did something happen?"

David came running up the stairs, pale as a sheet. I stared at him, then put both my hands on his shoulders.

"I got it. I figured out his pattern."

David looked surprised. "You what?"

"It was when I thought about the thing at the theater; you know when we sat there with Melanie, and how it took all the patience I could muster. That's when it hit me. What's the definition of patience?"

David stared at me like I had gone mad.

"It's the capacity to accept or tolerate delay, trouble, or suffering without getting angry or upset," I answered my own question.

"And? I am not quite following here," he said.

"Patience. She needed to endure it. Melanie did, or we would all die. If she got upset, we'd die, all of us."

"Because her blood pressure would rise, yes," he said.

"Okay, let's go back to Adam," I said. "He was holding Allyson's picture in his hand when he went into the school with the gun. We both agree he was put up to it by the Leech, that he had kidnapped

Allyson and made Adam do it, or he'd kill Allyson. That's the theory, right?"

"Right."

"So, why did he do it?"

"To protect Allyson," David said.

"For love," I said.

David nodded. "Yes, for love."

"And the people at the hotel who we believe were poisoned with champagne?"

"What about them?"

"They were celebrating, having a great time when they were killed."

"That's true. What are you getting at?"

"And the nursing home, what does that represent?" I asked.

David looked confused. "Old people? Aging? Resting?"

"Exactly. Peace."

I stared at David, waiting for him to get there too. He didn't seem to.

"So, what are you saying?" he asked. "I'm not sure I follow."

"We have Love, Joy, Peace, and Patience," I said.

"And?"

"Love, Joy, Peace, and Patience. Didn't you go to church as a child?"

He scoffed. "A few times, maybe."

"It's the Fruits of the Spirit. It's biblical. From Galatians 5, I just looked it up. There are nine Fruits of the Spirit. They are Love, Joy, Peace, Patience, Kindness, Goodness, Faithfulness, Gentleness, and Self-control. All the fruits are in contrast to the works of the flesh."

David stared at me, his eyes wide open, mouth gaping slightly.

"I know it sounds mad," I said.

"Oh, thank God," he said, breathing, relieved, "because, for a minute there, I was worried you couldn't hear it."

"Nevertheless, I believe it is his pattern. He is killing the Fruits of the Spirit, so to speak, one after another, letting evil win, telling us good will never triumph; the flesh is too strong."

"Okay, okay," David said and reached out his arms. "Before you go all Bible camp on me. Let's say you're right. I've promised to indulge you, so that's what I'm doing. Let's say this guy is killing the Fruits of the Spirit, destroying all goodness, then what is he up to next?"

"Kindness," I said. "He's reached kindness."

Chapter Seventy-Five

"I THINK I may have found something too," David said. He had told me to come with him downstairs to his office, and now I stepped inside, and he closed the door behind me. The room was packed with computer screens and looked like a hacker's den.

"Is this your office?" I asked and touched one of the keyboards gently. David looked terrified at my gesture, and I removed my hand.

"Yeah, well," he said and sat down in his office chair and rolled to one of the screens. "I work from home."

I realized I knew nothing about the man that was my father and felt a little bit embarrassed. I hadn't even asked what he did for a living. I had been so busy being angry with him and punishing him.

"What do you do?" I asked.

He sent me a wry look. "I can't tell you, or I'll have to kill you."

"Very funny."

"I'm in Cyber Security. Companies pay me to find their weak spots and possible breaches in their security. I help them detect it, so they won't be hacked."

I stared at him. This was the last thing I would have imagined him doing. I guess I had been wrong about a lot of things.

"I see," I said, suddenly very interested. "What did you want to show me?"

"Chan3," he said and tapped on his keyboard, letting his fingers dance across it. "It's a website. Two months ago, a shooter who shot up an arcade in Wilmington posted a manifest in there. It is known to be a place where people like our Leech live out their fantasies and a place where you find likeminded people if you will."

"Okay, that's terrifying. And you think the Leech might be visiting that page too?"

"As soon as you said the part about him needing to live out the part of his nature where he was able to tell the world about his endeavors, that's when I thought about this webpage. Guys like him hide in plain sight, you know. And they can do that here. In places like these, they can brag all they want and post videos, and it'll never get seen by anyone but their peers, people who will be their fans. It's quite nasty. It's all user-created message boards. Each owner regulates their own board with no interference by the administrator. That's how they can keep it a secret. It was created as a free-speech friendly alternative to the supervised society we live in. It was created for people to be able to speak without being watched after what the creator defined as 'rapidly escalating surveillance on the net and loss of free speech.' Users create their own boards, and then they can pretty much post anything they like."

"But … there might be hundreds of these boards. How do we find his?"

David looked up at me. "You're not the only one who's been up all night."

He clicked something and opened it.

"It's encrypted," he said, "but I know how to get around that."

David tapped very fast on the keyboard, and I watched as he gained access to the message board.

"Now, I've narrowed it down to around five different boards based on geography. These guys think they can hide their IP addresses by sending it across the world, but they can't trick me. I can narrow them down to Florida, and these five are from here. So here we have them, five message boards that he might be a part of or even run himself. None of them store anything, so if it has been sent, then it's gone, kind of like Snapchat. Makes it harder to come after them later on. You'll have to be there right at the moment when it is broadcasted. I've created alerts for when anyone goes live in any of the five message boards, so if they start a broadcast, I'll be notified."

"So, now we wait? Is that it?"

David nodded. "That's about it, yes."

I exhaled, feeling tired, yet excited to finally be getting somewhere. "I'll get us some coffee."

Chapter Seventy-Six

EILEEN MADE us pancakes and scrambled eggs, and we ate together, all four of us. I kept staring at the pictures of Adam on the walls, wondering if I would ever get the chance to get to know the kid. He liked fishing; that much was obvious from the photos, and so did David. He was in all the pictures with him, holding up one big fish after another.

"I've filled the kayaks," Eileen said when we were halfway through. "So, they won't fly away in the storm, and then we can use the water to flush the toilets once the water is cut off. I'll also fill a couple of gallons of water and freeze them. We can use it for keeping things cold when the power goes out."

"I think you're overreacting, Mom. It looks like it'll make landfall down south," David said. "I watched the spaghetti models this morning, and they pretty much all agree that it'll hit Ft. Pierce. We'll be fine up here."

"Maybe," she said. "But it won't hurt to be prepared, just in case. I've stocked up on water and canned food, and bread, and toilet paper, so we won't need anything once it is over. You know how it takes a few days before everything works again. Once, I went two weeks without power. It's no fun; I tell you that. Even if it makes landfall down south, there's no harm in being prepared. I have life-jackets behind the couch in the living room in case of flooding. I'm filling the tubs with water and putting duct tape on the outside locks, so they won't be filled with sand again. I'll put all our important papers in the dishwasher, where they'll keep dry; let me know if you have any that need to be put in there with them. There's plenty of room. My neighbor will bring over sandbags later to guard the house."

I thought about my kids and whether they'd be fine too. Since they'd be north of the storm, they'd get hammered pretty severely. I reminded myself to call Chad later on and make sure he stayed on top of it. We needed to have a plan in place for them and my mom. I had talked to him about it earlier in the week, and we agreed they'd all go to Orlando and stay at a hotel there until it was over. Now, I wondered if I should go back home to be with them. I had grown up in Florida myself, so I was used to this, and had evacuated many times in my life, and often ridden big storms out in our house in Cocoa Beach as well, but for my kids who had grown up in Washington, it could be scary. They might need their mom there with them.

I sipped my coffee when David's phone rang, and he picked it up, walking outside on the porch for better reception. He came back a few seconds later, holding the phone tightly in his hand, his eyes staring into the air without really looking at anything in particular.

"That was the hospital," he said, looking like he could pass out.

"What is it, David? Is it Adam?" Eileen asked.

David nodded.

"What happened?" I asked.

"H-he ... he woke up."

"What?" Eileen shrieked. "What are you saying? Don't tease me, boy."

David nodded, smiling. "They said he woke up this morning and mumbled something to the nurse that she couldn't really under-stand. But his eyes were open, and he was looking at her. They called the doctor down, and he examined him, and he's fully awake now. They say it will take a little time before he'll make sense and be normal, but they believe he will be."

I clasped my mouth. "Oh, Lord. We should go see him."

David nodded. Sydney made a half-choked sound.

"Let's all go," she said. "Let me just grab my purse."

"I can't believe it," David said, panting happily.

For a second, I felt like hugging him, but I held myself back. I wasn't quite ready to go that far yet, and a second later, the moment was gone. Sydney came rushing down the stairs, holding her purse, wearing a hat, a wig, and sunglasses, so she wouldn't be recognized. Shortly later, we were all in the car, backing out of the driveway when David's phone beeped again. He looked at it, then glanced nervously at me.

"They're live in one of the message boards. Someone is making a live video right now."

Chapter Seventy-Seven

I JUMPED out of the car. David came up right behind me, and we hurried back inside and into his office downstairs. David found the message board and opened the live-feed on one of his big screens.

A swing set.

"What are we looking at?" I asked, confused.

David shook his head. "I don't know. It looks like a playground?"

"Look at the comments," I said. "People are tuning in and cheering him on. But for what?"

"The number is rapidly rising. Now it passed two hundred viewers from all over the world, look. I have them on the screen over here. They're pinging in from India, South Africa, The Maldives, even Sweden."

"What is he about to do?"

"That's hard to tell," David said.

"I have a feeling it can't be anything good. A playground means kids, right?"

David gave me a look of concern. "Usually, yes. Look, something is happening."

We watched while holding our breath as a flock of kids came out from a building and rushed onto the playground. People who were watching were commenting like crazy, saying nasty things about what they would do to the children. It made me sick to my stomach. Who were these people?

One child approached the camera and stood still for a few seconds while staring at it. He reached over and picked something up, and that was when my heart dropped.

I watched the kid open a Pixie Stick, then place the candy powder-filled straw in his mouth and pour in the contents.

Oh, dear God.

My eyes locked with David's for a brief second of panic. We needed to get to these children before it was too late.

"I think I know where it is," he said. He pointed at the building in the back on the screen. "That's Southside Elementary school. Adam used to go there. It's close to downtown Fernandina Beach on Jasmine Street."

Sydney came to the door. "Are we leaving or what? Dad?"

My eyes locked with David's. I saw the indecision in his.

"You go," I said. "I'll take care of this. You go see Adam."

"Are you sure?" David asked.

"Yes! Just GO!" I yelled louder than I wanted to. The pressure of the situation as I watched more kids come up to the boy and start to devour the candy made me stressed out. I fumbled with my phone and managed to finally dial nine-one-one while I rushed to my minivan and took off, trying to explain to dispatch that this was no joke, that I wasn't insane, that a bunch of kids were about to be poisoned at the elementary school and she should send police and first responders.

"We need ambulances," I ended up yelling as I sped down Jasmine Street toward the school, flooring the accelerator, blowing my horn at everyone who wouldn't get out of my way.

"We need plenty of them!"

Chapter Seventy-Eight

E.T. FELT GOOD. He was watching the live-feed on his screen and monitoring the comments along with the number of viewers. It was going up at a good and steady rate. Soon, it reached almost five hundred, much to his pleasure. Next thing, he was heading for a thousand. He knew it would be one of his best so far, and he had been right. There was just something about hurting children that sparked the views.

The first child had taken a Pixie Stick, and E.T. watched as he poured it into his mouth, completely unaware of what it really contained, what E.T. had mixed into the sugar.

Stupid, gullible children

Now, E.T. was anxiously waiting for more children to join this one, and he wasn't disappointed. Seconds later, another kid came up to the camera and grabbed an entire handful that he swallowed quickly while calling for the others. Soon, the camera was surrounded by little innocent faces, reaching into the bag, gulping the candy down happily like there was no tomorrow.

Which, in their case, there wasn't.

E.T. had gotten the idea from reading about how poisoned candy on Halloween was a myth and that it had actually never happened. For some inexplicable reason, people had just decided to fear Halloween candy and that strangers might put poison, or razor blades in it, or broken glass, or anything else that would hurt random children. But the fact was that it had never happened. The police had never documented actual cases of people randomly distributing poisoned goodies to children on Halloween. It was all just a collective fear, hysteria created by media and anxious parents. The only real story was of a child being killed by his own father in nineteen-seventy-four in Texas. The dad wanted to collect his life insurance and let him eat Pixie Sticks that were poisoned with cyanide. The rest was nothing but an urban legend. It was hysteria.

Up until now.

As of today, E.T. had made the nightmare come true. From now on, parents would never let children eat candy from strangers, especially not from the hands of a clown. It would go over in the history of terrifying stories to tell.

And it was all his doing.

E.T. chuckled as he watched the first kid collapse to the ground. Another followed, and seconds later, they were dropping like flies. Some were holding their stomachs and having seizures, their bodies trembling on the ground, while others simply fell down without any warning signs. It was eerie, like a horror movie, but even better.

Because it was real.

And the numbers were up. Now, E.T. had reached two thousand viewers, and it was rapidly climbing.

Five thousand, six, seven, eight ... could it be ... could he really reach that magical number and out-win all the others?

Nine ... ten ... eleven!

Eleven thousand people all over the globe had now tuned into his small live-feed and were commenting and cheering him on. That was it. This was what he had been waiting for. He had achieved his ultimate goal.

He was finally famous.

Chapter Seventy-Nine

"STOP! Get them away from the candy!"

I stormed toward the playground and jumped the fence. Two teachers were already attending to the children who had dropped to the ground. One of the teachers was crying hysterically. I ran to them. In the distance, I could hear sirens, which meant the lady at dispatch hadn't dared not to take me seriously, or maybe one of the teachers had managed to call it in as well, and they'd finally decided to send help.

It didn't matter. What mattered was that help was on its way. And we needed it. We needed it more than ever.

Twelve children had collapsed on the ground. A few others were throwing up or holding their stomachs, crying in pain. A girl had a Pixie Stick in her hand and was about to put it in her mouth when I stopped her and knocked it out of her hand. She started to cry help-lessly, while I hurried to the source of this.

A clown was sitting on the bench, a basket in his lap. His head was slumped, and he wasn't moving.

"Help is on the way," I said to the teachers, who were both whimpering and crying while watching the lifeless children. "Ambulances are coming. Police are on their way too. Should be here any second now."

"This one isn't breathing," one of them said. "He just stopped breathing. What do I do? I don't know what to do?"

"This one isn't breathing either," the other said, while frantically trying to perform CPR on the small body. "I don't know what to do!"

"Keep at it until help gets here, both of you," I said and threw myself over a lifeless kid. I turned him around and felt for a pulse. When there was none, I began pumping his chest and blowing air into his mouth. Nothing happened. The sirens were approaching while we fought for these children's lives until the paramedics came rushing in, carrying stretchers and wearing uniforms. Once they took over, I backed up. My hands were shaking, and I was crying heavily. The sight of all these lifeless children had overpowered me.

Who could be this evil? Was it really possible that anyone could do such a thing and still call himself human?

In a fit of rage, I turned to face the clown, remembering that I had watched it all go down on the video in David's office, like thousands of others who subscribed to this guy's videos. I approached him and put a set of fingers on his throat but found no pulse. I looked closer at his costume. There, in the middle of that curly red wig, I spotted a Go-Pro camera. I took in a deep breath, then stared directly into it.

"You can hide behind your cameras all you want to, you sick coward, but I will get you. Do you hear me? I will find you if it is the last thing I ever do."

As I stood, hunched above the camera, I finally got a closer look at the clown. Thinking that I recognized this man from somewhere, I took off the wig and held his face between my hands, trying to look behind the make-up, making completely sure I wasn't mistaken.

"Oh, dear God," I said and clasped my mouth. "Oh, my dear God."

Chapter Eighty

IT LOOKED LIKE A WARZONE. I sat down on the bench next to the dead clown and watched as they carried away the children one after another on stretchers. There was a lot of yelling, and it was complete chaos. Meanwhile, I couldn't keep my cool any longer. Shock had taken over me. Tears were streaming down my cheeks, and I could barely move.

This was worse than anything I had ever encountered in my days in the FBI. Way worse.

Finally, when all the children had gone away in ambulances, and the teachers had given the police their reports of what happened, a deputy came up to me. I recognized him as Deputy Williams, who had come to take my phone when I received the video from the nursing home.

"Miss Thomas?" he asked.

I looked up and met his eyes. Then I looked at the clown next to me, my voice quivering as I spoke:

"He's dead," I said. "He didn't deserve that."

Deputy Williams nodded and glanced at the clown. "The teachers said that the kids were eating candy from this basket in his lap. Do you have any idea where this came from?"

I shook my head. "I don't. I wish I did. Someone placed him here, knowing the kids would eat the candy. Because, of course, they would. They're kids. They don't know any better, right?"

"Right."

I sniffled and wiped a tear away with my hand, trying hard to get my composure back. It wasn't easy after what I had just witnessed, or with the guilt gnawing at me. Could I have reacted faster? What if I hadn't hesitated in the car when David said there was a live video broadcasting. I had considered for a few seconds not watching it and just going to see Adam. Why did I hesitate? Why did it take me so long to leave the house once I realized what was happening? I could have arrived seconds earlier. Why didn't I drive faster? If I had been seconds earlier, it could have saved lives. Or it might have, at least.

Children's lives.

They all have parents out there who don't even know yet, who don't know their lives have been altered forever. They'll never be the same after this. Losing a child is the worst thing you can possibly go through.

"You might want to take a closer look at the clown," I said to Williams with heaviness in my voice. "It's someone you know."

Deputy Williams did. He stood in front of the clown for a few seconds, looking at his face when the realization sank in.

"It's McMillen," I said. "Detective McMillen."

Deputy Williams looked terrified. I rose to my feet and walked away while he yelled for the paramedics to come. Soon, the other deputies were swarming McMillen, yelling and rushing the paramedics along. But I knew it was no use. The detective had been dead for a while.

Deputy Williams came up to me after they had removed the detective. He handed me a bottle of water, then took my entire statement, his hand shaking while he wrote on the notepad. I told him about the website where I saw the live-feed and how I knew everything. I didn't even try to make it sound less insane because I didn't care anymore. I had already heard that two of the children were declared dead on their way to the hospital, and I had a feeling several others would be as well.

It was unbearable.

"I should have stopped it," I mumbled over and over again while Williams scribbled on his pad. "This is all my fault. I could have stopped it."

Chapter Eighty-One

THEN:

"What are you doing?"

Marlene didn't stop to answer him. She had hoped he wouldn't be home yet when she got back, but he was. Bruce had been sitting in the living room, staring into thin air. Marlene stood in the doorway and watched him before she rushed up the stairs and dragged her suitcase down from atop the old armoire. She hadn't spoken a word to him, and she didn't want to either. She opened her drawer, grabbed her favorite shirts and tops, then threw them into the suitcase on the bed.

"A-are you packing?"

She paused for a second, then grabbed all her underwear and put it in next to the shirts with a snort.

"What's going on here?" he asked, raising his voice slightly. "Marlene? You won't even talk to me now?"

Marlene took a deep breath, then finally spoke in nearly a whisper: "I am leaving."

"You're leaving me?" he asked, his voice growing shrill.

She finally turned around and faced him, hiding her hands behind her back so he wouldn't see them trembling.

"Yes, Bruce. I am leaving you."

"But … but why? Is it because of all the lies they've told you?"

She stared into his eyes, then felt her heart drop. She had loved him so deeply and never thought anything could ever destroy that love.

"I have to, Bruce. For me. For Jack."

"But don't you see? That's exactly what they want. They want to split us apart. You're giving them exactly what they want."

"And just exactly who are *they* Bruce?" she asked. "The police? The DCF? Who is after you?"

He threw out his arms, annoyed. "All of them. They're making all this up; I'm telling you. I never did any of those things. And you know this, Marlene. You've known me for what … ten years? You know I would never do anything like this. Especially not to my own child. Why do you believe them and not me? I don't understand this, Marlene; I truly, honestly don't understand a thing of what is going on right now. It scares me, and I need you to help me get through this. I thought you and I were together in this. I thought we'd be there for one another. If you leave, then I have no one left. I'm all alone, Marlene."

She stared at him. His eyes were welling up with tears, and it was hard for her to watch. This was the man she had loved until just a few days ago. Before it all started, before they started saying all those things, before …

"It's not just what they've told me," she said. "There's more. Things about you that you thought I didn't know. Things you've been hiding from me that I don't think I can live with."

She slammed her suitcase shut and latched it, cursing this entire thing far away. Wishing herself back to a time when she didn't know any of all this, when her life was good and simple, when she had a son and a husband that she loved and trusted. She had everything she ever wanted in life. And now it was all gone. How could it be taken away so fast? How was it possible that things could change so drastically in the blink of an eye?

Bruce was sobbing behind her, and it felt devastating to her already broken heart. How had it come to this? They had been a happy couple; they were the ones who would make it if anyone would, they all said. They had been inseparable. So deeply in love that no one or anything could tear them apart. They had gone through so much together. And this was how it would all end?

She really didn't want it to be like this. She wanted to wake up from this nightmare now.

It's too late. You can't go back now.

He grabbed her arm as she tried to walk past him out of the bedroom, suitcase in her hand.

"What things, Marlene? Please, tell me. The least you can do is tell me."

She took a deep breath. This was exactly what she had hoped to avoid. She really didn't want to be there when he realized that she knew.

"They found some things. On your computer," she said.

"What things?"

She stared into his eyes, scrutinizing them, and for a second, she thought she saw an innocence in them that she knew and understood.

Could he really not know what she was talking about? Could he be innocent?

No, it was impossible.

She shook her head, then pulled her arm from his grip. She rushed down the stairs with him yelling behind her.

"What did they find on my computer? Dang it, Marlene. Tell me! Why can't you just say it?"

She stopped at the foot of the stairs, then looked up at him. He was angry now, his eyes ablaze.

"Try and think about it for a second, Bruce. What could they possibly find on your computer that would make them want to take your kid away, that would make your wife leave you? Don't play innocent. You know exactly what I'm talking about. Yes, I'm leaving you, and you know perfectly well why. Because I have to. I need to. Or I'll lose everything. They'll never let Jack back with me as long as I'm with you. I have to leave you to save myself."

She walked to the door and grabbed the handle. Bruce reached for a vase, grabbed it, and threw it after her. It shattered right as she slammed the door shut behind her, and she could hear him yell out in a fit of rage behind the closed door. Then she ran to her car and drove away as fast as she could, tires screeching on the asphalt, praising God under her breath for getting her out of there in time.

Chapter Eighty-Two

E.T. STARED at the screen on his computer. The face staring back at him made him shiver with anxiety. Her blue eyes were looking directly into the camera that he had placed on the clown's head. Her red hair in a ponytail dangled as she moved her head.

It was the footage from the playground that he was looking at, over and over again, constantly going back to the part where she approached McMillen on the bench and then pausing it as she stared directly into the camera and left him a message, knowing he'd be listening.

"I will get you," she said. "I will find you if it is the last thing I ever do."

E.T. listened to the message over and over again, then paused the footage and stared into her eyes.

"I'd like to see you try," he mumbled.

At first, he was angry when realizing she was watching his feed. It was the only way he could explain her presence at the playground so early — before the police came. It made him fearful. Was she breathing down his neck? Was she getting too close?

But then he had calmed himself down. So what if she had found out? Big deal. So what if she had somehow managed to gain access to his message board and was following his live-feed. It didn't mean she was anywhere close to catching him. He was still way ahead of her.

But the thought of her watching his work made him want to up his game. The very notion that she might think she was close to catching him made it even more fun. Thrilling. He had wanted to play games with her, to play cat and mouse, and now she had made an unexpected move. So what? He could handle that.

He could even use it to his benefit. He had a direct line to her now. All he needed was to use it the right way.

E.T. chuckled dryly while looking at her face on the screen. He grabbed the knife from the desk, then placed it against his bare chest. He then closed his eyes as he wrote the next word, biting down on his tongue in pain as the blood trickled down the skin of his stomach. Once he was done, he stared at the letters in the mirror, while the skin underneath throbbed and he panted in agitation.

KINDNESS

Chapter Eighty-Three

I WAS in no state to be driving. David called just as they had decided to let me go, and I asked him to come and pick me up. I couldn't stop crying, and my hands were shaking badly.

He arrived about ten minutes later with Sydney in the passenger seat. She jumped out of the car and ran to me, pulling me into a warm hug.

"It's not your fault; do you hear me? It is NOT your fault," she said over and over again.

I let it all out and cried in my sister's warm embrace, not knowing what else to do or how to even go on from there.

When Sydney let go of me, David took over. He helped me get into his car, and I gave Sydney the keys to my minivan, which she drove back to the house for me. Meanwhile, I took off with David, hiding my face in my hands, crying until I had no more tears. David didn't talk, and it was too late when I realized he wasn't taking me home, but to the hospital. He parked the car in the parking lot in front of the big glass entrance and looked at me.

"David ... I don't think ..."

"He's awake, Eva Rae. I want you to see who you are fighting for while trying to catch the real killer. I want you to look into his eyes and know who he is."

I stared at David, searching for all kinds of excuses not to go in, but couldn't find any that seemed valid enough.

"Please? He wants to meet you," David said. "He met Sydney earlier and knows who you are."

I felt my heart rate go up as I debated whether I wanted to go in or not. I still wasn't sure I was in any condition to meet my long-lost brother, and I wasn't sure I wanted him to see me like this the first time we met, but I guess I was curious. This was a big part of why I had come, wasn't it?

"All right," I said and opened the door. I stepped out and stared at the big hospital building in front of me. I wondered for a second about the poor children and their families who would be in there waiting for news.

I shook my head as we walked into the building, deciding that Sydney was right. I couldn't blame myself, even if it was hard not to. I could blame the Leech and focus on catching him. I could concentrate on what to do and not on what I should have done. It was the only way to move on.

"He doesn't say much still, and he keeps drifting in and out, so I can't promise that he'll be able to talk to you," David said as we approached his room. He opened the door and held it for me.

"Adam?"

David stepped inside his room first, and I came up right behind him, feeling nervous.

Adam blinked his eyes and looked at David, then smiled faintly.

"Dad."

David took his hand in his and smiled back. "I brought someone."

David stepped aside so Adam could see me.

"This is your other sister, Eva Rae."

I waved awkwardly. Adam chuckled weakly.

"I heard about you," he said out of breath. "You're the cop, right? FBI? That's so cool. Dad talks about you constantly, and I always wanted to meet you."

I almost teared up. David had told Adam about me? David had talked about me to him? I didn't realize. The thought made me blush.

I looked into the blue eyes of my brother. I studied the red hair and freckles. He looked so much like me; it took my breath away. I hadn't realized this until now, but he was my spitting image. Sydney was the odd one out, apparently, and that made me feel good. I had always been the only one who looked like this in my family.

"I am," I said. "And I want you to know that I believe your story. I believe in your innocence, Adam, and I am going to prove it."

Chapter Eighty-Four

"How much does he remember?"

David and I had gone out in the hallway to get some vending machine coffee while Adam rested. He got tired real fast and had trouble finding the right words, so we let him rest, and I decided that David could fill me in.

David shook his head and blew on his plastic cup. "Not much. He says he walked Allyson home on the night of the party and that they had made up on their way back. They weren't fighting anymore. Then, the next morning, he woke up and heard that she was gone. Her parents called our house and asked if she was there and she wasn't. And then he helped search for her. He was scared to death when he received a video. In the footage, he saw Allyson tied to a chair, crying. A knife was placed against her throat, and someone was standing behind her holding it. That someone's face couldn't be seen in the video, as it was cut off at his neck, but this person gave Adam the instructions. He said he had to walk into the school in the cafeteria and shoot as many as he could, or Allyson would die. He had placed a weapon in backpack, put it in a locker at the school and told Adam to go get it. During lunch, he was supposed to take it out and shoot. If he told anyone, Allyson would die. If he involved the police, Allyson would die. Adam was terrified and didn't know what else to do. He thought that by shooting up under the ceiling, he wouldn't hit anyone, and he could save her life and not hurt anyone. He was scared out of his wits, the poor kid."

I sipped my coffee, then looked up at David. "And the video? Did he save it anywhere? Is it still on his phone?"

David exhaled and shook his head. "It was sent through Snapchat by someone he didn't know."

I nodded. "Of course. In Snapchat, the video gets deleted once you've watched it. Doesn't leave a trace."

"If I had his phone, I might be able to find it," David said. "I've done similar stuff before. But I don't have his phone. The police took it as evidence."

"You've recreated Snapchat videos before?" I asked startled.

"For work," he said.

"One of these days, you need to tell me more about that work of yours. It sounds very interesting," I said.

"I'm not sure you'd understand," he said.

I widened my eyes and gave him a look. "Oh, really?"

He nodded. "Really. Besides, I'd have to kill you. I told you this."

I chuckled and sipped my coffee. I looked through the door to Adam's room that was ajar, and I could see Adam sleeping in his bed.

"But I take it that the police aren't taking his word for it," I asked.

David shook his head. "Nope. They're sticking to him being angry at Allyson, killing her, dumping her, and then shooting up the school. I can't blame them, really. It is the most obvious explanation."

"And the easy one," I said and threw my coffee cup into a trash bin.

David exhaled deeply.

"They're taking him in tomorrow," he said. "I just got word about it. They're transferring him to the infirmary at the prison. He's well enough to go, the doctor says."

My heart dropped when I heard this.

"You can't be serious?"

David lifted his eyebrows. "I'm afraid so."

"I can't believe it. We just got to see him. He just woke up. They can't take him away already, can they?"

"That's what they intend to."

"But ... we have to do something."

David shrugged, tearing up. "What can we possibly do?"

Chapter Eighty-Five

MATT DROVE the car into Publix parking lot and stopped the engine. All the buildings in the strip mall had boarded up their windows. Matt had been busy securing his mother's house all day, putting the shutters up, and starting up the generator to make sure it worked. He was planning on riding out the storm from there with his mom and Elijah. Damian was supposed to have made landfall down south this morning, but had made a sudden turn northward and was now headed up the coast instead, gaining strength across the Atlantic Ocean. It was forecasted to go up along the coast, and it was believed it would stay in the ocean, so they'd probably be fine where they were. He'd gone through worse than this one in his life. He sighed, then looked at the list his mother had given him when she asked him to go pick up a few things for her.

My mom is still cooking for me. My mom is still telling me what groceries to buy. This is embarrassing.

It wasn't like he had lived with her always. He used to live in his own condo across from the beach. But then a hurricane passed through and destroyed his condo, and his mom said he could move in with her until the roof was fixed. It was just supposed to be for a short period of time. But then he learned about Elijah, and as soon as the boy's mother died and he found himself alone with him, there was no way he could go back to his old life again. He had always thought it was temporary, but as he stared at the grocery list, he suddenly felt like he was suffocating. He couldn't stop thinking that maybe it wasn't temporary. Maybe this was till Elijah grew up and moved away. Maybe even then he wouldn't be able to leave his old mother because she'd need him around because by then she might be too old to take care of herself.

I am never getting out of that house, am I?

Matt hurried out of the car, grabbed a cart, and rolled it through the store, grabbing all the groceries on the list, knowing it almost by heart because it was pretty much the same stuff he bought for her every week. With a few exceptions, of course, since they were getting ready to hunker down while the storm passed them out in the ocean. People around him were hoarding batteries and water like there was no tomorrow.

He almost made it through without running into anyone he knew when he walked down the nearly empty cereal aisle and saw Chad standing in the middle of it, looking at a box of Cinnamon Toast Crunch.

Just turn around and walk the other way, Matt. Just turn now, and he won't see you.

Matt turned the cart, but it was too late.

"Hi there, buddy. Didn't see you over there."

Matt froze at the sound of Chad's voice, then turned and faced him with a smile.

"Yeah, well …"

"Stocking up for the hurricane?" he asked. "They say it might go up the coast now instead of hitting down south. They've already run out of bottled water. I got the last one, and there's no bread left. Forget about batteries; they're all out of those too."

"Yeah, well, the storm is still a day or so out, so I'm just grabbing some Special K for my mom."

"We'll go inland tonight," Chad said. "I promised Eva Rae that I would get off the island before everyone else if it looked like Damian would come our way. So, I guess I better do so, right? It's my first hurricane, so to be honest, I don't know anything about it. Guess it's a piece of cake for you who grew up around here, huh? I find it terrifying, yet people say they're only leaving if it's a direct hit or if it's more than a Cat3. Most people say they'll ride it out even if it is a four or a category five. Can you believe it? I would never dare to stay for a storm like that."

"I don't think it'll be too bad," Matt said. "Looks like it'll stay off the coast."

"I think I'll take the kids away no matter what. I heard someone say that it is moving faster than they expected it to today and that it might make landfall here on the East Coast by tomorrow night. I don't want to be here if it does. It is a beast of a storm right now. A Cat 4, they said this morning."

"Yeah, well, I feel pretty sure it'll stay out to sea. All the models say so. Only a few take it in over land."

Matt reached over and grabbed a box of Special K. He was about to leave when Chad chuckled.

"Can you believe the amount of sugar in this stuff? Eva Rae doesn't like me buying this for the kids, but hey, if she isn't here, she won't see it, am I right? And I guess you won't tell either."

Because I'm not with her anymore; is that what you want to say? Is that what you want to rub into my face, huh ... buddy?

Chad gave Matt a look of triumph that made everything explode inside of him. Chad then pushed his cart further down the aisle and disappeared, while Matt stood back, nostrils flaring.

Are you really gonna let that guy get to you this way? Are you going to let him win just like that?

Matt was about to yell something after him when he stopped himself. He took a deep breath to calm himself down, realizing he was way off.

This wasn't about Chad or any other guy for that matter. This was about himself and the fact that he had — once again — let go of the love of his life.

"This is not going to work," he mumbled to himself as he pushed the cart down the aisle. "It's about time I fight for her and for us."

Chapter Eighty-Six

David had gone to the hospital early, so I was eating breakfast with my sister and grandmother when they knocked on the door the next day. I braced myself, then walked to open it.

"Detective Foster? To what do I owe the honor?"

"Save it, Thomas," he said.

He nodded to the two deputies behind him, and they stepped forward. One of them grabbed me and turned me around while the other deputy cuffed me and Mirandized me. He hurt my wrists, but I refrained from complaining. I knew better than anyone how important it was to let them take you away without resisting. Protesting or resisting physically would only serve to make things worse for you.

"What's going on?" Sydney said as she came out to the door. She glanced at the detective, then at me and my cuffed hands with a concerned look in her eyes. "What are you doing?"

"They're taking me in," I said, trying to sound calm.

"Why?" Sydney asked. "Why are they taking you in? For what? H-how? I don't understand."

"You're under arrest for obstructing an ongoing investigation,"

Detective Foster said to me first, then addressed his deputies. "Go ahead and book her."

"But … wait," Sydney said. "Why? What has she done exactly?"

Detective Foster stopped and turned to look at Sydney. "Among many other things, she warned a suspect so he could get away."

"Who?"

"Adam Clarke. He wasn't in his hospital room when we came for him this morning," he said.

Sydney looked terrified. "Adam wasn't in his room, but …? Didn't you have a deputy supervising him?"

I sent her a smile to ensure her it was okay, but she didn't seem to understand. Instead, she kept protesting.

"You can't just come here and …"

"As a matter of fact, yes, they can," I said.

Sydney seemed like she wasn't sure she bought that entirely. "But … How do … what can I …?"

"Just get me a lawyer," I said. "That's all you can do to help me right now. That would actually be a great help."

She stood like she was frozen and stared at us.

"O-okay."

I tried to smile again, to assure her that I was going to be okay, but the deputies dragged me toward the car. They pressed my head down as they put me in the back of their cruiser. The last thing I saw as I was taken away was Sydney standing on the porch looking helpless, while Eileen came up behind her.

I just prayed Sydney would get me a good lawyer, and fast.

Chapter Eighty-Seven

"How DID you know that the candy was poisoned?"

I smiled as patiently as I could. We had been at it for four hours inside the interrogation room at the sheriff's office. I had told them everything that I knew over and over again. I was getting tired and just wanted to go home.

"I told you. I saw it on the live-feed."

"In some message board that is encrypted, yes; you told us that. We just wanted to see if you were ready to change your statement," Detective Foster said, "to something a little more believable."

Someone came to the door, and he got up to speak to them, then returned. He rubbed his forehead anxiously.

"They found cyanide in the candy," he said. "Just like in the champagne at the Ritz-Carlton." He pointed at me. "You knew this. You told Detective McMillen that the champagne was poisoned just like you knew the candy was. I don't understand how you could have known that? How did you know about the bomb in the theater?"

"That one was a coincidence," I said. "I happened to be there. But I do believe it was the work of the same guy."

"So, you say. What I really want to know is, where is Adam

Clarke?" he asked with an exhale. "We need to know. He's to be taken into custody, and you obstructed that. Obstructing a police investigation. That is a serious offense, Miss Thomas. You could go to federal prison for that. You notified a suspect that we were coming, and we believe you helped him escape. You visited him last night, and this morning, he was gone. This is serious, and you know it very well. When those that are sworn to protect the public violate their oath, they will be prosecuted for their misconduct. You violated the trust of the community you're supposed to serve, undermining our investigation, and put law enforcement officers in imminent danger, not to mention the public now that a murderer is back on the loose."

"You don't know that he is a murderer," I said, annoyed. I hated that they talked about my brother that way. "He's not convicted yet. And I'm telling you, he's innocent. You're looking for the wrong guy. Think about it; if all these events are connected, how can Adam be guilty? You said so yourself; there's a connection between the murders at the hotel and the children at the school. They both used cyanide. Have you checked McMillen's nails yet? I am certain several of them, if not all, are pulled out. It's his thing, you see? He can't help himself; he needs to brand his victims. It's his tell. But also his weakness. Think about it. Allyson's nails were pulled out too. So were Jeff Facer's. They were all his victims. You want to find who killed Detective McMillen? I'm telling you; it's the same guy."

Foster stared at me, then cleared his throat.

"All right. A suspected murderer, then," the detective said, completely ignoring most everything I had just told him. Still, I sensed I had gotten through to him somehow. He wasn't completely dismissing my theory, which was progress.

Just not enough. The Leech was still out there planning his next move, one that would have to top the previous one, if I knew him right.

One that attracted more viewers than ever.

"We need to know where Adam Clarke is," David said. "If you don't cooperate and help us find him, we'll have to charge you with obstructing our investigation. I see no other way."

"Go ahead," I said with a shrug. "Charge me."

Foster rose to his feet and gathered his papers, then looked down at me. "You'll go to prison, Miss Thomas. You won't get to see your children for a very long time. We're talking birthdays and Christmases, lots of them that you'll miss. Your oldest might be in college by the time you get out. Think about that and let me know when you're ready to tell me where he's hiding."

I stared at the door as it slammed shut behind him, my heart pounding in my chest. He had hit me where it hurt the most by talking about my children. Was it worth saving Adam if it meant my own children would lose their mother?

I sure hoped so.

Chapter Eighty-Eight

I WASN'T LET out until the next morning when Sydney came to the sheriff's office with her lawyer and posted my bail. The lawyer was taking my case now, he said, and he'd be in touch. Those were his last words to me right before he drove away in his big black Cadillac. I just prayed that he knew what he was doing.

David was waiting in the car, the engine running, as I got in. He was biting his nails and looked concerned.

The radio was on, and they were talking about Damian, the hurricane that had cheated all the forecasters and spaghetti models and not made landfall in south Florida as expected. Now, it was roaring up the coast, staying over the ocean but threatening to make landfall somewhere along the beaches.

As we drove across the bridge and back onto the island, I noticed all the houses were boarded up, and people were packing their cars, ready to get away. The host on the radio told us no one knew what path Damian would take, so it was time to make preparations and get inland just in case. The storm was growing in speed and strength, and there was no telling how much damage it could invoke if it made landfall.

"And even if it does stay out in the ocean, we can still expect hurricane-force winds and storm surge here in our county, and especially in low-lying areas like Amelia Island," he said.

Sydney turned it off. She looked at me in the back seat. "Now, will someone finally tell me what is going on? Where is Adam?"

I exhaled tiredly. I had barely slept at all in my cell. I had made one phone call to Chad and the kids the night before, and they had told me they left the island and Cocoa Beach and were staying at a hotel in Orlando, so I didn't have to worry about them. Christine had cried and said she missed me and that she was terrified that she was going to die in the storm. I told her she would be fine and that it was going to stay out in the ocean. Alex had thought it was the coolest thing ever and said that it was already blowing like crazy and that he wanted to play outside, but Dad wouldn't let him. Olivia had been quiet, and I knew that meant she was terrified too, but not able to tell me because she had to be the big sister. I missed them terribly and felt awful for being so far away during something as terrifying as this.

"It's okay, Syd," I said. "Didn't David tell you? We made sure Adam was taken away early in the morning while his guard was asleep. I don't know where to because then I would be lying in the interrogation room when they asked. So he didn't tell me. Where did you take him, David?"

David stopped biting his nails and looked at me in the rearview mirror. "That's the thing. I didn't."

"What do you mean?"

"I mean, I didn't take him away. Adam wasn't there when I went for him. He was already gone."

I could feel the blood drain from my face.

"He was what?"

"Gone. He wasn't in his bed. Deputy Corel was sound asleep, and I couldn't very well wake him up and ask him where he was. I just left instead."

"You've got to be kidding me," I said. "This can't be happening!"

"So … no one knows where Adam is right now?" Sydney asked, her voice getting shrill.

"That about sums it up," I said and glared out the window where a family was putting their dog in the back seat of the car.

Ready to evacuate.

"We haven't the faintest idea," I said, feeling the panic rise when thinking about my brother and where he could be. "Meanwhile, a hurricane is approaching, which means we need to find him. And fast."

Chapter Eighty-Nine

HE WAS WATCHING the house and saw the car drive up as she finally returned home. E.T. couldn't help feeling cheerful at the thought of Eva Rae Thomas spending the night in the slammer. Nothing could make him happier right now.

Except the thought of what he had in store for her.

You ain't seen nothing yet.

E.T. watched as Eva Rae Thomas's dad parked the car in the driveway, and Eva Rae got out. Her grandmother came out of the front door and greeted her with a hug on the porch. They had already boarded up their house with plywood, just like all their neighbors had. People were ready for the storm that was approaching.

At least they thought they were.

The winds had picked up, and the palm trees were wavering as gusts hit them with great force. Soon, it began to rain violently, making Eva Rae and her family rush inside the house and close the door.

E.T. could no longer see them and took off. From the trunk of his car, he could hear the boy groaning loudly behind the gag as he tried to scream for help and knock on the lid.

"Knock and holler all you want to," E.T. said and accelerated down the empty roads, rushing through the puddles that were already shaping in the low-lying areas. "No one can hear you over the raging winds and pounding rain. A hurricane is coming, a storm fiercer than anything this island has ever experienced. It's a beast of a storm. A beast, I tell ya."

Chapter Ninety

"You have twenty minutes. I'll be in the room, supervising the visit. You're not allowed to be alone with him."

Marlene nodded in agreement to the woman from DCF. The woman gave her a stern look like she wanted to make sure that Marlene knew she was watching her.

"He's in here," she said and opened the door to a small room with many windows. In there on the carpet, by a bunch of toys, sat Jack, playing with a truck, making noises with his mouth.

Marlene walked closer, then squatted next to him. Tears were piling up in her eyes, and she felt a huge knot in her throat. She hadn't seen her son in four weeks, and he looked so much older and taller already.

Bruce had been arrested was all she had heard. The child porn on his computer was enough to get him convicted, and he would be jailed for a long time was what her lawyer said. Meanwhile, the investigators were still trying to figure out Marlene's part in the matter, if she knew and closed her eyes to it, or if she took part in what happened to Jack. *The abuse* as they kept calling it. Marlene was going to fight them with all she had, and her

254

lawyer said she had a chance of getting him back, not a big one, but it was there.

Hope was all she had to cling to.

"Hi there, sweetie. What are you doing?" she asked, suddenly feeling estranged from her own son. She was suddenly terrified that he would start to cry or yell and that they'd think she was doing something wrong, that she was abusing him.

She had been going through every detail of her upbringing of the boy lately, wondering what could be interpreted as abuse. Back when she grabbed his arm because he wouldn't take a shower? Was that abuse? Had she hurt him?

It was her lawyer who had asked her to think about all the situations through his upbringing that they might use against her in the courtroom. Every little detail counted, he said.

What about the time she got frustrated with him in the car and yelled? Or the time when she pulled him out of his car seat, and he screamed because his foot got stuck and she didn't notice because she was in a hurry? And then when she looked at his leg, it had a bruise on it?

All of them, her lawyer had said. All of them needed to see the light of day so they could prepare properly for the court session and the attacks that might come.

"Sweetie? Jack? Hi there. It's me. It's your momma."

The boy didn't look up. He completely ignored her and kept playing with his truck, running it across the floor like she wasn't even in the room.

Hadn't he missed her at all?

Marlene looked back at the woman from DCF. "What's wrong with him? Why won't he talk to me?"

The woman answered with a shrug, then looked down at her pad in her lap. She glanced at her watch, then said:

"You have seventeen minutes left."

Marlene looked at her son again, then smiled. "Jack, how about we talk a little, huh? Mommy missed you so much, and I can't wait to be with you some more. Are you all right?"

The boy turned his back on her and continued playing. Marlene felt her heart sink. This was heartbreaking. Her own son didn't even want to look at her?

How did this happen?

"Jack? Don't you want to talk to me at all? I missed you, sweetie."

The boy finally lifted his eyes and glanced at her, his eyes suddenly ablaze. He rose to his feet and pointed his finger at her.

"You're evil. Stay away from me."

Marlene backed up, tears welling up in her eyes. She turned to look at the woman from DCF, then approached her. She didn't mean to, but it happened anyway. She couldn't hold it in anymore. All these months of frustration and anger were finally let out as she screamed at the woman and grabbed her arm:

"What have you done to him? My son never spoke to me like that before. What did you do to him? What did you do to my SON?"

Chapter Ninety-One

"So, what do you think happened to Adam?" Eileen asked and handed me a cup of coffee. I sipped it and sat down on a stool in the kitchen. Being back, even with the circumstances of my brother missing and a hurricane coming was still far better than being on the inside. I hoped I never had to spend a night like that again.

I shrugged and closed my eyes, letting the warm drink spark life into me again. Eileen pushed a plate of scrambled eggs and bacon in front of me, and I gulped it down so fast I almost choked. I hadn't eaten properly for a long time, and this was heaven-sent.

"I don't know. I know what I fear might have happened," I said.

"I mean he can't just have walked away on his own, can he?" she asked.

"It's possible," David said as he grabbed a cup and poured coffee into it. "But not very likely. It's just not Adam's style to run away from everything. Besides, where would he go?"

"So, we're assuming someone helped him?" Eileen asked.

I nodded and looked around the dark house. With the windows boarded up with plywood, it seemed smaller somehow.

"What are we going to do?" David asked me. "How do we find him?"

"In the middle of a hurricane?" Eileen asked. "I say we have to wait till it's blown over. It might make landfall in a few hours. We should stay inside. It's no time to run around or drive around for that matter."

David nodded. "She's right. Safety first. We have to wait and look for him when it's all over — when the storm has passed us."

I exhaled, exhausted. I really didn't like the thought of Adam out there all alone, on his own through all this. Hadn't he been through enough? The kid was fifteen, for crying out loud — same age as my Olivia. I would be scared half to death if she was out there all alone, and I could tell that David was too.

I didn't like this one bit.

As a wind gust blew down the street, a trash can tipped over and was blown down the road, making an awful noise outside. A fence by the neighbor's house was loose and banging in the wind. I stared at my phone, wondering if we'd lose both power and service during this storm when suddenly we heard noise outside coming from the porch. A second later, there was a rapid knock on the door. My eyes met Eileen's.

"Who's outside in this weather?" she asked.

"I'll go check," I said and walked to the door and opened it. Outside stood Chris, leaning on his crutches, an anxious look on his face.

"Chris? What the heck are you doing here? You know the storm is approaching, right? Come on in."

He moved forward, humping along on his crutches, and I closed the door behind him. He sat down in my grandmother's favorite recliner, the one she usually fell asleep in at night when she didn't want to go up the stairs to sleep, which was most nights, even if she didn't want to admit it.

"What's going on?" I asked, feeling uneasy. This couldn't be good. Not by the look on his face.

He reached into his pocket and pulled out a phone, then turned it on.

"There's something I need to show you," he said. "And you're not going to like it."

Chapter Ninety-Two

"I RECEIVED this video about an hour ago," Chris said and held up his phone. I grabbed it from his hand and turned on the video. As I saw Adam's strained face on the display, my heart dropped.

"What is this? Who sent it?"

"I don't know," Chris said. "But there's a message. It's for me, and I don't know what to do."

I played the video, my heart pounding in my chest as I saw the gun placed against Adam's temple and the strain on his face. He was gagged and blindfolded, so I couldn't see his eyes, but I didn't need to. Not to know just how scared he was, the poor kid.

"If you go to the police, he dies; if you tell anyone, he gets it. Do you understand?" the distorted voice in the video said.

I stopped it and looked at Chris.

"I can't do it," he said, choking up. "I simply refuse to."

"What does he want him to do?" David said, approaching us.

"To grab a gun and go shoot up one of the shelters while people are evacuated from the hurricane, thinking they're safe," I said with a deep sigh. This wasn't good. Remembering what happened to Allyson after the Leech sent a similar video to Adam, I had a feeling

Adam wasn't going to get out of this alive. No matter what Chris did or didn't do.

"I … I c-can't do it. I can't hurt anyone. I've never even shot a gun before," Chris said. "I don't know who or what this guy thinks I am. But I'm not the one he thinks I am. Look at me. I'm handicapped for crying out loud."

"That's probably why he chose you," I said. "Because no one will suspect this of you, of someone walking into the shelter on crutches."

"But …?"

Chris sent me a look of despair, his eyes were wet, and a tear escaped. It rolled down his cheek and landed on his lip.

"I can't do it," Chris said. "I came here to tell you that. I'm sorry, and I'll have to live with the guilt for the rest of my life if Adam dies, but I can't do it. If I could take Adam's place, I would, but I can't."

I placed a hand on Chris's shoulder. "Of course not. No one expects you to do what he is telling you to. No one. You did the right thing coming to me with this video."

"I know I might have doomed Adam by doing it," he said. "But I didn't know where else to turn. I figured you might be able to help."

"You did well, Chris," I said. "Are you staying here for the storm?"

He nodded. "My grandmother is back at the house. We're riding it out together."

Something heavy tipped over outside, and a loud noise emerged as it scrambled across the road. I opened the door and looked out. It was raining hard now, and there were already big puddles in the street. Water was rising quickly.

"I think you might want to get back to her as soon as possible, while you still can," I said and grabbed my phone and car keys. Chris humped out and down the steps. I watched him as he made it up the street, making sure he made it to his house up the street safely.

"Where do you think you're going?" Eileen asked, placing both hands on her hips.

"Out," I said. "I need to find Adam before it's too late."

I slammed the door shut before she or anyone else could protest, then rushed to my minivan, getting soaked during the few yards I had to go. A neighbor's tree was leaning dangerously close to a tipping point. I went online and looked at the hurricane app to see Damian's track. Now they were saying that it might make landfall on Amelia Island, right on our beach. I figured I had at least a couple of hours before it got really dangerous.

Chapter Ninety-Three

MR. JENKINS' street looked as deserted as the rest of the island, with its closed-up houses and plywood that was protecting the windows. All the yards were stripped of loose items, the trash bins had been secured inside, and a few loose palm-branches had fallen into the street, which I drove over. I stopped in front of his house, then ran up to the front door and knocked.

I hadn't expected this, but the door opened, and a woman appeared. I recognized her as his wife.

"Yes? How can I help you?"

"I'm looking for Mr. Jenkins," I said. "Is he here?"

She shook her head. Their daughter came up to her and looked at me shyly. "There's a storm coming," she said, sounding troubled.

"He should be back soon, though," Mrs. Jenkins said and looked at her watch. "It won't be long."

"Are you staying for the storm?" I asked.

She shook her head. Her daughter clung to her leg. I remembered being a child in Florida and facing evacuation and storms. It became easier once you had been through a few of them, but it was always scary. The worst part was when your parents told you to choose between your stuffed animals since you could only take your favorites. The thought of coming back and all your toys and the house being gone was scary as heck. The uncertainty was the worst, and then the waiting, for days often, before it was over.

"We're about to leave now, actually," she said. "Just packing up the last things. My husband said he'd take the other car and join us there later. He went to board up our summer cabin on the beach. We just bought it some six months ago and were going to use it mostly as a rental for extra income. But it is right across from the beach and will get hit hard. I'm just praying it won't be too expensive to fix it up afterward. Bruce has spent so many hours out there getting it ready, and now this happens. Why did you need to talk to him again? Was it important? I can try and get him on the phone. I think they still work."

"They do," I said, and raised my hand to stop her. I couldn't have her alert him that I was looking for him. That wouldn't end well. "But that won't be necessary. I'll just talk to him later. Maybe after the storm. Stay safe."

"You too," she said with a concerned look on her face. "I hope we have a home to come back to after this."

"I'm sure it'll be okay," I said, trying to sound reassuring for the child. This storm was big, and there was no telling what might happen to these houses. I feared for my grandmother's house most of all. It was old and in a low-lying area that would flood quickly.

I said goodbye to the two of them and wondered what their lives would be like if it turned out that Mr. Jenkins was the Leech, how much it was going to change that poor girl's life once she found out the truth. I knew a little about it from experience, but I had been an adult when I found out about my stepfather. She was a child, no more than five or maybe six years old.

The thought broke my heart.

I ran back across the driveway and got into my car, getting soaked on the way. A branch from a palm tree was ripped loose by the wind very close to me and flew through the air, landing on the front of my car with a loud bang. After the shock had dissipated and I could breathe again, I left it there to fall off as I accelerated down the street, driving toward the beach and the Jenkins' cabin.

Chapter Ninety-Four

THE WAVES WERE SLAMMING the sand and splashing over the dunes as I reached the beach. The small street between the houses and the dunes was already flooded in places, and it forced me to drive very slowly while my windshield wipers ran amok in front of my eyes, struggling to keep the water off. The pounding rain on the roof was maddeningly loud, and the wind gusts pulled at the car forcefully, making it hard to steer properly.

I parked in front of the Jenkins' summer cabin where I had seen him go on the night before he drove to the theater. I suspected this was where he kept Melanie and the armoire that he took down there and placed on the stage.

It could also very well be the same place he was keeping Adam.

I parked as close to the entrance as I could, then got out and ran as fast as possible toward the front door. I knocked, hard, then waited while the wind blew rain in my face and it was hard to stand still.

Nothing happened.

Realizing he probably wasn't going to open the door for me, I grabbed the handle but found the door locked. I snuck around the house, fighting the water and the winds, then found an old door in the back under the stairs that wasn't locked. I walked inside and closed it behind me, then shook off some of the water. I walked to a set of stairs and snuck up. I found myself in a kitchen that was very clearly still undergoing some serious renovation. Some parts were brand-new, while others, like counters and some of the cabinets, were missing.

I grabbed my gun from my ankle holster and held it up in front of me as I walked upstairs to what had to be the bedrooms. The windows had been boarded up already, and the house seemed ready for a storm. I continued up the stairs when I heard a sound and stopped. Holding my breath, I continued running up a few steps more, then walked into what was going to become a media room, furnished with a sofa, a big TV, and a futon. I walked to the first bedroom, pushed the door open, and looked inside, holding the gun out in front of me.

Clear.

I walked to the next, opened the door, and looked inside, just as something lunged at me. I shrieked and held my hand up to cover my face. Whatever it was, it landed on the floor next to me, then hurried out the door, and I realized it was a raccoon that had probably sought shelter from the storm inside the house.

Heart pounding in my chest, I returned to the hallway, then opened the door to the last bedroom and peeked inside.

It was empty too.

"Adam?" I called out, thinking if he was being hidden in a locked closet or somewhere, then maybe he would answer.

But no sound came.

I then ran down to the garage to see if Mr. Jenkins' car was there, but I found it empty as well. There were tire tracks, though, on the cement, and they were still wet. I realized he had already been here and left again, and probably taken Adam with him.

I was too late.

Chapter Ninety-Five

THE DRIVE back to my grandmother's house was terrifying, to put it mildly. The winds had picked up, and trees were falling next to me. Wooden parts from broken fences were flying around, and the water had begun to rise. Most of the roads were flooded, and my minivan was struggling to get through. Twice, I had to take a detour because I needed to travel a road that was impassable because of high waters. The pouring rain on my windshield made it hard to see ahead of me, and with the high waters, it was difficult to see what was the road and what wasn't. I drove into a ditch at one point and got stuck for a few minutes before my minivan managed to drag itself back up on the road.

I wasn't panicking yet, but it was close.

After a fifteen-minute drive that took more than an hour, I finally managed to get back to my grandmother's street. The driveway was flooded all the way up to the first step leading to the front porch.

I parked on the neighbor's front lawn and ran the last bit of the way, or rather dragged myself through the knee-high water, then finally reached the porch and made it to shelter.

"Moom!"

The sight that met me inside was maybe even more terrifying than what I had expected.

My children. All three of my children were there.

Alex was the first to throw himself at me, hugging my legs, asking to be held. I grabbed him in my arms while Christine and Olivia approached me as well. They looked pale and tired.

"Thank God, you're back."

Chad came out of the kitchen. He hurried to me and leaned over to kiss me, but I pulled away, then put Alex back down.

"W-what the …? Chad? What on Earth are you doing here? And with the kids?" I asked, barely able to find the words. I was fighting not to explode.

He exhaled, resigned. "The kids were scared. I was scared, and we didn't know what else to do. They wanted to see their mom, and frankly, I've never been in a hurricane before, so I had no idea what to do. Christine was crying for her mother, and all they wanted to do was to go make sure you were all right."

"Let me get this straight. You drove them here, to an island in the middle of the Atlantic Ocean during a hurricane?"

He nodded.

"Are you insane?

"I'm sorry. I didn't know what else to do."

"Chad, dammit. The entire area is about to flood. Have you seen how high the water is outside?"

"Yeah, well, we … I parked in one of the neighbor's driveways. We didn't know how bad it was until we got here, and it wasn't that bad about an hour ago. I thought we'd be safe here."

"The bridges have closed; there is no way off the island anymore. If anything happens, no one can come to our rescue since we were supposed to have evacuated. No one will come. This is not safe; this is dangerous, and you … you bring the *kids* here?"

"Yeah, well … I'm sorry, Eva Rae. I thought you'd be happy to see us. We had everything packed, and so I thought we might as well come up here. There was nothing to do at the hotel."

"Well, you thought wrong," I said, hissing at him. I felt like my blood was boiling and I couldn't stand looking at Chad right now.

Instead, I went outside on the porch where the water was now licking the top steps. It would only be a matter of time before the porch was flooded and with it the rest of the house.

Chad came out behind me. The trees in the neighboring yard were angled in the wind, and the storm was howling.

"I'm sorry, Eva Rae," he said. "How many times do you want me to say it?"

I bit my lip, shaking my head. "I just … argh … I was just so happy to know that you were all safe inland down south and I didn't have to worry about the kids."

"I didn't mean to …"

I turned around and faced him. I felt so confused, so frustrated that I wanted to scream.

"What do you want from me, Chad? Huh?" I yelled, trying to be heard above the howling winds.

"What do you mean, *what do I want from you?* I'll tell you what I want. I want you to say you love me. Because you do. I know you do. I see it in your eyes. You and me, we're not done yet, Eva Rae. Far from it. I still love you, and you still love me. We were meant to be together. There, I said it. Nothing should come between us anymore. No storms, no new boyfriends."

"Need I remind you that you were the one who had a new girl-friend first, huh?" I moaned. "For about a year without me knowing it, as I recall. You were the one who left overnight and didn't even have the decency to face me when you told me. You did that, Chad; you did all those things."

"And I am sorry for it. I hate myself for what I did to you and the kids. It's all I think about from when I wake up in the morning till I go to bed. How I messed up. How I destroyed everything. I didn't know how much I had, how rich I was till I lost it. And now, I want it back, yes. I want to make everything up to you. I want to love you the way you need to be loved. The way you deserve to be. Don't you understand, Eva Rae? It was always us; it has always been us."

I stared at my ex-husband on the porch, the wind grabbing his hair, the spraying water soaking it. He had never looked more

SAY YOU LOVE ME

vulnerable, never looked more fragile, yet determined. And I had never loved him more than in this moment.

Yet I had no way of telling him. Nothing was clear to me right now, especially my love life. No matter how much I wanted my family to get back together, I still couldn't let go of Matt, the man I had loved all my life. And this wasn't the time or the place.

"Argh!" I screamed in the wind. "Not now, Chad! Of all the times you could have chosen, you tell me this now? In the middle of a hurricane? Have you completely lost your mind?"

With that, I groaned loudly, then walked past him inside and slammed the door behind me. As I stepped into the kitchen, Eileen looked at me from the end of the room, and I saw the terror on her face. Water had started to seep up from underneath the floors.

Chapter Ninety-Six

"IT'S TIME TO LEAVE. We have to get out of here."

I stared at Eileen, who was trying to stop the water using towels.

"The water will just keep rising," I said, "and soon we'll have to be on the roof waiting for someone to come fetch us by boat. I don't think you want to sit on the roof in the middle of a hurricane. We are only on the front side of the storm; the back side is when there's a real risk for a surge. We can't be in this house when that happens."

Eileen shook her head. "There's a shelter at the elementary school for those who didn't evacuate the island in time. It's on higher ground, and the building is safe."

"Great," I said. "It's not that far away. Let's go."

Eileen gave me a faint smile. For the first time in the short while I had known her, she actually seemed her age. She was suddenly nothing but a tired and fragile old lady.

"I think I'd like to stay here. I don't want to leave my house."

"But ... Grandma?"

She gave me another smile. "That's the first time you've called me that; you do realize that, right?"

I looked down at the water coming in, soaking my grandmother's toes, then rushed into the living room where I found Chad with the children.

"There's a shelter at the elementary school," I said, heart throbbing in my chest. I needed to get those kids out of this house before it was too late. Then I'd deal with my stubborn old grandmother afterward.

"You should take the kids there now."

"I can't drive in this weather," Chad said. "Have you seen how high the water is outside? My car won't go through that much water."

"I'll take them … and Sydney," David said, coming up to me. "In my truck. It can go through anything."

"Thanks," I said relieved, thinking that if I trusted anyone to get my children safely through a hurricane, it would be him. "I appreciate it."

"But … what about you, Mom?" Olivia said. "You can't stay here? There's water coming up in the bathroom too."

"I'm going to try and help Grandma get out of here. I'll be right behind you, okay, sweetie?"

"I'm scared," Christine said, tears welling up in her eyes. Water was splashing against the plywood outside, the wind howling even louder, pulling at the wood.

I grabbed her and held her very tight. "Go now. I'll get to the shelter, and we'll meet there, okay? You're safe with your granddad. He has a very safe car, and he knows this area like the back of his hand."

"She's right," David said reassuringly and grabbed Christine's hand in his. "I do. Do you trust me?"

Christine thought it over for a second, then nodded.

I kissed her forehead, then sent them all on their way with the bunnies in their cage in the back. I stared at the big pick-up truck as it left the garage and drove slowly through the water, then wondered if I was ever going to see my family again.

Chapter Ninety-Seven

"I'M NOT LEAVING. And you can't make me."

I stared at the old woman in front of me. The water had reached her ankles now and was slowly rising inside the living room too. Still, I couldn't — for the life of me — convince her to leave with me.

I walked to the door and looked outside. My car was still on the grass next door, but the water was soon going to reach it as well. Once it did, I wouldn't be able to make it out anymore. So far, there were several lawns with no water on them that I could drive across as I had seen David do when he left with the kids. I had tried texting my children to ask how far they had gotten, but my messages weren't sent, and when I tried to call them, the phone was dead.

We had been cut off from the world.

I ran back into the kitchen where Eileen was trying to block the water with a kitchen table.

"You have to come now, Eileen. We need to leave now."

"It's my house, and if I want to go down with it, then it's my business, isn't it?" she said, hissing. "I'll go upstairs and ride out the rest of the storm."

"And if the water gets up there too? Then where will you go?"

"The roof," she said.

I stomped my foot. "Why do you have to be so stubborn?"

"That is my privilege. You go, Eva Rae. No one is stopping you."

"I'm not leaving you," I said, tears rolling down my cheek. "I refuse to leave you to die."

"Well, you have to," she said with a snort.

I stared at her, unable to grasp how anyone could be so stubborn. If I left her here, it would mean her certain death. No eighty-year-old woman would survive anything like this.

I shook my head.

"Nope."

Thinking she couldn't be very heavy, I ran to her, grabbed her around the legs, and lifted her into the air, then took off with her slung over my shoulder.

"I'm not letting you go," I said when she complained. "Not now. Not when I've just gotten to know you. It's as simple as that."

I kicked the door open and rushed outside where the water was splashing against the sides of the house, flooding the porch. Carrying my small grandmother on my shoulder, I walked through waist-high waters until I reached the neighboring house, whose yard was on higher ground, and where I had been clever enough to park the car. My grandmother was still yelling for me to let her go when I threw her into the back seat, jumped into the front, and prayed to God that it would start.

Once I heard the engine roar, I took off. I drove across the neighboring yards, going through puddles, water splashing the sides of the car, crashing through small fences, bushes, and even hitting a trash can on the way, but staying on dry ground for the most part. When we reached a section of the road that was still dry, I floored the minivan, leaving my grandmother's drowning house behind.

Chapter Ninety-Eight

THE DRY LAND didn't last long, though, and soon we were driving through water again, often having it splashing through the sides of the car. I couldn't stop thinking about my kids and praying they had made it to safety.

As I took a right turn, I reached an area with marshland, and as I drove through it cautiously, a strong current suddenly grabbed the car, and I lost control of it.

My grandmother screamed in the back as the car was pulled sideways off the road. I tried desperately to steer it back, but nothing worked. The car was being pulled by the rushing water, and I had no way of controlling where it went. All I could see out the windows was water and more water.

"It's getting submerged," my grandmother yelled from behind me. "The car is being pulled under!"

It all went by very fast, and I could barely react. Water was filling up inside the minivan and had soon reached my waist.

"Help!" Eileen screamed. "What do we do?"

"Stay calm," I said and rolled down the window next to me, letting even more water inside. "That's the most important thing right now — remaining calm. We have to wait for the car to be filled with water. Stay in the seat till the water reaches you, and you can't breathe anymore. Once it is completely full, we can get out. Then you hold your breath and swim to the surface. Can you do that for me, Grandma? Do you think you can do that?"

The water was now at my neckline, and I was stretching my neck to stay above it as long as possible. Eileen was fighting to breathe behind me. Water kept coming up, and I took one last look at her while holding the steering wheel, clutching it so I could use it to push me out of the car once it was time.

"Now, take in a deep breath, as deep as you can, and then we swim. It shouldn't take more than thirty seconds to get out and up to the surface. Do you hear me?"

She answered with a whimper but did as I told her to. I filled my lungs with precious air, just as the water reached my nostrils. I then took off my seatbelt and used the steering wheel to push myself out of the window. I remembered training for this in the FBI and was relieved to know what to do. I knew we wouldn't be able to open the doors because of the pressure put on them by the water outside. I also knew that the air in my lungs would help take me to the surface.

But training was one thing; reality was another. It was a lot harder than I thought. I could hardly see anything as I swam, and I didn't know what was up or down. I lost track of Eileen on the way and didn't even know if she made it out of the window.

Desperately, I turned in the water to see if I could find her, but she was gone. Panicking over this, I swam back toward the car but realized I was about to run out of air and continued upward. I could see the surface, but was struggling to make the air last. It was like in one of those dreams where you fight to get somewhere, but you keep going backward instead. I kept swimming and swimming, but it felt like I was sinking instead, and the surface was getting further and further away.

I had almost given up reaching the surface when something moved in the water above me, and I felt a forceful pull.

Chapter Ninety-Nine

I GASPED LOUDLY AND COUGHED. It felt like my lungs were on fire. I threw up water on the grass next to me.

Then I saw his face. His sweet eyes stared down at me.

"Eva Rae?"

"Matt?"

I almost screamed his name out when realizing it was him.

"Eva Rae," he said and held my face between his hands, his eyes looking nervously into mine. "Were you the only one in the car? Was there anyone else besides you in that car? The kids ... were they with you?"

I sat up straight then felt sick and threw up more water. I was disoriented, then I remembered.

"Eileen. Where is Eileen? Did she make it out? I can't see her anywhere; is she still down there?"

Matt stared at the water in front of us. He didn't think about it twice before he jumped in. While holding my breath, my heart racing in my chest, I glared nervously at the lake of water where Matt had gone in. I hadn't come this far to lose her now. I simply refused to.

Please, let her be all right. Please.

Matt suddenly reappeared, dragging Eileen's small body after him. I helped him pull her to dry ground, where I immediately performed CPR on her. I pressed on her chest, praying under my breath for her heart to beat and for her to start breathing.

Eileen coughed, and water came out of her. I breathed, relieved. Matt wasted no time. He took her in his arms and carried her to his pick-up truck, where he put her in the back seat. The wind was still howling, and the rain pouring down on us. I jumped in next to him in the front seat, and we took off, leaving my minivan submerged in the water.

"Where did you come from all of a sudden?" I asked, still gasping for air as the truck roared through and across the grass, staying on what little dry ground was left.

"I came back for you. I drove up into your grandmother's street just as you left. I saw your car take off across the lawns and followed you. My truck had trouble getting through the water on the way here, and it brushed me off the road. It took a while before I could get back on track. I made it over the bridge just before they closed it."

"You have no idea how glad I am that you came," I said.

"Me too," he said. "I almost didn't."

He made it to a drier road where we could actually see the asphalt and where the houses were still intact. We rushed across a small neighborhood until we reached Jasmine Street, and I breathed a sigh of relief. I could see the school in the distance and it looked intact and safe.

My heart beat faster as I thought about my family. When Matt parked the truck in front of the school, we lifted Eileen in our arms and carried her toward the front door while the strong winds pushed us back and the rain whipped our faces.

Chapter One Hundred

"Mom, what happened to you? You're soaked!"

I hugged both my daughters anyway and held them very tight to my body. Alex had found some kid he was playing with across the room. He gave me a quick hug, then ran back.

They had set up some beds in the commons and the gym, and a lot of islanders had sought shelter there the past few hours while the water rose, bringing chairs and sleeping bags. I was happy to see both Lauren and Chris there, along with Deputy Corel and Detective Foster, who were supervising the shelter and greeted me as we came in. Even Allyson's father, Ryan was there, sitting on a chair, hiding his face between his hands.

We placed my grandmother in one of the few beds there, and David pulled up a chair next to her to keep an eye on her. Meanwhile, I hugged and kissed my kids and gave Sydney a huge hug, thanking God for bringing all my loved ones to safety. It was hard to put into words how relieved I felt in this moment.

We were all safe.

Chad came toward me, but then he saw Matt and his smile froze.

I pointed at him, then at Matt. "You two behave. This is an

emergency situation, and the last thing I am having is you two fighting."

They both nodded in agreement, hopefully realizing this was not the time nor the place. Alex called for Chad to come to see something and he backed off. I sat down on the foot of my grandmother's bed with a deep exhale. Matt sat next to me. The storm howled outside, but inside, it was nice and calm.

"Listen," Matt said after a few minutes of silence that I used to gather myself. My hands were still shaking, and I was beginning to get cold in my wet clothes. I didn't have anything to change into, though, so there wasn't much I could do about it. Matt saw me shaking and found a blanket on the back of a chair that he wrapped around me. It helped.

I turned to look at him. I couldn't help smiling. His hair was beginning to dry, so it was pointing in all directions. He looked like a wet puppy.

Matt continued:

"I know I was the one who backed out and all, that I told you to go be with Chad and your family, but … well, I don't want that. I have to be completely honest with you and with myself. That's why I came here now. To tell you that I want to be with you. I love you, and I believe we belong together. I don't want to give you up, and I'll fight for you if I have to. Now, if you'd rather be with Chad, and you tell me so, then I'll respect that, of course, but …"

I shook my head with a chuckle.

"What?" he asked. "What's so funny?"

"Of all the times … you and Chad both choose to do this in the middle of a hurricane?"

Matt wrinkled his nose. "Chad? What did he do?"

I shook my head again. "Nothing. It's just that … well, to be honest with you, I'm not sure where I'm at right now. I haven't had a moment of peace to think about this. I think I have to wait before I can give you my answer — before I can tell you what is in our future. Can you live with that?"

Matt swallowed hard and looked away. He was disappointed. I couldn't blame him. I took his hand in mine.

"I love you. I really do," I said. "With every fiber of my being. I have never loved anyone more than I love you. That's the truth. But I have to think about my kids too. You know, I do."

I rose to my feet and walked away, tears welling up in my eyes, feeling even more confused than ever. I walked into the cafeteria where they had set up coffee pots and sandwiches, then grabbed a couple and devoured them before filling up on the warm coffee.

For a few minutes, I stood and sipped my cup while thinking about my future, when I spotted Chris and Lauren sitting on a bench, chatting away. In the doorway, a few feet from where they were seated stood Mr. Jenkins, glaring at them.

Chapter One Hundred One

"WE NEED to keep an eye on Chris," I said as I returned to my grandmother's bed. I had brought two coffees and handed David one of them since Matt had left.

"Why? What's going on?"

"Mr. Jenkins is here. I haven't seen his family, so I'm guessing they made it off the island in time. But if he is the Leech, then Chris is in danger."

David rose to his feet. He walked with me to the cafeteria, where I let him see for himself. Jenkins was on his phone now, texting. I grabbed my own phone from my pocket and thanked God for waterproof phones. I realized we had a signal there. That was a good sign. We weren't completely cut off from the world. The Internet even worked on my phone.

"Well, we can't let him get to him, then," David said. "We must keep a close eye on Jenkins. I'll take the first shift."

I left the cafeteria and went back to my grandmother, then laid down on an empty bed next to her. I felt like the room was spinning around me as a million thoughts overwhelmed my poor brain. Yet, I still somehow managed to fall asleep. After about two hours of deep, dreamless sleep, I opened my eyes. The noise from the wind outside had grown stronger and was like a constant howling in the air.

My grandmother was awake and sitting up.

"Eileen," I said. "How are you feeling?"

"I've had better days," she said and felt her head. "But I guess I'll be all right. Thanks to you."

I chuckled and sat up. Alex came to my bed and crawled up to me, then put his small arms around my neck.

"It's scary outside, Mommy."

"I know, baby. But in here, we're fine, remember? This is a safe shelter. We have police here and everything."

Alex nodded. "They say the eye will be over us soon. What does that mean?"

"That means we're halfway there. The storm is like a circle, right, and we're in the middle of it now. Listen?"

"I can't hear anything," he said with a sniffle.

"Exactly. In the eye, everything is completely still. There's no wind and no rain. But as soon as the eye is gone, it'll start again."

"I hear something now," Alex said. "What's that knocking?"

I took in a deep breath, remembering this from my childhood. "That's people banging on their pots and pans. It's an old tradition. Once the eye of the storm is over you, you go out on your porch or stand in your doorway and bang on pots and pans to let your neighbors know you're alive."

Alex gasped lightly. "Wow."

"I know. There are still people out there, but by the sound of it, they're okay."

"I wanna go bang on a pot," Alex said and jumped down.

I grabbed his arm.

"Oh, no, you don't. You stay inside; you hear me? Inside is safe."

"Okay."

Alex gave me a disappointed look then took off to be with his newfound friend. As he left, I spotted David walking up to me, a serious look on his face.

"What's up?" I asked, my heart rate going up as I sensed that something was very wrong.

"There's a new live video," he said and showed me his phone. "He just started it. And it's coming from inside this shelter."

Chapter One Hundred Two

"He's live right now," David said and showed me the screen. "Looks like it's in the cafeteria."

My heart pounded loudly in my chest. If the Leech had started a live-video, that meant he was planning on something happening, something that he wanted to capture on camera, and show to his fans. Could it have to do with what he tried to get Chris to do? Was he waiting for him to fulfill his demands? Had he gotten to him somehow and threatened him to do it anyway? To save Adam?

No matter what, it couldn't be good.

I didn't think about it twice, but I ran through the commons area toward the cafeteria. I ran into some lady on the way and made my excuses before hurrying on.

Inside the cafeteria, I stopped, panting and agitated. David came up behind me.

"Where is he?" I asked. "Where is Jenkins?"

"He was right here a minute ago when I left the cafeteria," David said. "He was standing over there, on his phone."

I scanned the area and the many people getting coffee and putting sandwiches on plates.

"Where is Chris?"

David exhaled. "He was with Lauren over there, but …"

I rushed to Lauren. "We're looking for Chris. Do you know where he went?"

She shook her head. "Maybe he went up to get something to eat?"

"I don't see him anywhere. Dang it."

"Did he talk to anyone before he left?" I asked.

She nodded. "There was this guy who came over. He said he wanted to talk to him and asked if he could come with him. They walked down that corridor."

I glanced in the direction she pointed, then hurried toward the opening. David looked at the screen, following the live-feed.

"He's in a corridor now. He's filming the brick walls."

"Is he saying anything? Is anyone commenting?" I asked.

"He just said that the video will start in a few minutes and urged his fans to hold on. He also said it'd be worth the wait, that he had something really grand planned."

I felt my heart skip a beat. Was he going to shoot inside the shelter? My kids were here. I couldn't let this happen. I couldn't let him hurt any more people.

I felt for my gun, then remembered it had been in the car, in my purse when we were submerged in water. It was probably gone. I realized I was no match for him if he had brought a weapon to the shelter. I couldn't stop him by myself.

I needed help.

Chapter One Hundred Three

I ASKED David to keep an eye out for them, while I hurried back to the media room where I had last seen Detective Foster. But as I opened the doors and walked in, I couldn't see him. I couldn't find Deputy Corel either. I walked through the library and into another corridor when I spotted a leg in the doorway to the bathroom.

Oh, no!

I ran to the door and pulled it open. On the floor lay Deputy Corel, motionless, his head resting on the tiles, his eyes wide open. A pool of blood surrounded him like a halo. My heart rate went up rapidly as I frantically checked for a pulse, but realized it was in vain. He was gone.

A patch of blood on his back caught my attention, and I realized his shirt had been ripped. As I looked closer, I could see that something was carved into the skin. It looked like letters, shaping a word:

GOODNESS

"Another Fruit of the Spirit," I mumbled.

I stared at the dead deputy, wondering why the Leech had carved the word into the man's body when he hadn't done that to any of his other victims.

Because he's sending you a message. He wants to make sure you know it was him. He knows you're on his trail.

Realizing this, I hurried back toward the cafeteria where I found David coming toward me.

"I haven't found them yet. I walked both of those corridors, but they were nowhere to be seen. The broadcast is showing just a white wall and a clock counting down. It started at ten minutes, and now there are six left."

"Six minutes till his big event, huh? We need to stop him," I said. "Before it's too late. I found Deputy Corel dead in the men's bathroom. He killed him and carved the word Goodness into his skin to make sure we knew this was his work. We need to find Detective Foster and tell him. He's armed; he can stop him, but I haven't been able to find him anywhere."

"Me either," David said. "I asked around, and no one seems to know where he is."

"I'll go down the east hallways and look inside all the classrooms if you take the ones on the west side," I said.

David nodded, then grabbed my arm. "Be careful, sweetheart."

I almost complained about his choice of word, but for the first time, I didn't mind. If I was completely honest, I actually kind of liked it.

I sent him half a smile.

"You too."

"DETECTIVE? FOSTER?"

I walked into a classroom and found a family of five sitting in there, eating their food. The kids were playing with toys on the floor. The parents looked worn out. They had that look in their eyes that told me they had lost everything in this storm, that they might be in safety but feared for what awaited them once they got back home. A house submerged in water?

"I'm sorry," I said. "I was looking for Detective Foster; have you seen him around?"

The mother shook her head. She was too tired even to say a

word. I left them and walked down the hallway until I met a man who looked like he had been through Hell and back.

"I'm looking for Detective Foster," I said. "Tall slim guy with brown hair. He wears a badge, have you seen him?"

The man stared at me, his eyes blank with shock. "It came from everywhere. The water was just there all of a sudden. We were doing all right till the water suddenly came up. My poor wife, she crawled up on the kitchen table till it collapsed and she ... she drowned on me."

I stared at the man, who obviously couldn't quite figure out what had happened.

"I keep walking these corridors because I don't know what else to do," he said. "I keep thinking she's back there waiting for me, but she's not. I can't seem to be able to sit still."

"I am so sorry," I said.

The man didn't say anymore, he just nodded, and then continued walking. My heart broken for him, I ran down the hall-way, looking into each and every classroom, yelling Foster's name, feeling more and more terrified as I went along. I knew the clock was ticking, and I couldn't really see how I was going to stop Jenkins in time.

That was when I saw Chris. He was standing by a big wall of artwork made by the school's children, leaning on his crutches. Seeing him made me breathe in relief.

"Chris!" I yelled and waved.

He looked up, then smiled.

"Are you okay?" I asked as I walked closer to him.

He nodded. "I'm okay."

I breathed, relieved when suddenly I sensed that everything was wrong. Out of the corner of my eye, I spotted someone, movement; someone was running down the hallway toward Chris.

It was Jenkins.

"Run, Chris, Run!" I shouted, even though I knew the boy couldn't because of his crutches. I sped up as I saw the man storm toward Chris and leap for him.

Chapter One Hundred Four

CHRIS DUCKED down as the man jumped him, and seconds later, they were rolling on the floor.

"Get off him," I yelled as I ran closer. "Get off him, you sick bastard!"

Chris managed to get out from beneath Jenkins and tried to get away, but Jenkins grabbed his legs and pulled him back. Chris yelled loudly as he was dragged back, and he received a punch to his face. Chris answered by driving something sharp into his neck. Jenkins stopped in the middle of a movement, blood gushing from his wound. Stunned, Jenkins stumbled backward and fell against the tiles. Chris shuffled backward, crabbing across the ground to get away from Jenkins.

I stopped in my tracks as I saw the man bleeding on the tiles and Chris, who was panting on the floor. My entire body was trembling as I watched Jenkins fight to breathe his last breaths, the blood spitting out of his throat.

Chris crawled closer to him, staring at Jenkins, probably making sure that he was actually dead.

"We should call for help," I said. I looked at Chris, and our eyes met.

Chris shook his head. He placed his hands on the floor and pushed himself up. "No. Let's not do that."

"Excuse me?"

Chris rose to his feet without any help from his crutches and stood in front of me, all five-foot-six-inches. I was suddenly very aware of the fact that he was extremely well trained.

"Let's not involve anyone else. This is just between you and me now."

He must have noticed my expression changing as the realization washed over me. So much information was running through my brain, bombarding me, all the things I missed, all the signs, all the alarms.

"Your face. Your disease … Cutis Laxa syndrome."

"Is a rare, inherited or acquired connective-tissue disorder in which the skin becomes inelastic and hangs loosely in folds. Patients develop a prematurely aged appearance," he said. "But it doesn't require me using crutches, no. That one I added for effect, sympathy, and well, so no one would suspect me. But yes. My disease makes me look like I'm forty, maybe even older with my sagging skin."

He watched me and I him. There was no use in pretending anymore. We both knew the truth.

"The hardest thing when growing up with something like this is the other's gaze. The children's mockery, even the adult ones. And the fact that you can't live a normal childhood or youth. You are automatically and involuntarily thrown into the adults' world. You miss one of the steps of your life. The one which, normally, is the most beautiful, the one where you're thoughtless, where you can meet others without being victim to judgment. As a child, I was called, Oldie or Grandpa. Kids feared me. Can you blame them? I looked like an old man at the age of four. They were scared of me, ran away if I tried to play with them. Once I was mistaken for a teacher at the school, or for a kid's father. I was even kicked off a school bus once because the driver didn't believe I was a kid. When suffering from Cutis Laxa, you must always justify yourself, at school, at work, everywhere. You have to answer the question: How old are you? Your worst enemy is the mirror. I look twenty-five years older than I am. In this society, where everything is based upon appearance and youth, I wanted to be young too. But how can I? I'm locked inside this old body and face. I was only nine when I started having jowls on my face; I was five when I developed the loose, floppy skin on my neck."

"But it also made it possible for you to pretend to be an adult," I said. "To go to bars and order beers and kidnap women, or to liquor stores and kidnap men like Jeff Facer, even though you're only fifteen in reality."

"You shouldn't have come here, Eva Rae Thomas," he said. "I mean, I am personally glad you did because you helped me push myself to get bigger than what I could ever have imagined. Do you know that I now have more than ten thousand subscribers to my page, huh? I'm finally as big as I wanted to be. I am finally being seen. The thing is, when you grow up like this, is that no one actually sees you. You're always hidden away. I grew up with my grandmother, and she'd keep me away from visitors so they wouldn't be scared when seeing me. She refused to take me into town because I might scare people. And once you do get to meet someone, sure, they'll stare at you for a few seconds until they realize it's impolite, and then they remove their glare and pretend like you're not there anymore. That's what most people have done my entire life, pretended like I wasn't there. The teachers won't call on me in class because then they'll have to actually look at me. See, I make them uncomfortable. Looking at me makes everyone uncomfortable, so they choose to ignore me. All my life, I've been ignored and overlooked, but not anymore. Now, they see me. Now, I am forcing the world to look at me."

"There are other ways of getting attention, you know," I said.

"Smile, Eva Rae Thomas," he said and lifted his phone. I realized he was filming me. "Our live video has just begun, and today, you're my very special guest of honor."

Chapter One Hundred Five

"You can try to run away," he said. "But where will you go? The storm is still raging outside, and in here, well ... we have your children and so many more innocent people, don't we?"

I exhaled. Chris kept filming me with his camera, and it made me uncomfortable.

"Where's Adam?" I asked. "What did you do to him?"

"I'm so glad you finally asked," Chris said and tapped on the phone's screen. "I know that my viewers all are wondering about the very same thing. And here he is. This is a live feed from a Go-Pro camera I have attached to his head. I am just gonna share the screen here, and now my viewers can see both us and his feed."

Chris turned the phone and showed me the screen.

"What am I looking at here?" I asked.

"This is live from a shelter on the mainland — Yulee Elementary School, where more than five hundred people have sought shelter from the storm. I've placed Adam there with them, and he knows he's not allowed to say anything to anyone about what is in his backpack. If he does, it blows, and everyone dies. This is a place where many homeless seek shelter or the poor who live in trailer parks, and many of them are children."

"You sent him in there with a bomb?" I asked, breathing nervously.

"Yes," he said. "And I have the switch here. The trigger."

Chris raised his hand and showed me a small device in his hand. "If I let go of this button here, then they all go."

"What do you want from me?" I asked, barely able to speak. I kept staring at the homemade device in his hand. The thought of poor Adam in that shelter waiting to be blown to pieces crushed me. He had to be so scared.

"I have a feeling you want me to do something, am I right?" I continued, my voice trembling. "What are we at now? I know that Adam was Love, the people at the Ritz-Carlton represented Joy, while the nursing home was Peace, Melanie at the theater was Patience, while McMillen was Kindness, and Deputy Corel, Goodness. But what about the rest? Next, we have faithfulness? Is that Adam?"

"You have done your homework, I can hear. Now, you mustn't be impatient. I'll get to that."

"Was it Jenkins?" I asked. "Was he faithfulness?"

Chris scoffed. "Dear Lord, no. He was nothing. Not important."

"Why did he attack you? Did he know what you were up to?" I asked.

"If you must know, I insulted him. He had a temper, you know. I simply told him it was his own fault, that everything that had happened was his own fault. Him losing his child, him losing his wife."

"Except it wasn't, was it?" I asked. "I was wondering about the texts between him and Allyson. He was a registered sex offender, and I read through his case files from back then. He had a son that he lost the rights to because they found child pornography on his computer. But he denied it till the very end. In everything I found, he said he was set up. He served time in prison, and when he got out, his wife had committed suicide. You are that son, aren't you? The one he lost?"

Chapter One Hundred Six

THEN:

"How are my chances, do you think?"

Marlene stared at Scott Hunter, her lawyer. It had been a long process, including several days in a courtroom where she had fought for her rights to be with her child. Now, they were standing outside the courtroom, waiting for the verdict.

Scott cleared his throat. "Well, it didn't help that you attacked the woman from the DCF who was sent to supervise your visit with your son; I can tell you that much. The judge won't look lightly at that. Security guards had to drag you out of there. It doesn't paint the picture of a stable and mentally capable mother. The opposition argued very well that you weren't mentally fit, that there was no way the abuse could have taken place without your knowledge. And especially with your son's extra challenges, his disease, they are arguing that you're simply unfit to take proper care of him. I'm sorry to say it, but it doesn't look very good, in my opinion."

And he was right. Marlene knew he was as soon as she stepped back inside the courtroom, and the judge looked down at her. He read the verdict, but she barely heard any of it. All she could think about was her poor son and whether she'd ever see him again.

How can the world be this cruel?

"I am so sorry," Scott said as they came back out. "We did what we could. But you must remember that they're only thinking about the well-being of the child."

Marlene looked up at him, tears in her eyes. "But … where will he go?"

Marlene heard a voice behind her, and she turned to look. Then her heart dropped like a heavy rock in her chest. In front of her stood her mother. She hadn't seen her much lately. Her mother didn't like Bruce and had told her not to marry him, or she might end up regretting it.

"You?" she asked. "What are you doing here?"

"The court has appointed your mother as the new guardian of Jack," Scott said. "I thought you'd be glad to know this."

Marlene's mother smiled, and Marlene's blood froze to ice. She knew her mother very well, and she also knew her to be the meanest woman she had ever met.

"You?" she hissed. "You did this? You told them that Bruce was abusing Jack? You fed them the details, the pictures, and the stories?" she asked, gasping for air. She knew her mother could be one of the most vicious people on this planet, but this … this she had never thought she would stoop so low.

"The boy needs a proper upbringing," she said. "You weren't giving him that. You were being sloppy. There was no discipline in that house. Bruce was unfit as a father and a husband."

"You poisoned Jack against us, telling him what to say; didn't you? You came to the house that day a couple of weeks ago. I let you use Bruce's computer because yours was broken and you needed to check your email, you said. You planted the file, didn't you? You told them about the bruises and gave them the pictures that you had taken when Jack came to visit because you knew you could use it against us, against Bruce. And now he's going to jail and I … I lost the rights to my own son."

Her mother smiled victoriously and lifted her purse. "Well, I told you that you shouldn't have married him; didn't I? You chose not to listen. You laid this upon yourself. You made your bed, dearest, and now you must lie in it."

Chapter One Hundred Seven

"You weren't abused by your dad at all, were you?" I asked.

"My grandmother told me to say those things to the people from DCF and the investigators, or I would end up in Hell, she said. She said I needed to come live with her because I needed discipline. She told me I was a punishment from God, that my mom was being punished by God for marrying my dad, and that was why I had been born a freak, like she called me. That was why I had gotten Cutis Laxa and had to be hidden away from the public. And she was the only one who knew how to handle someone like me properly."

"And she knew that, with your condition, your disease, you bruised easily, right?" I asked. "It could easily look like abuse to the outside world."

"Just a bump on the leg could cause severe swelling or even a fracture to the bone," he said. "I once fell and had a skull fracture. I began bleeding between the skull and my skin. The skull swelled so badly that I looked like E.T. That's what I started calling myself because that was how I felt. Like an alien freak. My grandmother changed my name to Christopher since she said she never approved of Jack; that was my mother's name for me, and as soon as I moved in with her, she started to try and drive the evilness out of me. She'd take me to her garage and whip me, telling me to repent of my sins."

Chris grabbed his shirt and lifted it. I gasped as I saw the deep furrows.

"If there is no pain, there is no gain, she said. In all pain, there is a purpose. I had to rebuke my fleshly desires so goodness could grow in me. But the thing is, goodness never wins, does it? Look at the world we live in. Look at this storm. No matter how hard you try, even you, Eva Rae Thomas, evil will always win inside of you. We try to maintain all these virtues, telling ourselves that we possess attributes like love. An undefeatable benevolence and unconquerable goodwill that always seeks the higher good for others, no matter their behavior. But that doesn't exist, does it? Because if we do one thing wrong, then we lose it. If we look like me, we never receive it."

"So, by forcing Adam to shoot up the school, you proved that love doesn't exist?" I asked.

"Everyone loved Adam. Everyone adored him. His family, the school ..."

"Allyson," I said.

Chris stopped. He gave me a look. "Yes, Allyson."

"You loved her too, didn't you? But the older you got, the more you realized you could never have her or any girl like her. Your anger and resentment grew toward Adam because he had everything that you wanted. That's why you did what you did to him. It wasn't to prove love doesn't exist, or that we are all basically evil; come on. That's just too far out. You wanted him dead because you were jealous. My guess is that Bruce Jenkins over here, your dad, was trying to get back in contact with you, and that was why he was texting with Allyson. He knew you two were close, and since you didn't want to talk to him, he tried to go through her. He texted her using a burner phone, so his wife wouldn't find out because she didn't know his story and he didn't want her to. It would ruin everything for him, and he knew no one would believe him. Adam thought she was dating someone behind his back, but once he got the entire story on the way home from the party, he was no longer angry. Now, before this happened, Allyson kept telling you to see your father, and you did. He told you everything, didn't he? He told you the truth about what your grandmother had done and how she had caused your mother, the only woman who ever loved you unconditionally and who really wanted you back, how she had killed herself in sorrow after having lost you. He told you everything, and you got so mad you killed your grandmother when you got back, am I right? I bet her body is still at the house."

Chris stared at me, his nostrils flaring. The look in his eyes was answer enough for me. I had figured him out, and he didn't like it one bit.

"And then you didn't want to stop there. You wanted to punish the world for what had happened to you, how your life had turned out. You came up with this Fruit of the Spirit idea and started planning, making sure you could get Adam and Allyson down first because you were so mad at them. But everyone had to tremble at the sound of your name, right? You studied killers and wanted to be famous like them. You wanted finally to be seen by the world and recognized for something. If nothing else, then for being the most dangerous killer this world has seen, and the cleverest one. You think you were so incredibly clever, keeping under the radar, but I've got news for you. It wasn't that ingenious. I've faced killers who were way out of your league."

I said the words, knowing it would anger him. All this guy wanted from me was to fear him, to acknowledge him as a master in his field, as the winner. That was why he sent me the video from the nursing home. That was why he had chosen me for whatever it was he wanted to do now. Because I was the expert. I was the one who could give him the recognition he had longed for his entire life.

But I wasn't giving it to him. I wasn't going to give him that pleasure.

Chapter One Hundred Eight

"WHERE IS EVA RAE?"

Matt walked up to Chad, who was playing with Alex and his firetruck. Matt wrinkled his forehead in concern.

"It's odd. I haven't seen her for hours. She wasn't in the cafeteria, and she's not with her grandmother either."

"Well, I haven't seen her in a while either," Chad said. He rose to his feet and looked worriedly at Matt.

"Well, where can she be if she's not here? You don't think something's happened to her, do you?"

Matt shook his head. "We're inside of a shelter. It's a safe building. What could possibly happen?"

Chad lifted his eyebrows. "It's Eva Rae we're talking about."

He had a point. Eva Rae could get herself in trouble anywhere. She didn't have to go outside the door.

"Boys," a voice said from behind them.

They turned and saw David. The look on his face made Matt's heart drop.

"What's wrong?" he asked.

"It's Eva Rae," David said. He stared at them, his eyes serious, then glared down at the phone in his hand. He lifted it so they could see the screen. A video was running. Eva Rae's face was on the display.

"She's in trouble."

Chapter One Hundred Nine

"WHAT IS it that you want me to do?" I asked.

The wind was pulling at the plywood on the windows, and the rain was pounding outside. I stared at Chris's wrinkled face, then down at the trigger in his hand, wondering how I was going to get it out of his grip without blowing up Adam.

That was when they showed up.

"Step away from her," I heard Matt say as they came running around the corner.

Oh, no.

"Get back," I said. "He has a backpack with a bomb at another shelter that he'll detonate. Adam is carrying the backpack."

"We know," David said and held up his phone. "We heard everything on your little live show. It was easy to find you when you're standing in front of the school's art wall."

The sight of the three men approaching made Chris smile. It wasn't a pleasant smile, and I got the feeling he was expecting them to come. I wondered if that was why he had chosen that place to stand when I found him. To make sure they would find him.

"Don't come closer," I told them.

Chad spotted Jenkins on the floor in a pool of blood and gasped. He looked away, and I could tell he was terrified.

"Better stay over there," I said. "Don't come any closer. I've got this under control."

"At least you think you do," Chris said.

Again with that smirk on his face.

Chris turned sideways and put his phone up on the wall, making it stick by using his pop socket on the back of the phone, making sure he could still film everything. Then he reached in the back of his pants and pulled out a gun.

"Don't you dare hurt her," Matt yelled. David held him back.

What happened next went down so fast, I barely blinked. Matt took one step forward, breaking out of David's grip, coming for me to protect me. Chris smiled at me, then lifted the gun and fired a shot at him. The bullet whistled through the air and, as I turned my head in terror, I saw Chad walk in front of Matt, taking the bullet for him.

The bullet blasted through his chest, and Chad fell to the floor, rag-doll limp.

Chapter One Hundred Ten

I SCREAMED MY HEART OUT, then hurried to him. I grabbed Chad in my arms and pulled his heavy body up while blood smeared my clothes. I cried and screamed as I held his head in my arms, unable to grasp what had really happened.

"No, no, no, please, Chad; please, Chad, don't leave me. Not like this, please, no!"

David and Matt both stood like they were frozen while I cried. Chris stood in front of me, smiling from ear to ear, while I lost it completely. I rose to my feet and ran toward him. That was when he did something I had never expected. He turned the gun around and handed it to me.

"Here," he said. "Go ahead. Shoot me. I know you want to."

I stared at the gun in this hand, then grabbed it without thinking. I pressed it against his forehead, my hands shaking, sweat springing from every pore in my body. Anger rose in me to an extent where I could barely see out of my eyes.

"Shoot me," Chris said. "Get your revenge for your husband — your *faithful* husband. I was aiming for your faithful boyfriend, but your husband — sorry *ex*-husband — turned out to be the real faithful one. Dying when saving someone else's life. What an example to us all."

My finger lingered on the trigger, and I moved it, determined to shoot, to kill him right there and then. I wanted to do it more than anything in this world.

"Just remember one thing," he said. "If you do shoot me, then I won't hold onto this button anymore, and the bomb will go off. Five hundred people, including your brother — your sweet brother representing gentleness — will lose their lives. Do you want that to happen? Or do you possess self-control enough to refrain from killing me? That's the last one, you see? Self-control. The question is, do you have it?"

I stared at him, snorting as I breathed. Never in my entire life had I been angrier. I could barely breathe, so badly did I want to kill him, to see him suffer.

But I couldn't. I couldn't when knowing it meant killing all those people.

I lowered the gun, my knuckles still white from the restraint. I glanced back at Chad lying on the floor, then sobbed.

Chris smiled and went in front of the camera, addressing his viewers. "And that, my viewers, is how it's done. I will now be able to walk out of here, untouched, because they don't dare to take me down. I will keep on killing because I am simply untouchable."

Thousands of comments poured in on the screen, lots of likes and cheers. I felt the taste of defeat in my mouth when Matt came up behind me. He grabbed the gun from my hand, turned it at Chris, and before I could protest, he pulled the trigger.

Chapter One Hundred Eleven

THE BULLET WENT through Chris's back. Blood spurted on the phone and camera as he grabbed his chest, then fell forward against the wall, trying to get a grip, reaching for something to hold onto, but soon slid to the ground. The switch fell out of his hand and rolled across the floor.

"NOO!" I yelled and glared at Matt. "You just killed all those people, and one of them was my brother!"

Matt handed me back the gun, then shook his head. He took the switch in his hand.

"When I was stationed overseas, I saw my share of remote triggers for IEDs. I've seen them use cell phones, radios, and garage door openers but common for them all is that they can't reach more than a mile," he said. "It's a lot further than a mile to the shelter on the mainland where Adam is. Chris knew this. He tricked you."

"But ...?"

Matt grabbed the phone from the wall and showed me the screen where Adam was sitting still on a bed, his camera still showing the many people at the shelter, walking back and forth, some sleeping, others eating. On the other side of the screen, Chris's fans were leaving, logging out of the message board, one faster than the other, till no one was watching anymore.

They got out of there while they could before their identities were revealed, the cowards.

I could barely breathe. I looked up at him, shaking my head. I fell to my knees, sobbing. Matt grabbed me in his arms. I cried loudly while he held me tight, rocking me back and forth. All I could see was Chad's dead eyes. The man I had loved, the man I had been married to for fifteen years, the man who had given me three children was gone.

Dead and gone.

What do I tell the children? How will I break this to them?

It didn't take many minutes before the hallway was filled with people. It wasn't until Detective Foster finally came with another of his deputies that they managed to get people away from there.

David and Sydney took care of the kids, while Matt carried me back to the common room where he put me in a bed and tucked a blanket around me. He sat there all night, holding my hand in his while Damian finished his raging outside.

Three days later

Chapter One Hundred Twelve

THE STORM DAMAGE WAS EXCESSIVE. It was the worst in history, they kept saying on the weather channel and the radio. Completely devastating. So many had lost their homes, and three people had lost their lives. Who could have known the storm would suddenly make landfall as a Cat5 storm on Amelia Island when all the models had said it would stay in the ocean?

No one could have predicted this, they kept saying. No one.

The flooding was the worst. My grandmother's house was underwater still three days later, and we were staying in rooms at the Ritz-Carlton Hotel, which had suffered little or almost no damage. The hotel had opened its doors for everyone who needed a place to stay while the island began its long road to recovery.

The kids were inconsolable. The loss of their father was a huge blow to them, and they couldn't stop crying.

Neither could I.

I missed him terribly already, and I found it hard to forgive myself for getting him involved in all this. For some reason, I also kept blaming Matt slightly for what happened. Chad had taken the bullet for him, for whatever reason that I was never going to know. And it tormented me. I couldn't help but think about it every time I looked at Matt, even though I tried not to. After all, it wasn't his fault. He had no say in what happened.

Three days after the storm, I packed up what little I had, and took the elevator down to the lobby with the kids and Matt. I found Detective Foster waiting for me downstairs. He came up to me, hat in his hand, and asked if he could have a word.

I walked to the side with him, away from the kids so they wouldn't hear. Foster had not once made me feel like I was making things up when I explained the story to him over and over again, even though he found it hard to understand, which I guess we all did. Luckily, I had so many people backing up my story by now that he knew he had to listen. The fact that they found Deputy Corel with the inscription on his back had made it easier as well.

"So ... you're ready to go home?" he asked.

"I can't wait," I said. "No offense, but it might take a while before I come back here."

"You still have your family here," he said.

I nodded. He was right. David, Adam, and my grandmother were determined to fix up the old house again and stay here, even though I had asked them to come to Cocoa Beach with me.

"Maybe when Mom isn't around anymore," David had said. "But this is her island. She wants to die here."

"And she almost did," I said.

"I know it's been a lot," Detective Foster said. "And I'm going to let you go in just a second. But first, I want to tell you that we finally managed to get into Christopher Hutching's house, or rather his grandmother's. And you were right. We did find her body there. It was in the bedroom upstairs, and it looked like Christopher had been sleeping with her dead body for quite some time."

"I had a feeling that was what you'd find," I said. "What else? Cyanide?"

"Yes, we found huge amounts of a cyanide-potassium powder that he had ordered online from China. It's amazing what you can buy and get away with doing online these days, huh?"

"It sure is," I said. "I'm sure it'll be a match to what was in the champagne and the candy sticks that killed those three kids at the school and made six of them very sick. You see the strangest things online. Have you any way of tracking the people who watched his feed?"

Foster shook his head. "I'm afraid not. But I have spoken to the FBI about it, and they might try. It's out of my hands. I know they're going to try and get the website closed down. There's been so much bad on it so far, and I know that its creator is asking to have it closed down. It's out of his hands since he created it so that the users were managing it, and he can't close it down himself. But it has been used for people who dream about becoming school shooters, as a place to talk to likeminded people."

"That is nasty," I said.

"We found the entire living room filled with cameras and computers, and on one of his computers, we found many of the videos he had made. Looks like he was keeping them for himself, as a scrapbook maybe."

"Sounds like him."

"We also found bomb-making manuals that he had downloaded on his computer, and all the fingernails he pulled off his victims in a jar. When going through the theater, we found a camera attached under the ceiling that he must have put up there. It was linked to one of his computers. Jenkins did take the armoire there because he volunteered backstage, but Christopher must have broken into the building at some point and placed Melanie in the closet with the vest strapped onto her body. We found out that he has been using his grandmother's blue car to drive around in, just like he used her savings to live off while all this went down. I feel convinced that we have enough evidence to make sure there is no doubt about his guilt, and you'll be glad to hear that we found the video he made for Adam, threatening him to do the shooting, and holding a knife to Allyson's throat. So, it's safe to say that Adam's in the clear. I suspect that we can close the case in a few months. Give the survivors some peace of mind." Foster put his hat back on. "Anyway, I just wanted to say goodbye and thank you. Without you, we would never have stopped him."

I smiled, half-choked, and watched him walk away. I still wasn't so sure me coming here had helped anything. On the contrary, I feared that the fact that I had been there had made Chris accelerate and maybe even worsened things. I wasn't sure. And I never would know now. I knew I had to accept that and move on, even though it was hard.

"You ready?"

I turned and faced David and Adam. As it turned out, Matt had been correct. The switch that Chris had held couldn't reach the shelter on the mainland where Adam had been. As soon as I told Foster about the bomb, he had some of his colleagues who guarded that shelter get to Adam and take it from him. The bag was filled with explosives, and they called for a bomb squad to come out and defuse the bomb. Luckily, nothing happened to it, and all the people at the shelter were safe, including Adam. Eileen was still in the hospital, but she was getting better, they said. She was in amazing shape for an eighty-year-old woman. I could only aspire to be as strong as she was once I reached that age.

"I am," I said. "We have everything, I believe. Kids, Matt …"

"Bunnies?" David asked.

I nodded, chuckling sadly while thinking about Chad again. It was his project with those bunnies. I realized it was still too painful to think about him. The ME still had his body, so it would take a little while before it was released, and we could have a proper funeral for him.

"Come back to visit us soon, will you?" Adam said and gave me a warm hug. "It's so cool to have not one, but two big sisters."

I swallowed the knot in my throat and hugged him back. As he let go, I walked to David and looked into his eyes.

"Listen," he said. "I know you wonder why I left back then. Why I took Sydney and left with her, leaving you behind. But the thing was, your mother wouldn't let me see the two of you. She was angry at me, and I fought her in court, but she won. I didn't know how to live my life without my two little girls, so I decided to take both of you. It wasn't a good solution; I have no trouble admitting to that. But you'll have to remember that I was desperate, and very young, a terrible combination. But once I did grab you, and wanted you to come with me, you wouldn't let me take you. You pulled out of my grip, and I went for Syd instead. It wasn't because I didn't want you, sweetie, because I did. I truly did. I have dreamt about seeing you again so many times, and I tried to get in contact with you, but your mom kept you away. I can't blame her for doing so; I really can't, but that's what happened. I loved you then, and I still do. What I'm trying to say is that … I'm glad to have you in my life again, and I hope you'll come to visit me every now and then and bring those sweet munchkins of yours with you. My grandkids."

His words brought tears to my eyes, and I fought to keep my composure. I pulled him into a hug and held him for a few seconds, then let go of him, wiping a tear away.

"It's okay … Dad. It's all water under the bridge now," I said, half choked. "I … I guess I forgive you."

He nodded, his eyes wet. "That means the world to me."

I chuckled, then pushed him lovingly. "All right. Enough of all this. You're making me sad again. Besides, I have to go now. See you soon, okay?"

I walked up toward Matt and the kids. Christine was holding the bunny cage in her hands, and I could barely see her behind it.

Matt put his arm around me, and we walked out to the valet parking where they brought out Matt's car that I only hoped could fit us all and the bunnies. I didn't have any suitcases since all my stuff had been destroyed in the flooding.

"I was thinking," Matt said as the car drove up. "I don't want to keep living with my mom for the rest of my life. How about we move in together?"

I stared at him, eyes wide open. "M-move in together? Now?"

He smiled. "Yes. Why not?"

"With all my kids … and Elijah?" I said.

"Yes."

The valet parking guy got out and handed Matt the keys. The kids got in, and I helped place the bunny cage in their laps. Olivia groaned loudly at the prospect of having to sit like that for three hours. I couldn't blame her. I closed their door. Matt looked at me over the top of the car.

"I know it's crazy, but we only live once, and I know I want to be with you. What do you say?"

"I ... I ... well ..." I exhaled deeply, then shrugged. I didn't know what to say. I could find a million reasons why not to do it — among them that it was too early and that I wasn't ready — but I couldn't stand the thought of hurting Matt again. I had no idea what I wanted right now, and all I wanted to do was go home. Still, I loved Matt, I really did, and I wanted him to feel that. So, instead of the truth, I told him what he wanted to hear.

"Sure, why not?"

That brought out a huge smile on Matt's lips.

"Perfect. I can't wait."

Matt jumped happily into the car. I remained outside of it for a few seconds while fighting the sensation that I was about to choke. I finally got into the car and sat down in my seat, strapping myself in, while my heart pounded loudly in my chest all the way home.

THE END

Want do know what happens next?
Get book 5 **LET ME GO** here:
https://readerlinks.com/l/776927

Afterword

Dear Reader,

Thank you for purchasing *Say You Love Me* (Eva Rae Thomas #4) I wrote this book while I was evacuated from Hurricane Dorian. And of course, I had to put a hurricane in the book. It was odd writing about it while waiting for it to approach our home and not knowing what we would come home to. By the time we left, it looked like it would be a direct hit on Cocoa Beach, and that scared me, to be honest. Luckily, we got off easy, and nothing happened to our home or even our town. Others weren't so lucky, especially not people in the Bahamas, as you probably know. It was truly devastating to see the pictures coming out of there in the days that followed.

As usual, a lot of the elements in this book are taken from real life. The webpage, for instance, that was created for people to be able to speak freely, but misused, exists. It has been closed down now, but they fear it'll just pop up somewhere else. Up until the shooting in El Paso, it was a real deal. The El Paso shooter posted his manifest there, and it was known to be a place where people who dreamt of shooting in public places like schools could talk to one another and cheer each other on, etc. It's a frightening thought that they can meet like that online and help each other along to do these things, counting kill-scores. It scares me like crazy.

You can read more about it in this article:

https://www.wsj.com/articles/inside-the-toxic-online-world-where-mass-shooters-thrive-11567608631

Being falsely accused of abusing your child has to be devastating. Nevertheless, it happens from time to time, and it is quite scary. It is mostly a parent accusing another in a custody battle, but there are other stories where both parents are accused. You can read a story here that is very similar to Bruce and Marlene's tragic story:

https://abcnews.go.com/Health/false-child-abuse-charges-trigger-murder-suicide-colorado/story?id=16074344

You might be surprised to know that dumpster-diving videos on YouTube are a real thing. I accidentally came across a couple and that's how I got the idea for the woman in my book. You can find a ton of them if you go on YouTube and search for dumpster diving.

Also, Cutis Laxa is a real disease. You can read more here:

https://metro.co.uk/2017/02/16/20-year-old-with-condition-which-makes-her-age-dramatically-undergoes-facelift-6449805/

Oh, yeah, and as you might have guessed, my own kids just got bunnies, and yes, they're constantly fighting about them and whose turn it is to clean the cage. The bunnies are cute, though, and like so much else when having kids, it is worth the struggle. They were of course with us when we evacuated as was our dog Snowball, the Goldendoodle.

Thank you once again for all your support. Don't forget to leave a review if you can.

Take care,

Willow

Tired of too many emails? Text the word: "willowrose" to 31996 to sign up to Willow's VIP text List to get a text alert with news about New Releases, Giveaways, Bargains and Free books from Willow.

To be the first to hear about new releases and bargains— from Willow Rose—sign up below to be on the VIP List. (I promise not to share your email with anyone else, and I won't clutter your inbox.)

- SIGN UP TO BE ON THE VIP LIST HERE :
http://readerlinks.com/l/415254

Tired of too many emails? Text the word: "willowrose" to 31996 to sign up to Willow's VIP text List to get a text alert with news about New Releases, Giveaways, Bargains and Free books from Willow.

FOLLOW WILLOW ROSE ON BOOKBUB:
https://www.bookbub.com/authors/willow-rose

Connect with Willow online:

https://www.amazon.com/Willow-Rose/e/B004X2WHBQ
https://www.facebook.com/willowredrose/
https://twitter.com/madamwillowrose
http://www.goodreads.com/author/show/
4804769.Willow_Rose
Http://www.willow-rose.net
madamewillowrose@gmail.com

Afterword

About the Author

Willow Rose is a multi-million-copy best-selling Author and an Amazon ALL-star Author of more than 80 novels. Her books are sold all over the world.

She writes Mystery, Thriller, Paranormal, Romance, Suspense, Horror, Supernatural thrillers, and Fantasy.

Willow's books are fast-paced, nail-biting page-turners with twists you won't see coming. That's why her fans call her The Queen of Plot Twists.

Several of her books have reached the Kindle top 10 of ALL books in the US, UK, and Canada. She has sold more than three million books all over the world.

Willow lives on Florida's Space Coast with her husband and two daughters. When she is not writing or reading, you will find her surfing and watch the dolphins play in the waves of the Atlantic Ocean.

Tired of too many emails? Text the word: "willowrose" to 31996 to sign up to Willow's VIP Text List to get a text alert with news about New Releases, Giveaways, Bargains and Free books from Willow.

Cover design by Juan Villar Padron,
https://www.juanjpadron.com

Special thanks to my editor Janell Parque
http://janellparque.blogspot.com/

———

**To be the first to hear about new releases and bargains
from Willow Rose, sign up below to be on the VIP List.** (I
promise not to share your email with anyone else, and I won't clutter
your inbox.)

- GO HERE TO SIGN UP TO BE ON THE VIP LIST :
http://readerlinks.com/l/415254

Tired of too many emails? Text the word: "willowrose" to
31996 to sign up to Willow's VIP text List to get a text alert with
news about New Releases, Giveaways, Bargains and Free books
from Willow.

Follow Willow Rose on BookBub:
https://www.bookbub.com/authors/willow-rose

Connect with Willow online:
https://www.amazon.com/Willow-Rose/e/B004X2WHBQ
https://www.facebook.com/willowredrose/
https://twitter.com/madamwillowrose
http://www.goodreads.com/author/show/
4804769.Willow_Rose
Http://www.willow-rose.net
madamewillowrose@gmail.com

CPSIA information can be obtained
at www.ICGtesting.com
Printed in the USA
LVHW092230090421
684042LV00028BA/750/J